THE YACHT

Also by Kayte Nunn

Rose's Vintage
Angel's Share
The Botanist's Daughter
The Forgotten Letters of Esther Durrant
The Silk House
The Last Reunion
The Only Child
The Palazzo

THE YACHT

KAYTE NUNN

NO EXIT PRESS

First published in Australia in 2026 by HarperCollins
First published in the UK in 2026 by No Exit Press,
an imprint of Bedford Square Publishers Ltd,
London, UK

noexit.co.uk
@noexitpress

A CIP catalogue record for this book is available from the British Library.

ISBN
978-1-83501-151-5 (Paperback)
978-1-83501-152-2 (eBook)

2 4 6 8 10 9 7 5 3 1

Printed and bound in Great Britain by
CPI Group (UK) Ltd, Croydon CR0 4YY

MIX
Paper | Supporting responsible forestry
FSC® C013604
FSC www.fsc.org

The manufacturer's authorised representative in the EU for product safety is Easy Access System Europe, Mustamäe tee 50, 10621 Tallinn, Estonia

gpsr.requests@easproject.com

Any port in a storm.
Proverb

Fluctuat nec mergitur.
She is tossed by the waves, but does not sink.

Prologue

THE SURVIVOR

She is frozen in place, afraid to breathe, as if she's playing that childhood party game where the music stops and the first to move, even an inch, is out.

But this is no party.

The static in her head clears and fragments of memory surface: broken glass, a hand wrapped around a wrist, soft lips on a bare neck, a line of pale skin peeking from beneath a bikini, light so blinding she has to screw up her eyes, the burn of ice-cold champagne sluicing her throat, beads of pearly-grey caviar popping in her mouth, salt in the air and on her skin, thumping bass and a disco beat, strobe lights in red and blue, wide-eyed faces staring at her …

Blood blooming like a flower in the water, curling and spreading until she is bathed in scarlet.

She has no idea if the blood is hers or someone else's, if it's real or a nightmare.

She claws at the jumble of images, but they drift away, feathers on a breeze, replaced by a surging pain that begins at her hairline and travels down her body, along her legs, all the way to her toes.

Everything hurts. Her eye sockets, the back of her skull, her neck, her chest, her limbs. She flinches and the movement sends another wave of agony rolling down her knees, along her shins and ankles. Liquid seems to slosh around her skull and she identifies the soreness at the back of her throat as the scour that comes from swallowing salt water.

A faint humming reaches her ears, then an insistent high-pitched whine followed by an intermittent beep. The smells of antiseptic and pine detergent fill her nostrils and she has an overwhelming urge to sneeze. Her face twitches, the urge passes, and there's a cool hand on her arm. She tries to speak, but the sound that comes out is as weak as a kitten's mew.

Then, without warning, there's a sharp sting on her skin and she is flooded with a delicious, spreading, honeyed buzz. The noises fade, her limbs loosen, and she is dragged down, down to the bottom of an ocean from which she may never surface.

Her last conscious thought, a razor blade slicing through the fog, is that someone wants her dead.

She just can't remember who.

www.seemallorca.com
Breaking news
1 July

Fatal Yacht Accident

One person is dead, two people are missing and several others have been hospitalised after a luxury yacht capsized in the Cala Torta area, on the north coast of the island.

According to Palma Air Sea Rescue Service, the incident occurred at around 2.30 am this morning. Sea conditions were rough at the time, with gusting to gale-force winds throughout the Balearics.

The search and rescue vessel and the Helimer 221 were still plucking survivors from the sea at 4 am. Several crew members and guests were able to swim to safety.

A number of those on board are being treated at Palma Hospital.

This is the latest tragedy to rock the tourist paradise and comes only weeks after the bodies of two young women were found, on separate beaches, to the west of the island.

There is no suggestion that the incidents are related, and tourism officials insist there is no threat to current holidaymakers or visitors.

An investigation is underway.

Chapter One

THE DECKIE

Everyone has an opinion on what Piper should be doing with her life. Her father was adamant that she should have gone straight to uni and 'got a qualification: your results could get you in anywhere you wanted'. (He didn't mind what kind of qualification, he just wanted her to have one, so her future would therefore be secured and he could stop worrying about her.) Lexie always encouraged her to continue with her singing, and to 'at least take a gap year and go find yourself, preferably somewhere warm'. Even her Auntie Cath weighed in, saying that a skill would be helpful. 'What about being a barista, darling? Everyone always seems to want a coffee, and you like early mornings.'

None of them has a clue what she's actually planning.

A small sign fixed to the exterior of a shipping container tells her that she has come to the right place. It probably once enjoyed a life on the high seas transporting Japanese electronics to Melbourne or shifting bales of fast fashion from Guangzhou or Shenzhen to Barcelona, but it is now firmly landlocked, though within tantalising sight of the water, tarted up with a lick of paint and converted to an office.

Inside is a small waiting room with three upright chairs and a tired-looking pot plant. There are two doors, likely to internal offices, and one small window without much of a view. Piper takes a seat as far away as possible from a manspreading, muscle-bound, twenty-something dude wearing khaki shorts and a collared shirt, the armpits dark with sweat. He shifts slightly in acknowledgement of her presence but doesn't attempt conversation.

She stares straight ahead, going over the answers to potential questions. Her papers are in the bag at her feet: CV, a medical certificate confirming her clean bill of health, and proof that she's completed the required five-day basic safety training. She resists the urge to check them again. Instead, she smooths back a loose strand of hair and tries not to fidget.

It was a long, hot walk from the hostel and she didn't think to bring any water. Scanning the tiny space, she spots a dispenser half hidden behind the plant and is about to help herself to a cup when one of the doors opens and an older man with grey chest hair sprouting from the neck of his shirt emerges. Aftershave comes off him in waves as he brushes past her, and she instinctively turns her head, seeking a pocket of fresher air, though there is none to be found.

'Peeper Smith?' a voice rings out through the open doorway. It takes Piper a second to respond: the woman has mispronounced her name, but she's not about to correct her.

'*Si.*' She gets to her feet and goes in.

The woman behind the desk looks over her glasses at Piper, who smiles in what she hopes is an approachable manner. Piper's Spanish is as basic as it comes, and she doesn't catch the woman's name when she introduces herself.

'Sit.' She motions to a seat and begins leafing through a stack of papers. She stops, looking at Piper again, her gaze crawling over every inch of her, assessing.

Piper is wearing a pale pink polo shirt tucked into tight white shorts, worn-in Sperry Topsiders on her feet. She's of average height, with delicate bone structure and unusually long, slim fingers that could be mistaken for those of a ballerina or a pianist, though in fact she is neither. Her fine, fair hair is secured in a ponytail, her make-up minimal – just enough to enhance her blue eyes – and her skin is lightly tanned, thanks to spending the past week in Palma.

The pretty girls get the best jobs, and she's not above using any means available to gain an advantage.

Piper pulls out a chair and sits, tucking her legs neatly to one side, back straight, holding her smile until it feels practically frozen in place. She clamps her knees together, willing them not to jiggle.

'Documents?' The woman holds out her hand impatiently, and Piper retrieves them from her bag. The medical certificate includes a complete tox screen (blood, urine, hair) done earlier in the week. There's zero tolerance for illegal drugs, at least among crew, not that it's an issue for her. She doesn't drink much these days, having necked far too many Cement Mixers (a noxious concoction of Bailey's Irish Cream and lime juice) on a particularly messy night last year.

The woman scans her CV. It's mostly accurate, save for a couple of key details, but then everyone fudges their experience and qualifications a little, right?

'It's all in order,' Piper tells her, surprised at how confident she sounds. 'And there is a reference there as well.'

'I require two.'

'I've only ever held one job,' she replies. 'At the sailing school. But I was there for four years, on weekends and in the holidays too.' She hopes this at least shows her sticking power, that the woman will overlook the absence of another to accompany it. 'And I've worked on a couple of day cruises since I arrived in Palma.' She hesitates. 'I could see if they'll vouch for me.'

The woman's upper lip flares, but she doesn't push the point. 'I've got nothing at the moment,' she says, flicking through the paperwork, ready to dismiss her.

Has Piper come too soon? 'I'm a fast learner. And very discreet,' she reassures her. Only one of these is true. The other has never been tested. 'I'm not afraid of hard work,' she continues. 'And I'm looking to make a career for myself. In yachting. It's my passion.'

The woman examines Piper more carefully, as if probing for a weakness. 'This is not about serving cocktails to Leonardo DiCaprio, you know.'

'Of course not.' Piper is solemn-faced.

The woman is about to speak again when her phone rings, and she excuses herself. The conversation is brief. 'How unfortunate. Get better soon.' She rings off and blows out an exasperated breath.

She narrows her eyes, then appears to make up her mind. 'Your timing is good. There might be a job, but I need someone used to working for VIPs. It is a very private family.'

Piper nods, as if she understands completely. 'I've taught several children of high-profile, high-net-worth families,' she says. 'Of course, I couldn't possibly say who.'

'Any tattoos?'

Piper shakes her head. Not anywhere obvious, anyway. It's a small, inconsequential lie. She'll tell far bigger ones soon enough.

'Take your shoes off.'

'Sorry?'

The woman seems irritated at Piper's hesitation, so she toes them off hurriedly.

The woman rises, leaning over her desk to get a better view, then sits down and scribbles something on a sticky note, handing it to Piper. 'Tell them I sent you.'

Piper glances at the note. It appears to be the name and address of a nail bar.

The woman gives her a condescending smile. 'If you're going to work on a superyacht, even as a deckhand, you'd better have a decent pedicure.'

It hadn't occurred to Piper that such details might matter, and she curses the oversight, but does this mean she has the job? Part of her thinks it should have been harder than this.

There's a point in most movies where the director goes for the dramatic close-up, and the actor must register a flash of conflicting emotions on their face while barely moving it. The most talented of them – Shailene Woodley, Florence Pugh and Kate Winslet spring to mind – make it seem effortless, their mobile features subtly changing to telegraph their inner thoughts. Piper is much better at poker faces, at summoning a blank expression that reveals nothing of her internal turmoil.

'The girl I had lined up is suddenly unable to work,' the woman says. 'You are here at the right time. There's a return flight back to London once a year. Six weeks' annual leave, though none during peak season. The owner intends to have friends stay on board from time to time when he's not using it, so would like a year-round crew.'

These details are of little importance to Piper. She doesn't expect to stay after the summer is over.

The woman mentions the salary. 'And of course, the owners generally tip the crew at their discretion at the end of the season. The yacht is called *Ambition*.'

Piper allows herself a smile that she hopes conveys amenability. She wants to look grateful, not gleeful.

'Welcome to the white boat world,' the woman says, a half-grin illuminating her harsh features. She stops as something occurs to her. 'You are not accident prone, I hope?'

Piper is composed. 'No, not at all.'

'Excellent. You will start tomorrow. Nine am sharp. Ask for Johannes. You're lucky; plenty of girls would kill to work on such a yacht. You will be a deckhand, but expected to fill in where required. A floater.' The word conjures up an unwelcome image, but Piper is not one for second thoughts.

The woman pushes a stapled wedge of paper towards her. 'An NDA. There's a non-disparagement clause in there too, to be clear. It's standard practice.'

'Of course.' Piper pretends to scan the tiny print, although in truth there is little that would prevent her from signing it.

'Strictly no posting images of the yacht or guests to social media, or anything that can link you to your place of employment.'

'Not even photos of the landscape?'

'None. And under no circumstances are you to talk to the media, of any kind.' The woman glares at her with such ferocity that Piper has to stop herself from saluting.

'Of course. I understand.' Piper leafs through the document. 'I am to consent to a polygraph, if required?' She tries to keep the incredulity from her voice. This is more involved than she expected.

'We like to cover all eventualities. It is for your protection too.'

'I see.' It won't come to that. She turns to the final page and takes the offered ballpoint.

'And don't be late.'

'Copy that.' Piper breathes out and beams at her. '*Gracias*. You won't regret it.'

The woman told Piper that she is lucky, but she doesn't know the half of it. Piper hasn't got to where she is through mere good timing, whatever the woman might think. No, getting a job on board *Ambition* is the result of more than a year of careful planning.

Chapter Two

THE ELDEST DAUGHTER

Melissa Silk tosses back her shoulder-length, old-money-blonde (according to her colourist) hair and fixes Angus with an icy glare that would make a more self-aware man quake. In one hand is a spike-heeled shoe; in the other, a heavy crystal perfume bottle. She weighs them in each palm, considering which will do the most damage, then winds up her right arm and lets the bottle fly.

She aims high (she isn't a total psycho; besides, she doesn't want blood on the peacock-hued Schumacher wallpaper) and it sails inches above his head, bouncing off the wall and coming to rest on the thick carpet with a muffled thump. As the star pitcher of her high school softball team, it's satisfying to see that she can still bring it.

'How fucking could you?' she seethes, her teeth gritted. Bailey and Carter are downstairs watching TV and she doesn't want to alert them to the stand-up fight their parents are about to have.

He looks at her with a faintly bemused expression, ever the absent professor. She once found it deeply appealing, but now it only irritates her to the core.

'I can't believe you're such a cliché.'

He holds up his hands in surrender. 'It's not what you think.'

A laugh escapes her. 'Not what I think? Tell me, what *am* I expected to think when I come home and find both of you in her room and only one of you wearing clothes?'

'Amelia was showing me the bikini she got on sale at Bloomingdale's. Wanted to know if it would be suitable. For the trip,' he explains, then stops for a second before continuing. 'I know it sounds ridiculous when I say it like that, but it's the truth, darling.'

Melissa snorts at this, especially at the endearment tacked on the end. 'Do you really think I'm that stupid?'

He shuffles his feet, perhaps only now seeing the benefit of saying nothing.

She sighs. 'You might be smart, Angus, but you're a complete dumbass in every other regard. Shitting on your own doorstep? While the children are here? With the help? She's *nineteen*, for chrissake.'

He ignores her remarks. 'How can I prove to you that I've done nothing wrong? You're reading far too much into the situation. To be honest, I'm concerned that you're becoming increasingly paranoid, darling.'

She purses her lips, then stops; she doesn't want to end up with a cat's bum mouth in ten years' time.

She watched the nanny-cam footage last week, the two of them in the living room while the kids were having their breakfast in the kitchen, Angus's hand sliding along Amelia's thigh, his face buried in her neck, exactly the way he used to touch Melissa when they were first married. In the early days of their relationship, he once quoted a line from Thomas Hardy: 'all romances end at marriage'. At the time, she thought he was kidding.

She deliberately came home from the office early today, half-hoping, half-dreading, that she would catch them out.

Perhaps even more than his appalling behaviour, she's pissed that he's created another mess for her to clean up. Quite possibly, that was the point. After all, there are surely plenty of starstruck MFA students only too willing to sleep with their English professor, an outlet for his libido that would be far more discreet and a whole lot less disruptive. She considers the possibility that he is acting out – rebuking her for spending so much time at work.

She can't fucking win.

Until recently, they still had sex twice a week – Wednesdays and Sundays, on the regular – and she had thought that part of their marriage pretty good, all things considered, but clearly it wasn't enough for him.

Christ, she wishes *she* had time for an affair, but the only things she's been casting lustful glances at recently are the cabins on her father's new boat (never to be referred to as a *yacht*, at least not by owners and guests). According to Sandrine, the beds are the same ones as in their favourite Parisian hotel. 'You will sleep like on a cloud,' she said when describing them to Melissa. At this point in time, Melissa thinks she could sleep on a bed of nails. She's exhausted, desperate for a vacation, and finding out that her husband is cheating, *again*, is more than she's got the energy to deal with right now. 'I'll pay her till the end of the month. She signed the NDA, didn't she? Of course, you will never speak to her again.'

Melissa vowed long ago that she wanted her children to grow up with two parents who stayed married to each other, made a point of telling Angus that. Not all step-parents are evil, but she has no wish for the kids to go through the shitshow that she and Rocco endured after their father remarried.

Now, in a rare moment of self-doubt, Melissa asks herself how much longer she can continue to cover up Angus's mistakes, keep papering over the cracks in their marriage for the sake of the children, for the sake of appearances. She really doesn't have the time or the bandwidth for a divorce, not with construction approvals dragging on and a global marketing strategy for Thyssen's new development to roll out.

Besides, as a fervent Catholic, Angus is sure to dig his heels in. He's one of those rare, old-fashioned beings who still believes that marriage is for life and that only an annulment, or becoming a widower, can end the holy union. Yes, he cherry-picks the tenets of his faith, choosing to ignore those regarding faithfulness and the sanctity of holy matrimony, but she's lost too many arguments to bother debating it anymore.

The bigger tragedy is that the kids really like Amelia, more than their own mom sometimes, it seems. And on top of that, good help is about as hard to find as a faithful husband.

'Get out. I can't stand to look at you right now.' She raises the shoe still in her hand, though she is loath to ruin a perfectly good pair of Jimmy Choos. Besides, her initial storm of rage has now subsided to a simmering, resigned fury.

He backs out of the room, and she calls after him, 'Did you at least pick up the dry-cleaning?'

No answer is forthcoming.

She retrieves the perfume bottle, holding it up to the light, checking the cut-glass facets. It belonged to her mother, and is one of the few things Melissa has to remember her by. She breathes out, relieved that it's not damaged, nor is the wallpaper. A small win in a day of losses.

She won't cry; she never cries. Not for her mother who died too soon, not for her husband's serial betrayals and certainly not for herself. She is better than this, and most definitely stronger.

She doesn't usually let herself drink on a weeknight, but Christ, she could murder a glass of wine right now. Before going in search of a bottle of pinot grigio, she reaches into her purse, flung on the bed earlier, and retrieves her cell phone, fingers flying as she brings up Sandrine's contact and types a message.

> Have been thinking about the nanny situation – C & B old enough not to require constant supervision. Okay if we share Amber while we're away?

Her father has never voiced any concern at her ability to juggle a 24/7 job, motherhood and marriage, though he refuses to countenance his third wife returning to her career. The double standard is astonishing.

Melissa hovers a thumb over the send button. She hates asking Sandrine for a favour, but she doesn't see what other option there is. She's never taken a vacation without help (or without spending several hours a day on email), but the children aren't toddlers anymore and they'll have the crew to help keep an eye on them. It wouldn't be a terrible idea for her to spend a bit more time with them, either, she acknowledges.

As she presses send on the message, not wanting to waste another minute debating it, the sound of a crash followed by a scream and then a groan reaches her from the hallway.

What the fuck now?

bluewater76: I can't believe more of them didn't perish – that was one helluva storm that blew through. Unprecedented for that time of year.

thoughtsandprayers: You know who believes in climate change? Insurance companies, that's who.

Chapter Three

THE TROPHY WIFE

Sandrine Thyssen snaps the final clasp on her rolling trunk and gets to her feet, resting her hands briefly on her hips. Beatrice or one of the maids would have packed for her had she wanted, but she prefers to see to this task herself. It gives her a small sense of control over her life.

They'll be away for a little over a month, including all of July. The trunk contains a rainbow of dresses, including her favourite Missoni mini, a slinky, sequinned Elie Saab number for anything formal that might arise, and a long white silk Oscar de la Renta gown painted with poppies and lilies of the valley that Gwyneth Paltrow was photographed wearing earlier that month. Sandrine would have returned it if she could, but decided in the end it was too much bother. There is also a draped sheath dress that's the result of a collab between a New York–based artist and an Australian designer (both women, she is pleased to note), in ombre shades of blue that reminds her of the changing hues of the ocean. It's divine, the kind of dress you might choose to be buried in, not that she's thinking that far ahead, but her beloved *maman* died two months ago and so death has been on her mind lately, one way or another.

A smaller suitcase and a Loro Piana weekender are on the bed, stuffed with La Perla underwear, colour-coordinated activewear sets, Ladakhi cashmere sweaters in case of cool evenings, two-hundred-dollar T-shirts still in their packaging, organic eyelet cotton cover-ups, a dozen skirts – both long and flowing and short and skin-tight – and a handful of never-worn gauzy shirts in sorbet hues. White, navy and khaki shorts, sea island cotton pyjamas, silk negligees in oyster and smoke, two hats (one a wide-brimmed Panama, one a logo-free ballcap) and a wardrobe of sunglasses in various styles – though she'll probably end up wearing her favourite aviators – are also neatly stowed. Then there are shoes, despite the fact that she will mostly be barefoot when on board: half a dozen pairs of sandals, strappy summer heels and casual but no less costly flip-flops.

Will it be enough? She twists the thin silver ring around her finger, one of the few things that reminds her of life before marriage. The ring was given to her by Hervé Boucher, director on *Espoir*, the first film she made, and although it looks cheap compared to the trio of emerald-cut diamonds set in platinum on her left hand, she continues to wear it. Jewels … how could she have overlooked that? She lobs a silk roll containing a diamond tennis bracelet, bangles, necklaces and assorted earrings – diamond, pearl, emerald, Cartier, Van Cleef and Garrard – into a tote.

She justifies the insane amount of clothing she now owns by telling herself she needs to look the part, never more so than in front of Evan's grown-up children, but she's always had a weakness for pretty things. If she was a more introspective kind of person, she would say it was a form of self-medication, but there are surely far worse transgressions than having an excess of beautiful clothes.

Evan commissioned the new vessel three years ago but had been thinking about it for far longer, the ultimate status symbol to cap his success. He wanted to name her the *Lady Sandrine*, but Sandrine vetoed that suggestion, despite knowing how much it would piss off his children, especially Melissa. Tempting as it was, she could do without giving them another reason to hate her.

She still can't believe that they're all coming, though she shouldn't be surprised – who wouldn't want to cruise around the Med on board a brand-new luxury yacht, not having to lift a finger or pay for a thing? Ten days with all of them together in a confined space, even a two-hundred-and-fifty-foot boat … She told a friend last week that she wasn't sure they'd all make it out alive, especially after the last time. She was only half-joking.

Melissa, Evan's eldest daughter, is thirty-one, married with two children, and is a VP at Thyssen Properties, the company founded by Evan's father, Rolf. Her brother Rocco, also from Evan's first marriage, is nearly a decade younger than Melissa. He suffers from access to a surfeit of money and a complete lack of his father's attention, and as a result is spoilt and utterly feckless, but also exceptionally charming.

It's Kitty, the product of Evan's short-lived second marriage, who Sandrine feels genuinely sorry for. She's grown up with a broken family, a distracted father and a much older half-sister who barely acknowledges her. She's also at an awkward age, the excruciatingly shy mid-teen years when you feel you are either too much or not enough, never considering you might be perfect exactly as you are, that one day you'll look back and think, *Why did I waste so much time worrying about what other people thought of me?* Sandrine remembers her own experience of those years well.

Sudden rain hurls itself against the tall windows that overlook Central Park, a summer storm that's been threatening all afternoon, and the attendant gloom feels ominous. Sandrine goes to turn on the lights, but before she can do so, the door opens and Evan appears, a light dusting of raindrops on his shoulders and hair, his tall frame filling the doorway. He's early, which is unusual; for the past few months he's been getting home later and later.

His phone is pressed to his ear and he mimes the wind-up sign while rolling his eyes ruefully at her. Evan is on his phone more often than he's not, and she's used to their conversations being punctuated by calls of varying urgency. The only time he turns his phone off is, well, never, not even at night. Sometimes she wakes in the early hours to find him scanning a stream of emails, tapping out replies with his thumbs.

Still on the call, he tosses his monogrammed wallet on the nightstand and catches sight of himself in the long mirror, one hand loosening the knot of his tie. He sucks in his stomach – he'd be the last to admit that he's vain, but age and his fondness for triple-cream cheese and French burgundy are the cause of a softening waist and slackening jawline.

He abruptly terminates the call and leans in to give Sandrine a fleeting kiss. She catches a whiff of stale alcohol, also a more regular occurrence recently. Client lunches, or so he claims. At least they'll be getting out of the country tomorrow and so he might wind down, even if only a little.

He raises an eyebrow at the tangled heap of swimwear on the bed. 'Bring the white one, you look as hot as fuck in that.'

She ignores the heavy-handed compliment, though it's something of a relief to hear it. Evan's been unable to perform recently, and she's been wondering how to raise the delicate subject of Viagra. Perhaps this trip will shake things up in the *boudoir*. 'Do you think the storm will mean a delay?' Her voice has the husky tone that helped make her one of France's most in-demand actresses before her marriage.

'Forecast for tomorrow is clear. Don't worry so much.'

'You're home early.'

He comes closer and wraps his arms around her waist. She breathes in, instinctively flattening her stomach, self-conscious about the softness there since having Max and despite her daily

Pilates routine. 'Tell me you weren't planning to see your lover?' He enjoys this, the teasing. He nuzzles her neck, at the pulse point just behind her ear, then catches the lobe between his teeth, pressing down on the tender flesh almost to the point of pain.

She stills, ignoring the barb. If she shows even the slightest weakness, he'll only bite harder, and she's made that mistake once too often.

'I think Max is up from his nap if you want to go see him.'

It is the right thing to say; he releases her, although not before giving her skin a playful pinch, a reminder that if ever he hears even the faintest whisper of betrayal, his retaliation will be swift and merciless. He demands absolute loyalty from everyone: his employees, his family, his inner circle and especially her.

'Maxie!' he booms, leaving a vacuum in his wake. He dotes on his baby son. Sandrine imagines he is trying to make up for not being around as much when his older children were growing up.

A second or two later, Evan puts his head around the door again. 'Did you remember Rocco's coming over?'

'Of course,' she replies. 'Beatrice should have prepared something light for us.'

Sandrine has been in Evan's life for four years and has spent numerous family occasions, from birthdays to Christmases, with Rocco, but Evan's son remains opaque, though certainly disapproving of her. Melissa revealed once in passing that Rocco used to have a movie poster of her on his bedroom wall – the one to promote *Geneviève*, where her hair was cut so short she looked like a boy, and they applied so much kohl around her eyes they appeared to be bruised.

Right on cue, the doorbell chimes faintly from below.

She zips up the case, hauling it off the bed, and checks her appearance in the mirror before heading downstairs.

Beatrice has already let him in.

Rocco looks up as she descends the stairs, his gaze lingering on her bare legs, and Sandrine feels a moment's disquiet, remembering the poster, wishing Melissa had never told her about it.

'Rocco, so pleased you could join us.' She beams a smile that only she can tell is fake, acting her way into the emotion.

5GuysNamedMoe: Did you see the size of the thing? Yachts are some of the biggest polluters on the planet; their carbon emissions are off the scale. Bezos's new $500 million floating gin palace emits the CO_2 equivalent of 1500 cars annually. They're morally indefensible. Not that the owners care.

Chapter Four

THE DECKIE

Piper reaches the end of the dock at precisely 8.58 am. She cranes her neck to take in the two-hundred-and-fifty feet of sleek white brilliance. Even though she knew what to expect, it still takes her breath away, the enormity of it – immaculate, dazzling, alluring, a clean-lined, streamlined, multi-million-dollar floating pleasure palace.

The ultimate status symbol for the ultra-wealthy – sheikhs, oligarchs and captains of industry who aren't afraid to flaunt their fortune – superyachts are the embodiment of power, privacy and privilege.

Unlike probably any other newbie deckhand, Piper has done her research: M/Y *Ambition* was designed by celebrated Norwegian naval architect Trond Jonssen, took three years (an accelerated schedule) to be built at Larsbergen in Bremen, the home of mega- and superyacht construction, and is about to make her maiden voyage with the proud owner on board.

Ambition has a top speed of around eighteen knots and a cruising speed of fifteen. There are three decks: the upper deck with a swimming pool, jacuzzi, gym, hammam steam room, bridge, captain's quarters, massage area with retractable roof, expansive sundeck and outdoor cinema. The main deck features a salon, outdoor dining to seat twenty, a wine cellar, an owner's office/retreat, a master suite and seven generous guest cabins. Each cabin is fitted out with an oversized mirror that morphs into a screen on command (linked, naturally, to every streaming and music service in existence), and in the adjoining bathrooms there are rainwater and steam showers that feature red and blue light therapy (red has anti-ageing benefits, blue is for skin purification, or so the bullshit goes).

The crew of twenty-six will sleep two, three or even four to a cramped cabin on the lower deck. Also on the lower deck, along with the laundry, is a large galley staffed by three chefs and of course the engines and the fuel tanks, which have a capacity of more than 100,000 gallons. Piper hasn't bothered to calculate how much it must cost to refuel, not to mention the carbon emissions.

One tender, four jet skis, two Seabobs and various other water toys are housed on the lower deck aft, near the swim platform. If she's lucky, she might get to take these out on the water.

Piper believes in being prepared. She has memorised it all, poring over the plans of an almost identical yacht on which *Ambition* is based. It proved impossible to access the actual plans, but she also read a couple of articles, including one in *Robb Report*, on the new build. She's confident there won't be substantive differences, but she should have enough time and opportunity to find out if there are.

Of course, there are far bigger boats out there, ones that come complete with helipads, concert halls and even submersibles, but *Ambition*'s razor-sharp lines and glossy white hull make for a heart-stopping sight nonetheless, and she dwarfs every other vessel on the Palma dock.

Piper gets out her phone and sends her sister a brief text.

Guess who just got a job on a brand-new two-fifty-footer? Px

She signs off with a boat emoji.

She won't get a reply, but she sends it anyway. This was Lexie's dream; it feels strange that Piper is now the one living it.

Putting her phone away, Piper slips off her shoes and catches sight of her newly polished shell-pink toes. They are clean and pure, in marked contrast with the water in the dock, bottle-green and oily, slicks from the yacht engines forming a toxic rainbow on the surface.

She's about to push past the 'PRIVATE, NO boarding, NO paparazzi' notice strung across the *passerelle* when a delivery truck pulls up and a man unloads a large crate containing several elaborate flower arrangements. '*Ambition*?' he asks, looking directly at her.

She nods. Might as well make herself useful from the start. She signs for the flowers and as he hands them over, the heady aroma of hothouse blooms mixes with the smell of diesel, making her queasy.

Abandoning her suitcase on the dock for the time being, she turns back to the yacht and steps on board. There's an unfamiliar flutter in her belly and she swallows twice to calm her nerves. There's no going back now.

She gets no further than the threshold of the main salon before being stopped.

'You can put those down there.' The voice is terse, accented – Australian? New Zealand? – and belongs to a young woman with an impressively even tan and honey-blonde hair caught up in a messy bun. She blows her fringe out of her eyes at the same time as the tortoiseshell frames of her glasses slide down her nose.

Piper does as the girl asks and then steps forward, hand outstretched in greeting, but she has already turned away, bending down to stow crystal champagne flutes in a cupboard.

Piper coughs slightly to let her know she's still there.

'Oh.' She turns around again. 'Do you need me to sign? Just put Tamara on the sheet.'

'I'm not from the florist; I'm one of the new deckhands. Piper. I was told to ask for Johannes?' Piper flashes her most amiable but humble smile (she's practised in the mirror until it is second nature).

Tamara pushes her glasses back up onto the bridge of her nose for a better look. 'Sorry.' She sweeps an arm around the salon at the cluster of boxes and wrapping materials in various stages of unpacking. 'All of this should have arrived last week, but, well, you know how it is … There's always last-minute pandemonium.'

Piper nods as if she does know, though she hasn't the faintest idea how things work on a yacht of this size.

'You'll probably find Johannes by the swim deck, jerking off over all his new toys.' A fleeting grin crosses her face.

'Thanks. I might go grab my luggage first,' Piper says, remembering that her suitcase is still on the dock, sweltering in the Spanish sun. It's as old as the hills, doesn't contain much of value, and there are security cameras surveilling every inch of the marina, but still, she'd prefer not to risk leaving it there any longer than necessary.

* * *

Piper doesn't find Johannes, and is instead intercepted by a short, wire-spectacled, balding man, sweat beading on his forehead. Knife-creased khaki shorts reach beyond his knees, the ubiquitous polo shirt stretched over a barrel chest. He is carrying a clipboard and has an air of distracted efficiency. He holds up a hand as she approaches. 'Who the hell are you?' Behind the glasses, his eyes are jet beads and they flick, suspiciously, over Piper.

She smiles and introduces herself.

The man consults his clipboard. 'I am expecting a Penny. Not a Piper.'

'She had an unfortunate accident. The agency sent me in her place.' Piper shows him the paperwork from the crewing agency. 'It was a last-minute thing, maybe something got lost in translation?'

'I will have to call and check,' he says but seems to accept it. 'Walker,' he barks. '*Chef d'equipe*.'

'Very pleased to meet you, Mr Walker. I can't tell you how excited I am to be here.' She does her best to be ingratiating, but he responds with a look of withering disdain, riffles through a sheaf of papers attached to his clipboard and extracts a stapled document.

'It's just Walker.' He hands her the document. 'There will be no excuse for not recognising a family member or guest, for not greeting them by name and for not being aware of their preferences, their favourite beverages and so on, without having to ask. Please note that Mrs Thyssen prefers not to be spoken to by the crew; she will indicate if she needs something. All crew are here to create a frictionless experience for the family and their guests. You are paid to notice things, and also to not notice many other things. Do you understand?'

Piper gives him a murmur of assent. She can't imagine a life where you never have to rub up against anything inconvenient, never feel the lack of anything, where there is someone else to take care of your every desire, wish or whim. Let alone being such an arsehole that you insist the crew don't directly speak to you. She can't decide if she'd love it (the having every desire catered to, that is) or if, like eating too many sweets, it would make her feel sick.

Sweat trickles down the back of her neck as she looks at the paper. Jeez. The document runs to nearly a dozen pages. There is a list of rules: be friendly but not familiar, never address the female guests as ma'am, never touch the guests, especially the children, unless you are helping them in or out of the water … it goes on.

Then she turns to the specific guest details, starting with the owner, Evan Thyssen. The photo is flattering, from a time when he had more hair and fewer lines bracketing his mouth and eyes. The document lists his likes, dislikes, what time he generally turns in for the night. It's nothing if not comprehensive.

Then his wife. Third wife, Piper reminds herself. French. A former actress who famously retired just before she married Evan. Sandrine Furneaux, or Thyssen, as she is now known, is thin and nervy as a greyhound, beautiful, glamorous. The photo shows her with a low chignon that perfectly showcases her high cheekbones and generous, bee-stung lips. She's wearing heavy gold earrings and a necklace so thick it makes Piper think of a noose. She can't imagine what Sandrine sees in Evan – well, aside from the fact that he's ridiculously rich, of course. For plenty of people, it seems, money and power are everything.

There's no picture of the baby, but there is one of the nanny. Amber Cameron-Bruce. Young, with soft eyes and no make-up, the kind of fair skin that belongs on a misty Scottish heath.

'Discretion on board is essential.' Walker's American accent cuts into her thoughts. 'That means strictly no photography, no social media content that could be linked to the yacht. You are not to send pictures or information relating to the family, however trivial, to anyone, anywhere. Is that clear?' He scowls at her over his glasses, and his nose twitches as if he's smelled something unpleasant, but perhaps it's merely the thought that someone might disobey him. 'If you are found to have broken these rules for whatever reason, you will be escorted off the vessel. Immediately.' Despite his short stature, he's intimidating. 'Follow me. I will get someone to show you to your cabin.'

As they walk towards the bow, moving through the interior, Piper has to pick her jaw up off the floor. Light streams in through the floor-to-ceiling windows, offering expansive views of the water. She notes the humidor, the home cinema, the wine cellar, the iPad-controlled 20,000-watt sound and lighting system.

It's even more luxe than she imagined. The interiors look as though Ralph Lauren has moved in: artfully faded printed fabrics, alligator steamer trunks, brass fittings, aged chesterfields, bookcases filled with leather-bound volumes that have probably never been opened. There are chairs covered in buttery tobacco-coloured leather, and in the main dining salon a delicate chandelier is suspended above an impressively long glossy maple wood table. She resists the urge to reach out and stroke one of the throws tossed casually across an armchair, though it's undoubtedly cashmere or vicuña. She glances upwards: the double-height vaulted ceiling is painted with a cloudscape that would make Michelangelo envious.

It is an elevated, very American view of classic country house décor and although it feels slightly at odds with the Mediterranean setting, the effect is of an expensive, beautiful cocoon from the world's harsh realities.

They continue, passing a smaller room – a snug – complete with fireplace (surely fake; an out-of-control shipboard blaze is a sailor's worst fear) and an enormous map of the world. The map is based on the one onboard Barry Diller and Diane von Fürstenberg's yacht, *Eos*, (so she has read) and stretches the length of one wall.

Walker points to the guest cabins, stopping to open one of the doors and ushering her inside. 'The Owners' Suite,' he says, giving her a sidelong glance to see her reaction.

If he means to impress her, he succeeds. Snowy linen, thistle-down throws, plump pillows in shades of dove grey and sea green glow against the rich timber, sparkling glass and soft lighting. As her toes sink into the thick carpet, her mind boggles at the insane luxury of it all, unable to fathom how much it must have cost: the art, the craftsmanship, the attention to materials and detail. She's never been in such proximity to this kind of conspicuous wealth in her life, but for some people – the family that owns this yacht, for example – it is probably unremarkable.

'There are the haves, and then there are the have-yachts,' Walker says drily.

She's not sure how to respond to that, so says nothing. Give her the exhilaration of a wide ocean, a boat under sail, the wind tearing her eyes, grabbing at her hair and chapping her skin … Something raw and real. Nature's powerful force trumps anything manufactured, every time. All the same, who can fail to be seduced by a little (or in this case, a lot of) luxury?

* * *

'Johannes, take this girl off my hands, will you, and show her the ropes? I've got better things to get on with.'

They have reached the swim platform.

Johannes looks fit and strong, his chest filling out a navy polo, tanned legs emerging from white shorts. He greets her, showing perfect teeth. With a set of choppers like that, quids in he isn't a Brit.

'Piper,' she introduces herself. 'New deckie.'

'Johannes. Good to meet you.' His accent gives the game away, even if his name hadn't already. He takes her hand in his, grips it firmly. 'How long have you been working on superyachts?'

'Er, this will be my first time.' No sense in pretending anything different.

'A greenie?' A frown ripples across his tanned forehead, his dark curls ruffled by the breeze. He is far too good-looking, and in an effort to stop herself from staring, Piper glances at the pristine teak decking, catching sight of his bare feet, as brown as the rest of him, clocking the neatly trimmed nails. It seems the owner likes all the crew, male or female, to be pedicured. '*Jesu Christos*. I told them to send me someone with experience.'

'I've been around boats all my life,' she assures him. 'Although much smaller sailing dinghies mostly.'

'It's not the same.'

She stands her ground. 'I'm a fast learner.'

'Well, there is no time to make changes.' He sighs and leads her down a series of narrow stairs until they reach the crew area, basically a table fixed around built-in seating, which is open to the galley. 'You're down here,' he says, indicating a door at the end of a narrow corridor on the starboard side. 'Last on the left.' These spaces are tiny, especially when compared to the sumptuous guest cabins, but she doesn't care; it's still exciting, if a little surreal, to be on board.

When Johannes opens the door and she sees the mess, her initial reaction is irritation. As someone for whom everything has a place – shipshape, if you like – the flotsam of bras, shorts, crumpled uniform shirts, half-empty tubes of sunscreen, hair straighteners and wadded make-up remover pads is an affront. 'Mm. Cosy.' Her lips twitch involuntarily.

'Uh yeah, I guess you get the top one. You'll be sharing with Ruby.'

He ducks out briefly, returning with a large carrier bag. 'Your uniform. Hopefully it fits. If not …' He shrugs. 'Bathroom's down the hall. I'll see you on deck in fifteen minutes. The family arrives tomorrow afternoon and there's so much still to be done. You'd think a brand-new boat wouldn't need much attention, but you'd be wrong.' He sounds cheerful enough about it though, whistling as he leaves. She is semi-reassured by his chill manner.

Piper places the few clothes she brought with her on the shelves of an empty locker – shorts, a handful of T-shirts in plain colours, slides, once-white trainers, a couple of going-out tops and tight skirts, a baseball cap, a faded pink hoodie with CREW printed across the front that used to be Lexie's, and a small toiletries bag.

She upends the carrier bag, shorts and polo tops spilling out. There's even a notepad and a pen – quite a nice one – with the name *Ambition* inscribed in a curlicue script. She's pulling a navy and white uniform polo shirt over her head when footsteps sound from the corridor. She hasn't bothered to close the cabin door and turns to see a figure in chef's whites.

'Hey.'

'Oh. Hi.' She tugs her top down, caught out.

'Liam. Head chef.' He's Scottish, with pale skin, a strong jaw, high cheekbones and a generous mouth. His energy is intense, but she meets his gaze without flinching.

'Piper. Deckhand.' Dressed now, she thrusts out her hand.

He takes it in his, gripping her fingers for a moment longer than necessary.

According to Lexie, yacht chefs are a law unto themselves, mavericks incapable of working as part of a brigade, spat out by the restaurants they trained in, talented but temperamental fuck-ups who work best alone. Alcoholics and/or coke addicts, too, most of them. She wonders what, if any, of this is true of Liam.

'Have we met?' He runs the hand that just touched hers through curls the colour of polished copper.

'I doubt it,' she says lightly.

He doesn't seem convinced by her denial.

She could tell him that maybe they saw each other at a port-side bar, or perhaps he spotted her on the beach where she's spent the past few days, but she doesn't. The less said, the fewer questions she'll have to answer. She plans to keep to herself as much as possible. Besides, attractive men can be the most dangerous – they're not used to hearing the word no.

He squints. 'I'm sure we have. I'd never forget a face like yours.'

'Is that your best line? You're going to have to try harder than that.' She pretends to be amused.

'You know, most people who come to work on yachts are running away from something.'

'Not me. I just love being on the water.'

Chapter Five

THE TROPHY WIFE

'Sorry, sorry!' Bursting through the glass doors, Rocco arrives at Teterboro's private jet lounge with minutes to spare, trailed by another young man of a similar age, his looks as brilliantly fair as Rocco's are dark. Both men are well groomed and casually well dressed, with the frisky energy of puppies. Evan, who has been on calls since they left the apartment, frowns slightly at his eldest son, and for a second Sandrine can't help but compare his greying temples, receding hairline and the cluster of lines fanning out from his eyes to the boys' smooth, elastic complexions.

When they first met, Sandrine, besotted, didn't give too much thought to their thirty-two-year age difference, but it is a reminder that she is married to an older man. The past couple of years have aged him, she sees with startling clarity.

'I know, I know … wheels up at six.' Rocco runs his fingers through a floppy fringe, dropping his bags at his feet. 'We met up at Socialista last night after dinner and I'm afraid we didn't get in until the sparrows were chirping, did we, Ju?' Rocco spent several years at boarding school in England and a hint of a well-modulated British accent slips past the American one every so often. 'So it's been a slow day. And the traffic out of the city … horrendous.' He rolls the *rr* in exaggeration.

Sandrine is fond of Rocco's best friend – he softens Rocco's entitled edges and she's grateful that another outsider is joining them. Despite being married to Evan, she still sometimes feels like an interloper when the rest of the family are around.

'There might have been tequila involved,' Julian admits, trying but failing to look shame-faced. 'I think my skull is wired together.'

The two boys lean in to offer Sandrine kisses with a continental flourish. Say what you like about them, they both have lovely manners.

Kitty puts her phone down for the first time since they picked her up from her mother's on the way to the airport. Rocco grins, flopping down next to his sister. 'Ready for your Hot Girl Summer?'

Kitty rolls her eyes.

Julian winks at her, but she takes a book from her bag – a collector's edition of Virginia Woolf's *To the Lighthouse* – and pretends to be absorbed in it. 'Hel-lo,' he says slowly, gaze tracking over her bare legs as she self-consciously crosses and uncrosses them, twisting one around the other. 'Someone's all grown up.'

Kitty flicks her attention away from the page. Sandrine can see that she's trying to be cool, but the rising tide of colour in her cheeks gives her away.

'Knock it off.' A faint frown mars Rocco's smooth forehead. 'That's my sister, buddy.'

'Hi.' Julian waves at Amber, sitting opposite, a sleeping Max cradled in her arms. She, too, blushes in response, lowering her head to the baby. Despite the noise of the two boys' arrival, Max doesn't stir. Sandrine is grateful that he is such an easy baby, though she is well aware that having a full-time, British-trained nanny probably helps. The young woman is a stickler for routine, and Sandrine has to admit that it appears to work.

Evan finishes his phone call and greets the new arrivals. 'About time.' He slaps a palm on Rocco's shoulder, then takes Julian's outstretched hand in a fierce grip. 'Pleased you're able to join us once again, young man. It's been a while, hasn't it? Three years since we were in the Caribbean?'

'Wouldn't miss it for the world, sir,' Julian replies, looking relieved when Evan releases the handshake. 'Schwab were happy to give me a few weeks off.'

Julian works for one of the big four brokerage firms, employed as much for his ability to charm the wealthy elderly as his skill in picking stocks and managing a portfolio. Rocco, on the other hand, is on year three – or is it four? – of a so-called 'gap year'.

'I think you'll both be impressed,' Evan says, warming to his subject. 'She's not the biggest, or the fastest: I'm not interested in a dick-measuring competition, but she's certainly a beauty.'

Sandrine suppresses a smile and doesn't call bullshit on this. Her husband is as obsessed with status as the next successful man.

'I respect that, sir.' Julian is really good at sucking up.

Evan continues to hold the floor as he lists the features, bow thrusters and engines, cruising speed and top speed. 'The range is phenomenal for a vessel of its size, and the engines are some of the quietest ever designed.' He's found a receptive audience in the two young men. 'And her lines …' He's about to continue when a staff member approaches and quietly informs them that they are free to board.

'What's happened to Mel and the munchkins?' Rocco asks. Sandrine finds the description bizarre – it makes Evan's eldest daughter and her family sound like a pop band for kids – but maybe something is getting lost in translation. Her English is good, but the nuance occasionally bypasses her, leaving her baffled. 'And the Prof?'

'They're coming a day later now,' Sandrine says. 'Angus sprained his ankle last night, so he's in doubt.'

Rocco smirks. He and Evan secretly refer to Melissa's husband as 'Accidental Angus', for he always seems to be injuring one part of himself or another. Last winter he broke his arm sledding with the kids right before President's Day weekend in Aspen, and in the spring he ruptured a hamstring playing tennis. Sandrine has also heard him referred to as 'Asshole Angus', but she can't remember who came up with that.

'It's a bad sprain apparently; he might have torn something. He tripped on the stairs in their apartment. According to Melissa, he's strapped up and in a boot and, in her words, "mad as hell".'

Melissa told Sandrine through gritted teeth on the phone the previous evening that her assistant has managed to get her and the kids on a flight to Palma via Barcelona the next day. Melissa sounded more annoyed by the fact that they were having to fly commercial than worried about Angus's injury.

Evan was also irritated, because it would mess with their sailing plans, but Sandrine was able to calm him down, saying they could all do with a day to get over the jet lag in any case.

Max wakes up the minute they're airborne, screaming his head off at the noise of the jet engines. Amber tries rocking and patting him, but he redoubles his efforts. Soon his little face is red and tears squeeze from a pair of swollen eyes. Evan has earphones in and is absorbed in something on his laptop. He's never done the day-to-day care, wouldn't dream of changing a diaper. 'I'll take him,' Sandrine tells Amber once the seatbelt lights have been turned off. 'Perhaps his ears – the change in air pressure?' She checks that the other three, who are in a group of seats across from her and Evan, aren't paying attention, then unbuttons her blouse, shielding herself with a scarf.

Evan shoots her a sideways glance but doesn't say anything. He isn't completely thrilled that she's still breastfeeding Max, but she's held firm on the topic, taking a small satisfaction in the fact that only she can do this for her child.

Max latches on with the force of a suction hose, his eyelids flutter shut and for a while the cabin is mercifully quiet.

binkiebear90: They were all living a lie, the whole lot of them.

Chapter Six

THE YOUNGEST DAUGHTER

Kitty is having trouble concentrating.

She places the book down on the table in front of her, marking the page with the silver bookmark that Sandrine and her dad gave her last Christmas. It's in the shape of a kingfisher and she would hate to lose it. Sandrine undoubtedly chose it, and it's typical of her – thoughtful, subtle and perfect. She almost wishes her father's new wife wasn't so nice. What's that phrase? Oh yeah, toxic positivity. Sandrine is always so damn encouraging, it makes Kitty want to gag.

She'd really like a reason to despise her, but she can't deny that Christmases and life in general have improved immeasurably since Sandrine became a part of the Thyssen family. She can't tell her mom that, though. Kitty makes a point of saying as little as possible about her dad's new wife, instinctively keeping the two halves of her family separate.

Her mom gave her a ring-bound notebook for this vacation with a pink cover and the words 'Be yourself, everyone else is taken' on the front. This tells you all you need to know about Claire, who Kitty both loves and finds completely *cringe*. But at least she lives in the real world, where people have to worry about making rent and how much the repairs on their vehicle are going to cost, unlike Sandrine and her dad, not to mention

Melissa and Rocco. The most troubling item on their agendas is probably whether they can get a table at Carbone that night. Her dad's wealth is obscene, though not something that her friends know anything about. She's grateful her mom changed both their names when her parents split, though sometimes she wishes Claire hadn't signed such a miserly prenup.

They're two hours into the journey from New York to Mallorca and the plane ride is becoming increasingly bumpy. Though she wouldn't dream of admitting it to anyone, Julian's proximity is making Kitty feel even more awkward than normal. She's hyper-conscious of the way she crosses her legs, how she responds to questions, the pitch of her laugh whenever someone says anything even slightly funny. Being self-conscious around other people, even family, is an affliction she can't seem to grow out of.

Their last big family yachting vacation was three years ago, one she can't forget. She would have bailed from this trip, but her mother insisted. She had better not be expected to share a cabin with Bailey and Carter. Much as she adores them, she needs her own space, and she hates being lumped in with the 'kids' when she's nearly fifteen. Plus, at their ages – eight and six – they're likely to wake up at dawn, when the one thing she is looking forward to is being able to sleep in.

She's in no man's land, stranded between the youngest members of the family and the fully-fledged adults. At least she packed plenty of books – if things are really dull, she can escape into another world entirely.

The irony of wanting to avoid a situation that most people would dream of – a glamorous floating palace with every whim catered to, sunny days, blue skies and crystal-clear waters – fails to occur to her, though if it did, she would remind herself to check her fucking privilege.

Given half a chance, she'd prefer to spend the steamy summer break in New York, roaming the city's air-conditioned art galleries or holed up in her room. Her skin never tans, excess makes her deeply uncomfortable, especially when she thinks about the carbon emissions (which isn't as often as it probably should be), and she doesn't especially like being around too many people.

Spending weeks on end with family 24/7 isn't going to be easy, but vacationing in a place where she'll be expected to strip down to a bathing suit on the regular will be nothing short of excruciating.

She reclines her seat and closes her eyes, but that only makes the turbulence feel even more alarming. Rocco had better not spend the whole trip teasing her. She's still burning with embarrassment at his comment about Hot Girls. Can't he see that she's a total *gorgon*?

If only she had an ounce of Melissa's ballsy spirit, or the innate, cool elegance of Sandrine, a woman who has probably never felt out of place for a single second of her life. Maybe it's a French thing, or a particular sheen that one acquires as an actress, or both? Kitty, with her broad swimmer's shoulders, over-large knees (who *has* those?) and general awkwardness, has little hope of ever resembling her impossibly chic stepmother.

She turns her head to stare out the window and tries not to be so painfully, *cellularly* aware of Julian only inches from her, his thigh so tantalisingly close to hers that she can feel the heat coming off it, the atoms in her body practically jostling each other in response to his particular magnetic charge.

The plane gives a sudden lurch sideways, rattling the fuselage, and with a gasp, Kitty grabs the closest thing to her, recoiling when she realises that it is Julian's forearm. She can feel the heat rising in her chest as her eyes meet Sandrine's across the passageway. Sandrine gives her an amused smile and Kitty lets go of Julian's arm as if she's burned herself on his muscular, tanned skin. 'Sorry,' she murmurs.

'It's only a little turbulence,' he replies. 'Don't stress.' Then he leans in and whispers, 'You can hold on to me anytime if it makes you feel better.'

Kitty blushes furiously. She hates that she likes him – he is the epitome of rotten privilege – but she can't help herself.

Rocco, sitting opposite Julian, looks up from his phone. 'Everything okay, Puss?'

She nods and is saved from further scrutiny by the arrival of a plate of smoked salmon and cucumber sandwiches. 'A late snack before we turn down the lights for the rest of the flight,' the uniformed steward says.

'Remember these, Roc?' she comments, lighting up as a bottle of lemon soda is placed in front of her. They've served these cute little bottles on Dad's plane for as long as she can remember. She takes a sip and the bubbles fizz in her nostrils like sherbet. She decides she will allow herself one triangle of sandwich. Some food might help to settle her nervous stomach.

'You're such a traditionalist.' He says it like it's a bad thing and a little of her pleasure deflates.

'Nothing wrong with that,' Julian says.

Honestly, if she wasn't such a stupendous dork, she could kiss him in gratitude. Instead, she can only wrap her lips around the straw and shoot a defiant look at her brother. She tries not to think about kissing Julian, unimaginable as such a thing is. She's never kissed a boy, not like that, with tongues and everything. The thought is thrilling, but also faintly revolting. She sneaks a sideways look at Julian to find that he's still grinning at her, and an unfamiliar bolt of pleasure rockets through her, making her shift in her seat.

Maybe this vacation will be more promising than she dared dream: perhaps it will be *her* summer. How cool would it be to have something to tell her friends when school goes back in the fall, something to show off in addition to a few more freckles and a summary of the books she's read?

Gah! She's an idiot. Julian's seven years older than her and she's always been the annoying kid sister, a pet that he throws an occasional bone to but who otherwise probably never enters his thoughts. He's almost certainly got a girlfriend, someone totally cool and undoubtedly beautiful.

The thought depresses her and she puts the bottle of *limonata* down and picks up a sandwich. She extracts a piece of the salmon filling and lets the delicate, smoky flavour flood her mouth.

Chapter Seven

THE PATRIARCH

Evan Thyssen is trying to ignore the bouncing of the Gulfstream G700 as it is buffeted by winds somewhere over the Atlantic Ocean, but it is causing him to mistype the figures in the spreadsheet he's amending. 'Goddammit!' He grabs the slim silver laptop before it slides onto the floor. No matter how he parses it, the figures are worse than ever. He's often said that working in real estate development is like walking a tightrope across Niagara during a hurricane, but it's never felt more so than right now.

He's also trying to ignore the sharp pain in his chest. He's had it on and off for the past few weeks, but nothing showed up at his last physical, though he was warned to ease off the steak, butter and red wine and get more vegetables into his diet. His physician also suggested that although Evan handles stress better than the average Joe (he's never considered himself the average Joe), he might want to think about strategies to lower his adrenal response. Trouble is, Evan's never been able to sit still long enough to succeed at meditation (one of the few things he's failed at), and he's not the type to get into yoga or Pilates, no matter how much Sandrine might sing their praises. His idea of switching off, when he finally puts his phone down

– usually around midnight – is two fingers of an eighteen-year-old Macallan, straight up.

On the upside, his blood pressure is just the right side of normal, and he's far from obese, so there's nothing much to worry about, right? Not even a little chest pain, which was most likely caused by the spicy shrimp he ate for lunch.

He's been pushing hard for the past month as delays have piled on top of delays. The loans are becoming increasingly tricky to service, and his relationship with his bankers is on shaky ground. For their last meeting, they suggested convening in their offices, instead of coming to him as they usually did, a sure sign that the balance of power has shifted. He's been up against it before, but never as precariously as this. Even Sandrine has noticed his preoccupation, and he snapped at her more than once in the lead-up to this trip. He hates losing control, never mind letting anyone else see the swamp of doubt and uncertainty under the bullish facade he presents to the world.

Nothing, however, is going to take away from the anticipation of finally getting to see, touch and experience his expensive new toy. He feels like a kid on Christmas Eve, can't wait to watch her put through her paces. If he hadn't been needed in New York he would have been there the minute she arrived at the dock in Palma. *Ambition* was sailed by a skeleton crew from the shipyard in Germany, and the boat should be well sea-tested, any niggles ironed out by the time she got to the Balearics.

Ambition is the result of years of dreaming and countless hours of back-and-forth with Jonssen, the sombre, exacting Norwegian designer whose work he's always admired. Together they have achieved a vessel of elegance and beauty, equipped with the latest maritime technology. The waste heat recovery system and hybrid-electric propulsion mean it's one of the most environmentally efficient boats on the water, and it has a shallow draft, meaning it can access many of the smaller ports and anchorages that other boats of a similar size cannot. Importantly, *Ambition* will tell the world he's someone to take notice of, someone who has *arrived*.

He has every confidence in *Ambition*'s captain, having poached the experienced (not to mention damn attractive) sailor six months earlier. He'd had his eye on her since Sonny Verstoffen made the mistake of lending him his boat for a week in the Caribbean late last year. Evan is unapologetically avaricious, and everyone has their price.

It's important to have everyone together this summer in celebration of all that he's achieved.

He is annoyed that Melissa couldn't make the trip with them from the start. It's typical of that over-educated English husband of hers to go and injure himself the day before one of the most important family vacations they've had in years. Evan's chest gives another painful twinge and he stretches, thinking it might be a muscle cramp. She'd better not be any later than the day behind schedule she's promised, with or without the professor. He needs her forensic attention to detail to fine-tune the submission for the new multi-million-dollar, one-million-square-foot hotel, casino, residential and entertainment complex they're planning on the far west side of the city. It's the biggest deal in the company's history, and comes with the greatest risk.

There's no doubt in his mind that Melissa will devote at least several hours a day to business during this vacation, even if her kids are with her. She's a workhorse; he's always been able to rely on her.

He glances around the cabin. Kitty is gazing out of the window, while Rocco and Julian are laugh-snorting over something on a screen they are swapping between them. Sandrine is looking for something in her purse, her brows knitted together in concentration, a stray lock of hair falling across her face. He fails to catch her eye. Ever since Max was born, he's sensed an absence, as though some part of her is not entirely with him.

Max is fast asleep in a bassinet next to his nanny, dark curls peeking out from under the blankets. Evan is not afraid to admit that he has his favourites among his offspring, and Max coming relatively late in his life, at a time when he thought he was long past the little kid stage, has proved to be a delight. Plus, he doesn't answer back, though that won't be the case for too much longer.

He glances back to his wife again. He's given her everything she ever wanted – a beautiful baby, homes around the world, a glamorous, exciting life … so why does he increasingly sense her dissatisfaction?

darkmother: She had to know what was really going on – no one's that blind or ignorant. They were *married* for godssake.

helpmeRhonda: Evan Thyssen is a bully, and Thyssen Properties is one of the dodgiest developers in Manhattan. Everyone in the industry knows it.

Chapter Eight

THE DECKIE

When Piper returns to the swim platform, transformed by her uniform (which is only a little roomy) into a bona fide crew member, Johannes hands her a bean-shaped metal disc no bigger than an earring. 'This might be a little different from those you've used before. It should fit into your ear, but if you need another size, just let me know. We've got a selection. Walker loves his tech.'

She fits the metal device into her ear and finds it surprisingly comfortable, as if it's not even there.

'They're hyper-sensitive,' he continues, 'and you never know who's listening in, so be careful what you say. Make sure you charge it when you're on a break, and try not to lose it – you'll absolutely piss Walker off if that happens.'

'Copy that.'

'The beach towels should be somewhere.' He points to the dim recesses of the storage area. 'Just keep opening boxes. Shake them out, roll them up tight and put them in this locker here.' He gestures to a wall of cupboards behind him. 'In an ideal world we would run them through the laundry, but …' He shrugs, passing her a Stanley knife, the blade glinting in the sunlight. 'Too much to do here.'

'On it,' she says, taking the knife from him and stepping past a pair of shiny new jet skis.

She finds the towels on her third attempt and is soon sweating in the heat, wrestling with yards of plastic wrapping.

'Hey, Pip.'

'Yeah?' She's taken aback by the familiarity – she hadn't told him to call her that, had she? – but chooses not to comment on it.

Johannes peers into the windowless storage room. 'You coming? We've been summoned to the main salon. All-crew meeting.'

She hasn't heard anything through her earpiece and it's only as she's hurrying along behind Johannes that she wonders if she's forgotten to turn it on.

The main salon is filled almost to capacity with more than twenty crew, nearly all young, all good-looking: healthy, fit, tanned, the men clean-shaven, the women's mostly long hair tied back in perky ponytails. She spots the captain, identifiable by the stripes on her uniform and her overarching air of authority. Next to her are the officer of the watch, the purser, first officer and chief engineer. Everyone else either sits on chairs or the floor. The crew-to-guest ratio is mind-boggling – there must be more than two crew for every expected guest. Superyachts are probably one of the few places on Earth where this is not considered ridiculous (at least not by the people who own them).

'For those of you I've yet to meet, I'm Captain Christine Bird – Captain Chrissie to the crew – and ultimately, the buck stops with me.' Her accent is American, her hair a streaky silver crop and her skin deeply tanned. The deep lines radiating from her blue-green eyes speak to a life spent squinting at a horizon. Piper gets the unmistakeable feeling that the captain has a ton of experience and a razor-sharp bullshit detector. She clears her throat. 'First things first: I cannot stress highly enough that we take safety for all on board – family *and* crew – extremely seriously.'

Piper read somewhere that working on yachts is more dangerous than working on an oil rig. There was a news story last year about a young English bosun who went missing from a tender at night. After a perfunctory search, the captain simply scattered a few flowers on the water and handed the bosun's belongings to the local police. The complicated registration and ownership of the yacht in question made it almost impossible to find out what really happened to the deceased man.

Only slightly less alarming is reading about young women (and some men too) who experience sexual harassment, both from other crew or owners and their guests. When they complain, they are simply replaced. And then there are the back-to-back shifts, long hours, impossible demands and cramped working and living conditions … Sure, the money is good, and it might appear to an outsider to be a glamorous job, but the reality is far from it. Yet still, young people flock to the Med in search of adventure, excitement and stories they might one day keep from their children, possibly even their spouses. Piper, however, is here for rather more complicated reasons.

The captain hands over to Johannes, who explains the protocols in the event of an emergency, reminding them about the man-overboard procedure and what to do if the warning sirens go off, where to gather, the chain of command.

When he's finished, everyone gets to their feet and the meeting breaks up.

'Piper?' The captain at least is well informed. 'Welcome aboard.' Her handshake is bone-crushing.

'Thank you, Captain. I'm looking forward to my time here.'

'Work hard, get on with your crewmates, don't draw attention to yourself and you'll do just fine.' She flashes a brief smile.

'Absolutely.'

The captain turns to another crew member and Piper is dismissed.

She can sense Liam's eyes on her from across the room but pretends not to notice.

As the crew disperses, she trails Johannes to the swim deck, returning to the monotonous but strangely soothing task of rolling and stacking towels. An hour or so later, the sun is directly overhead, turning the storage area into a furnace, and Piper has to wipe stinging sweat out of her eyes every few minutes. She empties another box, stows the towels and uses the knife to break the box down flat. When she's finished, she wedges the knife under a pile of towels so it won't get lost and steps out into the sunshine with an armful of cardboard. She's overheated and parched, and the water glints in invitation. She would like nothing more than to strip off her damp shirt and dive in, dark oily water be damned.

Johannes nods at her, indicating that she should take the cardboard to the dock. 'Then have a break,' he says. Piper doesn't need to be told twice.

The temperature drops as she goes inside; it's so cold from the air conditioning that goosebumps form on her arms and her polo shirt soon feels clammy. Still, she's not about to complain about being out of the midday heat.

The crew mess, adjacent to the galley, has seating for ten with a banquette along one wall, but there are only a couple of people there when Piper arrives. A tray of unidentifiable meat – pulled pork or beef perhaps – a couple of salads, a plate of wraps and a number of hot-sauce bottles are strewn across the table.

'Help yourself,' says Tamara, pausing between bites of a wrap that's spilling its contents onto the plate beneath it.

'Thanks.' Piper takes a plate and a wrap and piles on meat, lettuce, avocado and a squeeze of chilli sauce before folding it into a neat-ish parcel. 'Is there anything to drink?'

Tamara waves towards the galley. 'First fridge. Soda, or water.'

Liam is at the far end of a work bench, head bent over an enormous fish, a filleting knife flashing in his right hand as he deftly separates flesh from bone. He glances up as she approaches the fridge but soon returns to his task.

When Piper returns to the mess area, there's another girl sitting next to Tamara. 'Hi,' she says, taking a seat opposite them.

'Ruby – Piper, Piper – Ruby,' Tamara says, introducing them. 'You guys are roomies. You're both English, right?'

Piper nods and grunts indecipherably, her mouth too full of water to reply properly.

'Nice to meet you, Piper.' Ruby is pretty (it's an unspoken but very necessary requirement of the job) and tanned, with caramel-streaked hair, a tip-tilted nose and an expression of curiosity in her wide-set eyes. 'Whereabouts?'

'Whereabouts what?'

'Whereabouts in England are you from?' Ruby asks.

'Oh, right. Southampton.' Piper swallows the falsehood along with a bite of her wrap. She's starving – breakfast was an apple, pinched from the bowl on the hostel's reception desk. She senses Liam across the galley, listening to their conversation, and it makes her self-conscious.

'Cool. I'm from Brighton.' There is spinach between Ruby's teeth. 'Not too far away. You worked in yachting for long?'

Piper shakes her head but doesn't offer any further information, taking another bite of her wrap instead.

'This is my third year. I love it, as long as I'm not always stuck in the laundry.' Ruby grimaces. 'You'll get the hang of it all in no time. Just remember what they say ...'

'What's that?'

'Don't screw the crew!' She dissolves into giggles.

'Pity you didn't remember that on our last boat,' Tamara says, smirking.

Piper smiles weakly. Getting involved with anyone on board is the last thing on her mind.

Ruby flips over her phone on the table in front of her, wiping a smear of mayonnaise from the screen. 'What's your number?'

'I'm sorry?'

'So I can add you to the crew WhatsApp group, silly.' She leans towards Piper, adding in a low voice, 'Well, the stews' and deckies' chat. The chefs have their own.' She frowns. 'I think.'

Piper reels off a newly memorised string of numbers and Ruby types it in.

'Thanks.' Piper opens her mouth to ask another question, but Tamara shushes them both, putting her hand to her ear.

'Copy that,' Tamara says good-naturedly. 'On my way.' She gathers up her plate and water bottle and hurries out of the mess area.

Has Piper still not worked out the earpiece? Or is it that the yacht's comms system can also be directed to a specific person? She pulls the bean out of her ear and checks it. There is a tiny light shining from it, so all seems okay. She wolfs down the rest of her lunch while Ruby fills her in on all things Walker. 'He's been with the family for years.' She tells Piper that she's worked for the Thyssens before, on a yacht that they chartered. 'I was pretty green then, and I've been on a few different yachts since, but I was asked to come to work on *Ambition*, which was flattering really. Mr Thyssen likes familiar people around him. Such a shame about Penny – she was a fun chick. We worked together on our last yacht – I was the one who recommended her for this job. You're one of only a handful of new crew on board, I think, apart from Haruki. He's a dedicated sushi *itamae*, a brilliant chef. Apparently, Mrs Thyssen has a thing for Japanese food, so Mr Thyssen poached him from one of the top restaurants in New York. If we're lucky there might be leftovers.'

But Piper's got much more on her mind than leftover sushi.

Chapter Nine

THE DETECTIVE

Sub-inspector Luis Perez of Mallorca's Policía Nacional is at his desk, in the brutalist concrete building that houses the Balearic headquarters, when the call comes in. He likes to get to work early and is the only one around to answer the insistent ringing.

Dressed in a tight black shirt and even tighter pants (he doesn't spend all those hours at the gym for nothing), he has a five o'clock shadow that starts to appear at noon, a hairline he refuses to believe is receding, and hawkish, deep-set eyes that fasten on details others miss.

He's out of sorts this morning because his mother called just after dawn (like him, she is an inveterate early riser), complaining that he never visits, that his father's health is worsening, that if he's not careful Papa will be cold in the ground and Luis will be sorry he hasn't come home sooner. Also, why hasn't he brought his girlfriend to meet them yet, is he ashamed of them? Emotional blackmail at 6 am. She's a master at it. He regrets telling them about Estrella, especially since he called time on the relationship a week after he moved to Palma. Before ending the call, his mother extracted a promise from him to visit as soon as he gets more than two days off. Which won't be until at least the end of September. The feeling that he's somehow failing, that he's not a good son, is hard to shake.

Luis was drafted to Mallorca from the mainland six weeks ago to cover the busy summer season. Last year there were well-publicised protests against mass tourism, residents angry that there weren't the resources to cope with so many visitors, and there's a chance the simmering tension between locals and tourists could erupt again at any time.

So far, he's dealt with a few cases of drink spiking, a couple of bar fights and reports of organised gangs of pickpockets. Not exactly what he got into policing for. The Balearics might have the highest crime rate in all of Spain, but it's generally minor stuff. Small-time theft, traffic infringements, drug possession, amateur break-ins and so on are dealt with by the Policía Local. Palma is, on all counts, far safer than a handful of other Spanish cities.

On the other hand, the scenery is nice, and he's discovered a sweet coastal running route that starts and ends at a cafe that sells the best espresso in Palma. It's run by an Australian. Who knew they could make such great coffee?

Last week, however, the body of a young woman washed up on a beach a few kilometres from the capital, and so far, efforts to identify her have failed. Luis and his colleagues have been working with the water police division to find out if anyone saw anything out of the ordinary, but with thousands of tourists swarming the island over summer, it's going to take a while.

Now the person on the end of the line – male, gabbling in broken Spanish, agitated – wants to report the discovery of a body while he was beach fishing. 'Washed up at the high tide line. A woman.'

'Where did you say this is?' he asks, scribbling the unfamiliar name on a notepad. His breath comes a little faster, adrenaline spiking as he takes down the details. 'Are you there now? Good. Stay there and someone will be with you shortly.'

Chapter Ten

THE DECKIE

Two black Mercedes SUVs approach the dock, their windows tinted so dark that they give no clue as to who is inside. Not that it matters; everyone on board knows who it is. The crew has been on alert since they received word that the plane touched down forty minutes earlier.

'Family arriving, everyone to their positions.'

Piper jumps: Walker's voice is loud in her ear. It's as though he's standing right beside her. She has straightened her ponytail, reapplied deodorant and washed her face in an effort to make herself presentable. Only the captain and Walker are required to welcome the family, but she's ready to help Johannes and the other deckies deal with the luggage.

She couldn't help it: as soon as she heard that the family were on their way, her breathing quickened, as if she'd sprinted up the dock herself. Her palms are clammy, whether from the squeegee she's been using to clean the windows or from anticipation, she can't tell. She fixes her gaze out to the horizon, using the hazy blue line between ocean and sky to steady herself. *They're just like everyone else*, she tells herself, knowing it's a lie.

'Hey, put that away before the family sees you.' Johannes comes to where Piper is standing, paused in the act of window-cleaning, staring at the dock. She nods and goes to the locker, hurrying to put the squeegee away. When she returns, the group is approaching.

Piper mentally counts heads. Seven of them in total; five fewer than she was led to expect, according to the information Walker gave out.

The men are wearing shorts, leather belts, polo shirts, boat shoes, dark glasses and ball caps, a Hamptons/Hyannis Port uniform favoured by a certain strata of New Yorkers on vacation. She's seen variations of it all over a number of Insta and TikTok accounts.

She immediately spots Evan Thyssen, two steps in front of everyone else, phone jammed against his left ear. He is basketballer tall, solidly built, with a heavy-set jaw. She reminds herself of one of her father's oft-used expressions: *A cat may look at a king.*

Sandrine Thyssen, even from this distance, is every inch the glamorous movie star in a pale linen suit, her face shielded by an enormous floppy straw hat, an Hermès Kelly bag tucked in the crook of her elbow. A couple of years ago, Piper spent one lost weekend when it was too stormy to sail immersed in a movie marathon: *Ne M'oublie Pas*, *Diabolique* and *Mer d'Etoiles*, all starring the then Sandrine Furneaux. Piper's boyfriend at the time had a thing for sexy French actresses. Seeing Sandrine now, in the flesh, is perhaps even more disconcerting than clapping eyes on Evan Thyssen.

Behind Sandrine comes a trio of younger people: two male, one female.

The girl, long-limbed and broad-shouldered, must be Kitty. Piper hasn't seen a recent photo of her – her socials are locked down tight, and even the photo on the crib sheet doesn't really look like her. At this distance she appears older than fourteen, with her bug-eyed, blue-lensed sunglasses perched on her distinctively hawkish Thyssen nose and an oversized water bottle dangling from one hand. She's dressed in the kind of anonymous clothes – loose jeans that hang low on her hip bones and a shrunken T-shirt showing several inches of midriff – that don't look expensive but undoubtedly are.

It's a moment before Piper recognises the first male. Her throat closes over, making it nearly impossible to swallow. Evan's son Rocco is much like his father, although slimmer, rangy and loose as an athlete. Long before Piper knew she had the job, she scoured his social media, finding a feed full of rich frat-boy antics involving copious amounts of alcohol, the flexing of various muscles (biceps and pecs mostly) and the presence of mainly blonde girls wearing very few clothes but always oversized, opaque sunglasses, rendering them both unreadable and almost interchangeable.

The second male is familiar from Rocco's socials. He's grown into his nose and his Adam's apple is less pronounced, his chest broader and his hair better cut, but it's definitely him: Rocco's best friend, Julian. He was with the family on their annual ski trip to Aspen last winter, and also on the family's last yacht vacation, three years earlier.

She forces herself to take slow breaths, in and out, as she studies the two young men.

They are as preppy as the Ralph Lauren interior, Rocco in black and khaki with tan deck shoes, Julian in a pair of raspberry-coloured twill shorts and a Madras check short-sleeved shirt. It fascinates her how some people manage to effortlessly assimilate into their surroundings, how they manage to look like they *belong*.

'As soon as they're on board, we'll go and get the bags,' Johannes says, interrupting Piper's thoughts. She turns away from the dock, but not before she's seen the final members of the party – a young woman wearing an unattractive beige uniform that must be stifling in this heat and pushing a baby in a stroller, an oversized tote bag over one shoulder. There's not much of the infant on view, save for a wayward curl of dark hair and a flash of cheek and button nose as they draw level, but she's certain it is Max, Evan and Sandrine's baby son, and the woman is almost certainly the nanny. Piper hopes for her sake that she isn't forced to wear that uniform for the entire holiday, though she wouldn't be surprised if she was.

Two other deckies join Piper and Johannes and they all stand aside as the group sweeps up the *passerelle* and disappears into the yacht's chilled interior.

Close up, the family is, without exception, glossy, in a way that only lots of money – bespoke, exclusive, organic everything – can achieve. They also radiate astonishingly good health and exquisite dental work, which they flash in the deckies' direction as they pass, although their attention skates right over the crew, Piper included. Instead, they are taking in the new yacht amid murmurings of delight. At least they're not so jaded that they aren't impressed.

Piper reminds herself that to them the crew aren't individuals, they're interchangeable, replaceable minions, living, breathing robots there to clean and polish and squeegee, to serve drinks and clear plates and plump cushions, to anticipate the family's every need, all with a smile on their attractive but forgettable faces.

A few minutes later, a van pulls up at the end of the dock and the driver begins to unload the luggage. Piper can't believe so few people could bring so much – it looks as though there's enough for a rugby team on a three-month tour. It takes four of them several trips to get everything on board and Piper is soon sweating with the effort. The suitcases are without a single scuff or scratch, so pristine that she wouldn't be surprised if this was their first outing.

Piper has already memorised the occupants of each guest cabin, not to mention the yacht's layout, but she follows Tamara obediently, pretending to listen as she tells them who is staying where.

'Mr Thyssen's eldest daughter and her family are arriving tomorrow,' Tamara explains as they pass their cabins.

That's why there weren't as many guests in the party as she had been expecting.

'They will join the boat by tender,' Johannes adds.

'Copy that,' Piper replies, grunting as she deposits the last of the bags into the cabins. She's fit and strong for her size, but this is more heavy lifting than she's done in a while. She'd better be able to haul the lines when it's time to depart. It's becoming increasingly clear that there's a world of difference between handling tiny racing yachts that skate over the water like insects and this behemoth.

She goes to leave and catches sight of Tamara's worried face. 'Everything okay?'

'I don't know how we're going to get this all unpacked in time.'

'Need a hand?' It's not strictly Piper's job, but she can't resist the opportunity.

Tamara nods gratefully and Piper goes into the owner's suite and opens the largest of the suitcases. Actually, it's more a steamer trunk than a suitcase, with reinforced battens and brass clips. Anyone would think this was the *Titanic*, she laughs to herself, then sobers up, remembering how that went down. Literally.

As she unwraps slithery silk from layers of tissue paper, eases thin-strapped sandals from their shoe bags, unrolls jewellery pouches (gawping at the rings and necklaces casually tucked within them) and re-folds cotton T-shirts still with their tags attached, she can't help but wonder how it must feel to own so many beautiful things, let alone never having to worry about paying a bill or whether you can afford to buy groceries that week.

Johannes's voice sounds in her ear. 'Piper? Where the hell are you? We're about to depart the dock.'

Chapter Eleven

THE TROPHY WIFE

It's a relief to escape the searing heat of the Mallorcan sun and enter the air-conditioned interior. Sandrine is curious to see the full effects of the designer's work. Evan oversaw much of the process; she was either trying to get pregnant or was pregnant and nauseous when most of the decisions were made. Besides, she more than had her hands full with the remodelling of their weekender on Long Island, a former seventeenth-century English barn they'd had shipped over from England.

Walker, Evan's obsequious major-domo, greets them as two crew members offer iced towels, bottled water and champagne – Laurent Perrier Rosé, her favourite. She accepts a glass.

Walker takes them on a tour, using an iPad to demonstrate the functions of the various spaces throughout the interior. 'Each of you has one of these in your cabins,' he says. 'You can use them to communicate with myself or any other member of the crew, as well as to change the lighting, music and so on. There's also one in each of the main rooms, the salon and the gym, with your own personal one-touch fingerprint-enabled login, so we'll always know who requires what and where you are.'

The interiors are impressive. The main salon is light and airy, with panoramic floor-to-ceiling windows, and the furnishings cleverly combine traditional, antique and contemporary elements. Sandrine is relieved to find that it is understated and luxurious. As she spies the bar area, set slightly apart from the main salon, fitted out with a dark wood counter, a foxed mirror backdrop, art deco crystal chandeliers, forest-green tiles and leather stools, she almost laughs aloud. The designers have modelled it on one of Evan's favourite places, the J-Bar at Aspen's Hotel Jerome. It's slightly incongruous in this setting but he seems delighted by it, running a proprietary finger along the length of glossy maple burl.

Walker ushers them into the gym and spa area, which is kitted out with two weights racks, a pair of Peloton bikes and a Pilates reformer bed. 'There is a personal trainer and a bodywork-slash-beauty therapist on call 24/7.'

They pass an infrared sauna and a secluded open-air massage station, where gentle music plays from hidden speakers. When they reach the sun deck, a vast cushioned area that surrounds a circular swimming pool, Julian and Rocco fling themselves down. 'We'll check out the rest of the boat by ourselves,' Julian says, closing his eyes. 'I'm exhausted.'

A look of annoyance flits across Evan's face, but he simply nods while Walker produces a bottle of sunscreen and places it at Julian's side. Sandrine keeps her expression neutral. Kitty has also slipped away; Sandrine would bet that she stayed behind in the library, keen to check out the contents. No doubt the designer was briefed on everyone's reading habits, such is the attention to detail.

'Do you have a preferred time for lunch?' Walker asks.

Evan glances at Sandrine, raising an enquiring eyebrow.

'In half an hour, perhaps?' she suggests, her low voice carrying effortlessly over the thunks from below as deckhands corral the luggage and bring it on board.

'Hear that, boys?' Evan says. 'One-thirty sharp.'

'Sure, Dad,' Rocco replies.

They continue the tour, arriving eventually at the owner's suite and Sandrine sees the excitement grow on Evan's face. 'You go in first,' he says.

A gasp escapes her when she sees it. There, above an enormous bed, which is made up with soft linen and a fluffy down comforter, is a painting of a young woman in a broad-brimmed hat, standing in a field of flowers. 'Jean-Pierre Cassigneul,' she breathes, taking it in, feeling the emotion behind the blurred lines. It's a drop in the ocean compared to the value of the artworks that grace their homes in New York and the Hamptons, not to mention Thyssen's corporate offices, but the fact that Evan went to the trouble to find this is touching.

'You like it, huh?' he asks, nuzzling her neck.

'*J'adore*,' she whispers huskily. 'How did you know?'

'Remember on our honeymoon in Paris? We went to the gallery … where was it? Somewhere in the Marais? You told me then that looking at his work turned your heart inside out. That the women he painted seem so melancholy, as if their life was waiting for them somewhere else.'

Sandrine blinks. 'I said that?' It's an uncanny echo of her current situation.

When they met, she was charmed by Evan's solicitous attention, boundless energy and incisive mind, not to mention the fact that he was, even for an older man, pretty sensational *dans la chambre*. She was also overcome by the desire for a baby, fearful that her ovaries were withering, and considered herself far too conventional to contemplate going it alone.

However, after four years together, the rose-tinted glasses are clearer and she sometimes wonders if she made a pact with the devil (as well as having signed a water-tight prenup that will give her practically nothing if she leaves him within ten years). Evan is now so caught up in the minutiae of his business that she feels relegated to an afterthought, and with every year that passes, the use-by date on her acting career races ever closer, if indeed it hasn't already arrived.

'Well?' Evan is looking at her expectantly.

Surprising her with this painting is proof that he does pay attention, and she is flooded with remorse. She has been self-absorbed and ungrateful. 'You are so thoughtful. I love it, and you.' She kisses him full on the lips, almost managing to convince herself that last part is still true.

texanforeveryoung89: I never thought Sandrine Furneaux was especially talented, or as beautiful as everyone said she was, but to get herself mixed up in THAT family. She didn't deserve everything that happened to her.

Chapter Twelve

THE DECKIE

The thrum of the engines rises up from the deck, vibrating through the soles of Piper's bare feet, as though a sleeping beast has been awakened. She is waiting, as instructed, to haul in the bow line as they prepare to leave the dock. She wipes her palms on her shorts, knees slightly flexed, muscles tensed. She's hauled in lines hundreds of times before, but she doesn't want to screw this up.

She waves a fly from her face and attempts to refocus. The shout from the dock takes her by surprise and she looks up just in time to see the heavy rope being released. Instinctively reaching forward, she fumbles, painfully twisting her middle finger, but manages to hold on and begins hauling in the line, leaning backwards as she braces herself against the weight of it. There's more shouting as the remaining lines are brought on board and then the power of the engine increases, the sound rising to a low-timbred rumble and the water beneath churning white.

She finishes the job, curling the rope neatly on the dock, and stands as the Palma marina disappears in their wake, the yachts still at anchor becoming ever smaller.

As always, the sight of the receding shoreline sets something loose in her, a release from land-locked cares, a sense of freedom and possibility.

Anything can happen at sea.

'Pip! Get yourself down to the galley and help the stews run plates to the table for lunch.' Johannes's voice crackles in her ear. 'Oh, and nicely done, by the way.'

'Copy that.' She's passed the first test.

The galley is almost obscured by steam as Liam and another chef battle with a malfunctioning dishwasher. 'Service!' he barks when Piper arrives. 'Get those plates out of here now, before they're ruined.' An array of shallow bowls on the long bench are filled with a bright green chilled soup. Another chef is bent over them, using tweezers to place tiny, delicate white flowers on the surface with focused precision. He points to the ones that are ready to go – 'Away!' – and Piper takes this as her cue to lift one in each hand. The surface of the soup trembles. She's no waitress and is grateful that the yacht is ploughing smoothly through the water, with little movement reaching them on this level.

'No spilling!' Liam yells.

She reaches the upper deck without incident, although she's questioning the design decision to place the galley so far from the dining area. She steadies herself. Serving at the table will bring her in close proximity to the family. Beads of sweat collect on her upper lip, but she hasn't a free hand to wipe them away. Tamara glances back at her, brows knitting together when she registers that Piper has stopped. 'Remember, the women first, then the men,' she hisses.

Piper nods and they both step forward.

The hum of chatter doesn't pause for a second as they place the soup bowls in front of the women. Piper's hand gives only the briefest of tremors as she deposits her bowl in front of Sandrine. She is so close that she can smell the woman's perfume, even the shampoo she must have used that morning. It feels unnervingly intimate to be just inches away from someone she's only ever seen on a screen until today. Sandrine's skin isn't quite as flawless in the unforgiving sunlight, but if she's had cosmetic surgery, it's so subtle as to be barely noticeable – just a slight fullness in the lips, a smoother forehead than one might expect.

Ruby and another stew follow close behind, serving the remaining guests. Ruby bumps into Piper, causing her to stumble. 'Oh my god, sorry!' she whispers.

Piper swallows the automatic impulse to protest, keeping her eyes lowered and her thoughts to herself. Tamara gives them both a signal to stand to one side. No one, save for Kitty, who tilts her head at the disturbance, pays them the slightest attention.

Piper overhears snatches of conversation. 'The Jonsons are here?' … 'Why don't you tell them that we can see them when we're next in port? Where is it we're heading to first? Soller? Or Porto Christo?' … 'They're such a bore, do we really have to?'

She surreptitiously studies each of them in turn, greedy for details. Sandrine is carefully spooning her soup, though she hasn't touched the bread that's within arm's reach.

'I thought the point of coming to Mallorca was to get away from everyone we know in New York,' Sandrine says in an undertone.

'Too late, I already said we'd love to see them,' Evan replies.

Piper watches as Kitty self-consciously flips her hair over her shoulders. Julian is angled towards Sandrine and is attempting to engage her in conversation.

'Why would you do that, Dad?' Rocco asks, tearing at a piece of bread and scattering crumbs everywhere. 'The Jonsons only want to come and check out the boat so they can boast to all their friends about having been on board.'

Evan's eyes flick constantly towards his phone, which lies face-down next to his fork. He's going for seconds of bread, soaking a piece in a dish of deep green olive oil. His advanced age is glaringly obvious in the harsh light. Oil drips onto his chin.

There's no sign of the baby, or the nanny, not that Piper would have expected her to be seated with the family.

Evan's phone vibrates with a notification and Piper can see his hand twitch in response, but after a look from Sandrine, he ignores it, reaching for more bread instead.

When most of the soup has been consumed, Piper, Ruby and the other stews, who have been standing by at a discreet distance, step forward to clear the plates before returning a minute or so later with platters of cold seafood: lobster tails, giant prawns, pale grey oysters and translucent slices of smoked salmon.

'We've got the rest of this, thanks,' Tamara whispers to Piper as they set down the last of the platters.

'No problem,' she murmurs, turning to leave. She would have liked more opportunity to listen in on the conversation but reminds herself that as long as she keeps her eyes and ears open she'll pick up a lot.

Chapter Thirteen

THE SURVIVOR

The next time she wakes, there's a light shining in her eyes, one of those pencil beams that doctors use to check your pupils. It blinds her to everything else. She flinches as it flicks from one eye to the other, and a murmur comes from somewhere above. She smells peppermints.

A whoosh of air, a door opening.

'Any change?'

The voice is husky, with an accent she can't place. She pretends she's still unconscious, though her reaction to the light has probably given her away.

'No.'

'When do you expect—'

'It's anyone's guess. But I'd say it will be some time before she's ready to talk. Her injuries, the swelling of the brain …'

A sigh that's somewhere between frustration and resignation.

'My concern is for the wellbeing of my patient. Everything else will have to wait. Has anyone else …?'

'Most of the other survivors aren't in as bad shape as she is. But no one can tell us much. They were all taken by complete surprise. They say they had no warning at all. She's lucky to be alive.'

'Even the captain?'

'She has given a statement.'

'And the owner? Any sign?'

There is a pause. She strains to hear, but whatever information the pair of them might share, it is communicated silently.

'You do not have to stay. It could be hours, days even. Someone will contact you the minute she wakes, I assure you.' The voice is firm.

She hears the clink of metal and the beeping sound is turned down. Then, footsteps, the door squeaking on its hinges, and she supposes they've left the room. The door shuts with a bang that startles her.

She wiggles her toes experimentally, makes the slightest curl of her fingers. Even that hurts. She opens her eyes a crack and things come into focus. Dim lights, the vague outline of a window, shades drawn. Something blinking orange on a square box to her left. She's up high, in an unfamiliar bed. The mattress crackles at the slightest movement. She blinks and a dark shape in the corner moves.

She freezes. She had thought she was alone.

'Hello there.'

Chapter Fourteen

THE YOUNGEST DAUGHTER

Kitty pushes a couple of enormous shrimp (a contradiction in terms that makes her smile) around on her plate, eventually burying them under a mound of salad. She calculates that she's eaten two shrimp, a cherry tomato, three slices of cucumber, four chunks of avocado (good fats are okay, right?) and about half a cup of shredded romaine. She doesn't want to draw attention to herself by asking if there is dressing on the salad, so she adds fifty calories to her daily tally in case there is.

If she can sneak away and spend forty-five minutes on the treadmill later, she'll be able to eat some steak (roughly the size of her palm) with a big serving of green veggies at dinner. Kitty knows all about eating disorders and she *definitely* does not have one, but it's important to keep track of what you eat.

Sometimes she wonders what it would be like not to think about food all the time, what space might be freed up in her mind for other, more useful thoughts. Sometimes she could almost scream with the pressure to be perfect.

'Pass the bread will you, sis?' Rocco motions towards the basket across the table. Kitty can't remember the last time she ate bread. She claims gluten gives her a stomach ache, but that's mainly to stop her mom forcing doughnuts on her. Giving up pizza was one of the hardest things she's ever done, but goddamn, she's proud of herself for sticking to it for nearly a year now.

'Not hungry, Kitty-Kat?' Julian asks, spearing another shrimp from the plate on the table.

Oh god. Why did he have to notice?

'I'm good,' she says, blushing furiously. 'Being on the water makes me a little queasy, at least to start with. I'm sure I'll be fine by tomorrow.'

'Uh-huh,' he says, spearing another fat shrimp and dipping it in a rose-tinted mayo that must contain at least fifty calories per teaspoon. 'You don't know what you're missing. This sauce is everything. Try it.' He holds his fork out to her and she has no choice but to take it.

'Mm. Not bad,' she admits, mentally adding another ten minutes to her treadmill schedule. She's rewarded with a grin of such frank approval from him that it's almost worth it.

When everyone's finished, Sandrine says she's going to rest, and Evan says he has a few calls to make. *What's new?* Kitty thinks. She's planning to retrieve her book from her cabin, but Rocco insists they go up to the sundeck. 'Come on, Kit.' His expression is so genuine that she finds herself agreeing. It's not until they get up to leave, Julian saying they'll go and change into swim shorts, that she realises she will also be expected to put on a bathing suit.

As she rises, excusing herself, she considers her options. Unlike Rocco, who has a generous allowance from their father, Kitty's mom insists on banking most of the monthly support payment she receives, saving it for Kitty's college fund. Kitty suspects her dad will pay her tuition fees and living expenses when she does eventually go to college, but there's no point in debating this with her mom.

She brought last year's bathing suit, which has worn dangerously thin in the butt and barely covers her now, and a new forest-green halter-neck that her mom picked up in a Neiman's sale, which she hasn't even tried on yet.

She knows she'll never hear the end of it if she doesn't join Rocco and Julian, so when she reaches her cabin, she shimmies out of her clothes and pulls out the green bathing suit. She holds it up dubiously: there's so little fabric she's surprised it passed her mom's strict eye. Taking off her underwear, she steps one leg in and then the other, sucking in her stomach as she pulls the one-piece up her legs and onto her body, before casting around for a full-length mirror.

Dammit. She can't believe whoever fitted out *Ambition* forgot to install a mirror in the cabins. The one that turns into a TV screen is set so high as to be worse than useless. She opens a wardrobe door in case there is one on the back of it. Nope. She adjusts the elastic under her arms and then pulls down what she can to cover her behind. She has no idea what she looks like, which is terrifying, but also strangely liberating.

At the last minute, she throws on an oversized T-shirt and winds her hair into a topknot. Grabbing her book and a pair of sunglasses, she leaves her discarded clothes on the cabin floor and takes the stairs to the sundeck two at a time.

When she gets there Rocco and Julian are splashing each other, soaking the deck and laughing. They barely seem to notice her arrival. She spies a cluster of sun loungers, each with a rolled towel placed on the end, and sidles around the edge of the pool towards them. Suntan lotion and an ice bucket filled with water bottles sit nearby. A stewardess materialises as if from thin air and Rocco and Julian each call for a beer.

'Nothing for me, thanks,' Kitty says, self-consciously dropping her book on one of the loungers.

'Come and join us,' Julian says and she feels herself go hot all over.

'Give me a minute.' She manages to sound almost normal. Grabbing a bottle of Ambre Solaire, she sprays it on her arms and legs, and then smears some lotion from a smaller bottle specifically for the face onto her cheeks and forehead. It's scorching in the sun, even hotter with Julian's attention focused on her.

She is saved from further scrutiny by the arrival of the drinks and seizes the chance to strip off her T-shirt and slide into the opposite end of the pool, away from the boys. She sinks below the surface until the water reaches her neck. It's deliciously cool and worth the potential embarrassment of being seen in her bathing suit. She glances down: her newly acquired breasts are in danger of spilling out, thanks to the extra buoyancy provided by the water. She makes a quick adjustment and then leans back against the pool's edge in what she hopes is a nonchalant manner, giving herself a crick neck. She's sure she's already as red as a beet.

Rocco and Julian ignore her, gossiping about a mutual friend of theirs who is spending the summer doing an internship at a law firm in the city. 'Who would do that,' Rocco asks, sounding incredulous, 'when you could be in the Med?'

'On Daddy's yacht,' Julian finishes and they go off into deep-voiced guffaws, amused by their schoolboy humour.

'It's the Balearics, actually,' Kitty says, sotto voce.

'The what?' Julian asks.

God, don't they even know where they are?

Julian slips a fraction in her estimation. She repeats herself.

'You know what I meant,' Rocco retorts, annoyed with her for showing him up. 'It's still the Med, smartass.'

Kitty ducks under the water in an attempt to cool her boiling face and avoid Rocco's glare. When she surfaces, blinking, they are both staring at her. 'What?'

'Er ...' Julian points to her front. 'You're flashing the nip, darling.'

'What?' She looks down to see that her bathing suit has slipped, revealing one entire breast. 'Oh god! Oh Jesus!'

Rocco sniggers. 'It's okay, Kitty-Kat, don't sweat it. But you might want to readjust ...'

She is a flaming ball of embarrassment as she hauls up the sodden fabric, turning her back on the two boys. 'Sorry. Sorry. Sorry!' Heat builds behind her eyes and her throat is so thick she can hardly get the words out.

'It's only a boob, Kit.' Rocco dissolves into mocking laughter. 'And it's not like there's much to see anyway.'

In utter mortification, she climbs out of the pool and stumbles towards the lounger, grabbing a towel to cover herself.

Julian effortlessly swings himself out of the pool and comes to sit next to her.

'Go away!' she cries.

But he grabs her wrist and forces her to look at him. 'It's okay, sweetheart. I'm sorry we laughed, and I'm sorry for your dumbass brother. There are worse things to happen at sea, now aren't there? Half of Europe sunbathes topless anyhow.' She smiles despite herself and the shame eases a little. Perhaps she was getting upset over nothing. Someone more sophisticated than her would have laughed it off. She studies the tanned skin of Julian's muscled arm, wishing she might memorise every freckle and mole. A line of poetry comes to her, and she thinks of the beauty of dappled things ... of pied beauty. And once again, she finds herself completely tongue-tied.

Chapter Fifteen

THE DECKIE

Piper hoses down the windows at midships on the starboard side before drying them off with a chammy, polishing until they are streak-free. Her arms ache with the effort. In addition to the acres of glass, there are also miles of marine-grade stainless steel that need attention. It's late afternoon but still baking hot, though a slight northerly breeze has picked up, taking the edge off the temperature.

As far as she can tell, only the younger members of the party, Rocco, Julian and Kitty, are on deck above her, cooling off in the pool. She can hear the occasional shriek and splash over the thump of the music they've put on.

They dropped the anchor about an hour ago, having cruised the short distance southwest of Palma to Portals Vells, a pretty little horseshoe-shaped cove.

There is a handful of people at the shoreline, colourful umbrellas and sun loungers dotting the beach, behind which lies a heavily forested hinterland. The sea beneath the yacht is a mesmerising crystalline turquoise, so clear that Piper can see the sandy bottom as she peers over the railing. She'd kill to jump in the water right now but unfortunately that's not an option.

Johannes and a couple of the other deckhands have gone to get out the jet skis for the younger members of the group.

Mr and Mrs Thyssen and the nanny are nowhere to be seen; Piper presumes they are taking a siesta after their long journey. Not all three together, obviously, although with people like this you never knew.

She wipes the sweat from her forehead with the back of her arm and squints up at the sparkling glass. Johannes said she could take a couple of hours' break when this was done, and the temptation to go to her bunk and crash is strong, but she wants to explore. Returning the squeegee and chammy to the cleaning stores at the yacht's stern, she walks at a quick clip along the port side. It always helps to look as though you know where you're going.

Pausing halfway down the external stairs to the lower deck, she peeks into the interior dining room where Evan, Captain Bird and Walker are huddled over a large sheet of paper spread out on the vast table, their heads so close they are almost touching. The window is open, but they don't appear to notice her. They are plotting the course, discussing the best places to call in at over the next few days.

'The forecast is good, so my recommendation would be to head west and then continue on north,' says Captain Bird. 'We'll make a complete circumnavigation of the island, then head to Menorca and on to Ibiza, as requested.'

Evan nods. 'She's performing well?' he asks.

'A few minor issues, but nothing we can't handle,' the captain reassures him.

'I didn't get the chance to say so earlier' – Evan turns to Walker now – 'but you've done a wonderful job. Truly. You've thought of everything.' Piper spots an ice bucket and some champagne flutes nearby. 'I knew I could trust you to get it done right.'

Walker inclines his head and a satisfied expression crosses his normally impassive features. 'Thank you, sir. Always a pleasure.' He lifts the bottle from the ice bucket and expertly uncorks it with the gentlest of pops. He pours a glass for Evan, then offers one to the captain, who shakes her head. He takes it himself instead. 'To *Ambition*!' he says, raising the glass in Evan's direction.

'To *Ambition*!' Evan repeats.

They knock back their champagne with such enthusiasm that Piper almost expects Walker to bang his hands on the table as they finish their glasses. Clearly, the zero tolerance for alcohol among the crew doesn't extend to Walker.

Instead, he refills their empty glasses and they resume studying the chart.

'I'd perhaps suggest a day at the Blue Cave,' says Walker, pointing to a spot on the chart. 'I can arrange for a dive boat to meet us there. Your open water licence is still current, I checked.'

Evan nods. 'Rocco and Julian will want to do that, I'm sure.'

'Of course.'

Diving? Surely not? She's desperate to keep eavesdropping, but Ruby appears below, pushing a small trolley stacked with linen and towels, so Piper hurries down the remaining stairs.

She wants to get to know every inch of this boat. She's on the lowest deck now, and when she is almost at the engine room, she spots an anonymous door.

It's exactly where she expected it to be. Named after Lazarus, the lazarette can be as small as a locker or, as is the case on a yacht of this size, as large as a cabin. Fun fact: its original purpose was to store the dead bodies of notable passengers or crew who might have died on a voyage, so they could be returned to their loved ones for burial. Less-important corpses were thrown over the side. On large-rigged sailing ships, the lazarette was often situated at the stern in order to minimise the smell of decomposing bodies. The tradition to include such a space remains, and although it is mainly used now for storing equipment or garbage, the name has stuck.

'Hey, what are you doing?'

She freezes, turning around slowly.

It's Liam, regarding her with a hostile expression.

'Sorry, I got lost.' Dammit, it would have been more convincing to have said that Johannes sent her down there. Too late now.

'What were you hoping to find?'

'Er, my bunk?' Putting on a ditzy act is the only way to handle this. 'I've obviously got no sense of direction.' She waves her hands in a comic pantomime.

'Turn around and head to the port side.' He's not flirty with her now.

'Copy that.' With no other option, she does as he suggests.

She finds her cabin easily and flops down on her bunk. As her eyes close, her blood seems to pulse through her skin.

She's on the brink of sleep when it occurs to her. Engineers are usually the only crew required in that part of the vessel. So what was the chef doing there?

Chapter Sixteen

THE SURVIVOR

The reek of aftershave wafts towards her. She sneezes, and pain ricochets through her body at the sudden movement. She can no longer pretend she's asleep.

Her heart flutters, a moth in a jar.

'*Señora.*' He drags a chair over to the bed, scraping it across the floor with a screech that goes right through her. 'My name is Luis Perez. I am a sub-inspector of the Policía Nacional and I am based here, in Palma.' He speaks softly, less an interrogation, more a caress. 'Blink if you can hear me.'

Almost without thinking, her eyelids flutter.

'Do you know where you are?'

She doesn't move.

'You are lucky to be alive.'

She blinks once more and gets an impression of dark hair, liquid eyes that have a hint of sympathy in them, strong eyebrows, clear skin. A crisp shirt, open at the neck, the sleeves carefully rolled to reveal muscular forearms. Young. Fit. Handsome.

Her throat is still raw, swollen from the sea water, and she tries but fails to swallow, making a gulping noise that sounds as if she's about to vomit.

The officer's eyes widen and he casts around for a bowl, a sick bag, something to contain what might be about to spew from her mouth.

'I'm not so sure about that,' she eventually croaks.

'What do you remember?' he asks, offering her a cup with a paper straw in it.

She gives her head a tiny shake, refuses the drink. 'What do you mean?'

'What's the last thing you can remember?'

Her head pounds and flashes of a scene come back to her. It's a while before she replies. 'A party, I think. There was music playing, someone on the decks, outside. People dancing. It was a hot night. We were on the water.' She pauses, exhausted with the effort of talking, remembering. 'Where am I now?'

'Very good.' He seems pleased, but doesn't answer her question. 'Do you recall who else was there?'

She shakes her head. She has a vague sense of being surrounded by people, but no individuals stand out.

'Please. It's important.' He leans towards her, elbows propped on his knees, the hair on his arms grazing the white plastic of the chair in a way that makes her think of curlicue doodles. He's attractive, in a machismo kind of way. He breathes out slowly, as if considering his words. 'Let's start from the beginning: can you tell me your name?'

Chapter Seventeen

THE TROPHY WIFE

Sandrine goes to the dressing room and idly begins pulling open the shallow drawers in front of her. Their luggage has already been unpacked and neatly folded. She's still not used to having someone do such personal tasks for her, and tries not to think about a stranger's hands touching her most intimate apparel.

She could take a jet ski, zip over to the beach she can see through the stateroom window and enjoy the feeling of sand between her toes, salt water on her bare skin ... but she'd be doing it alone. Evan made it clear he would be occupied for the rest of the afternoon.

She rolls her shoulders, stiff after the long flight. Maybe she could get a massage? Didn't Walker say there was a qualified therapist on board? She need only press a button on the iPad and someone would be waiting with strong hands and warm oil.

Paralysed by indecision, she goes to the bed and flops onto the plush comforter. She lets out a tiny sigh as millions of goose feathers cushion her body.

Should she go and see if Max has woken from his nap? He's in a cabin with Amber, who has perhaps taken advantage of a little time to relax herself. No, Sandrine decides, better not to disturb them. It's probably a good thing that Max isn't walking yet. He is crawling, finally, but shows no signs of hauling himself up on the furniture to balance precariously on his chunky legs.

Amber, lovely, sensible Amber, has allayed some of her concerns, telling her that by the time Max is eighteen, no one will be able to tell whether he walked early or late, talked early or late. But she's glad that he's relatively contained; curious toddlers and boats are not a good mix.

Restless, she rises from the bed, goes to one of the closets and selects a navy and white bikini, covering it up with a gauzy kaftan that at least veils the softened flesh of her stomach.

A lounger in the shade with a margarita for company is what she needs, she decides. She normally disapproves of day drinking, but they're on vacation, so it doesn't count, right? Perhaps she can persuade Evan to go for a spin on the jet skis later. They're both demons for speed.

They met at a charity drive day at a racetrack in upstate New York. She had been invited along by a friend who worked for one of the sponsors. After being given instructions from professional drivers in the morning, there was a race. Sandrine's hand shot up when they asked for participants, and Evan's hand went up at the same time. She caught his eye, and he raised his eyebrows in a clear challenge. She didn't look away.

They were to complete ten laps of the three-and-a-half-mile track, driving vintage Porsches. The fastest lap time and fastest overall time won a small trophy, but bragging rights were what they were really competing for.

Sandrine watched as the first few drivers took their turn, her nerves jangling. She began to wonder whether she should perhaps gracefully back out, but then she caught sight of Evan and changed her mind. There was something about the way he'd looked at her earlier that made her want to at least try to beat him, to show him that she wasn't to be underestimated, not by anyone.

She'd been confident enough in the practice laps, but now (with her instructor by her side) her knuckles were white, her foot hovering over the accelerator.

Afterwards, she could hardly recall the course, how she made the turns, though she will always remember the gasp from the instructor as she took the first bend a fraction too fast, the car's rear end fishtailing behind them, almost losing traction entirely.

The moment she crossed the finish line, she knew she'd driven practically out of her skin, but had no idea if it would be enough. At the very least, she hoped she hadn't embarrassed herself.

Evan was the first to congratulate her as she walked to the viewing area, unsteady as a baby giraffe, thanks to the adrenaline surging through her veins. 'You smoked it,' he said, handing her a glass of champagne.

She remembers shrugging, pretending nonchalance, though inside she was weak with relief.

'And not a hair out of place,' said Johnny, the friend who invited her.

Evan won the fastest lap time, a blistering full second ahead of the rest of the field, but it was Sandrine who took out the best overall time.

Of course, that was all in the past – Evan discourages her from driving now. 'Not in the city, honey. There's a reason you have a driver at your disposal.'

It's been a long time since she felt as proud of herself as she had that day.

carracoeur: Mistakes were made, big mistakes. No doubt about it. There will be an enquiry into the incident and then the truth will come out, mark my words.

Chapter Eighteen

THE DECKIE

'Pip, there are streaks on the windows on the starboard side,' Johannes calls to her. 'Can you go over them again?'

'Of course,' she says, irritated. She wants to correct him on her name, but she's already done so twice and he's taken absolutely no notice.

It's her favourite time of day. Dawn, with a lingering, wispy sea mist. The air is cool, creamy-soft against her skin, and the water is as still and clear as a millpond. The air smells fresh, salty, and she inhales deeply, closing her eyes for a second.

Paradise, heaven, nirvana. Bliss, if only she didn't have to work.

At this hour, the beach is a clean stretch of golden sand, but soon it will become scattered with a confetti of coloured towels and umbrellas. A handful of other boats have anchored at Portals Vells overnight, but *Ambition* overshadows them, an obscene Goliath dominating the landscape.

A lick of breeze raises goosebumps on her arms. There are certain places where bad things seem more likely to happen: an isolated house teetering on the edge of a cliff, a snowy chalet at the top of a mountain, a tumbledown cabin in the woods, a desolate moorland, a lonely highway, a cellar, a tunnel ... but a brand-new, shiny superyacht in the middle of a crystal-blue ocean? Hardly.

Who is she kidding? Bad shit can happen anywhere, even in the most idyllic places, places that might seem like paradise but for some are closer to hell. She should know.

As if reading her thoughts, a fish explodes from the water, its scales flashing, quicksilver in the light. Something larger is chasing it.

Without realising, she has stopped cleaning, the squeegee suspended in mid-air.

'Here. Let me show you.' Johannes has reappeared. He takes hold of her wrist and directs her arm in a sweeping motion, demonstrating the technique.

Piper grits her teeth. Johannes is a perfectionist, but she will put up with it. For now, anyway. Her arms already feel like they might drop off. At this rate, she'll be cleaning windows in her dreams. It's her third day on board, but so far she's only had one opportunity to explore the vessel. Every other minute of her time has been spoken for: helping to load and re-house the jet skis, ferrying stacks of wet towels to the laundry and running plates to and from the table.

'Let me see.' He stands back, hands on hips as she wipes off the squeegee before making long, even strokes across the glass.

Really, is it necessary for him to micromanage her? He doesn't seem to be doing it to any of the other deckies, nor does he seem to feel the need to touch them as he demonstrates.

'Right,' he says, finally satisfied with her progress. 'Carry on.'

A voice in her earpiece lets the crew know that the final guests have landed at Palma Airport and will be driven to rendezvous with the yacht at Portals Vells. Captain Bird asks Johannes to be ready to collect them by tender, reminding him to take two junior life jackets.

It must be Melissa, Evan's eldest daughter. Married. Two children. VP Marketing and Strategy for Thyssen Properties. The photos Piper's seen show that Melissa has the same strong jawline and wide brow as her father, the profiles she's read tell of a hard-working businesswoman keen to take over the business one day, with the phrases 'tough as nails' and 'chip off the old block' appearing more than once.

Melissa runs marathons in her spare time. For charity. Of course she does. She's not one of those women who relies solely on her youth and beauty to get by in the world. She does at least *contribute*, Piper reminds herself, though it doesn't make her a good person. Far from it.

The captain confirms that there will be three to pick up. 'Repeat. Three passengers. Mrs Silk and the two children.'

According to the information on the document Walker gave her, Melissa was to be accompanied by her husband and nanny as well as her children. Piper wonders what's changed.

* * *

Half an hour later, a black limo pulls up in front of the beach. There are a few tourists sunning themselves on loungers and kids splashing in the shallows now, and a small crowd has gathered to check out the tender that Johannes and another deckie have taken to pick them up. Piper isn't surprised: it's a beautiful timber-hulled speedboat modelled on the classic Italian Riva Aquarama design, complete with a jaunty flag fluttering from the stern.

A trio of tiny stick figures emerge from the limo and the tall one, most likely Melissa, shields her eyes, gazing out to sea. Piper watches as Johannes waves to them from where the tender wallows in knee-deep water.

Another deckie heads towards them and they wade out to the tender, pant legs rolled. Johannes helps them aboard, lifting the children clear of the water. The limo driver and the deckie have the unenviable task of transferring their suitcases and cabin bags, a process that takes strength and skilful manoeuvring.

Eventually, they set off and a short minute or two later, the tender approaches the swim platform where Piper stands ready to help them. 'Welcome to *Ambition*.'

Melissa Silk is wearing a grey airline T-shirt that's at least three sizes too big. Her hair is scraped off her face and her make-up, if she was wearing any, has long since rubbed off. Her skin, aside from the purple rings under her eyes, is the colour of cottage cheese. 'God, I can't believe he spent *millions* on this boat and didn't think it worth bothering with a helipad,' she gripes. There's no softness in her expression. She must resent having to arrive so dishevelled and travel-worn, looking, quite frankly, like shit. In the unforgiving morning light she barely resembles the polished person from her corporate headshots.

Beside her, sitting on the wide back seat of the tender, are two children with sandy hair and gap-toothed grins. They're as energetic as their mother is tired, squirming in their seats until Melissa reprimands them, warning that they are in danger of falling in if they don't sit still and wait their turn.

'Come on there, buddy, let's get you aboard,' Piper says to the boy, extending an arm. 'Grab my forearm and I'll take yours – it's the strongest grip.'

He does as she asks and soon Piper has both children on the transom, reminding them to keep their life jackets on until they're inside.

'But we're both good swimmers,' the girl complains. 'Don't treat us like babies. Mom?'

Melissa is either too distracted or can't be bothered to get into an argument. She hands the kids an iced washcloth from the tray that Piper offers, then takes two for herself, using one on her face and draping the other across the back of her neck. 'Where's my dad?' she asks.

Evan hasn't come to the platform to greet Melissa.

'I believe Mr and Mrs Thyssen are having breakfast on the main deck,' Johannes replies.

'Shall I show you up?' Piper asks, remembering at the last minute that they are not to use 'ma'am' when addressing the female guests.

'No. Take me to my cabin. I need to clean up first.' The smile that accompanies her words is brittle and Piper is surprised to see a flash of something else, anguish or perhaps simply exhaustion. She looks as though she has the weight of the world on her shoulders, not like someone about to start a no-expense-spared European vacation on Daddy's new superyacht. Piper couldn't care less.

'And the children?'

'I'm hungry, Mom,' the boy says, hanging off Melissa's arm.

'Why don't I send them up to see their grandfather?' Johannes suggests. 'Do you like pancakes? The chef makes the best ones – with honeycomb butter.' He widens his eyes and grins at them, a natural with kids.

The boy is sold, but the girl seems suspicious. 'Honeycomb?' she asks, her little nose wrinkling. 'I hope there aren't bees on board. That would be really dumb.'

'No, no, of course not!' Johannes takes her seriously. 'There is nothing that can sting you on this boat, I promise.'

'My cabin?' Melissa asks, impatient now.

'Of course, come this way. Your luggage should already be there,' Piper says, having seen one of the other deckies hustle the suitcases up the stairs ahead of them.

Piper leads Melissa towards the second-largest cabin. It's at the bow, which can mean it's subject to more movement in rough weather, unlike the main cabin, which is amidships. As with everything, there's a hierarchy.

'Here you are. The children are just next door,' Piper says, indicating the door beyond. 'May I arrange for anything to be sent in for you?'

'Coffee.' Melissa correctly assumes that all crew on board will be apprised of how she takes it.

'Right away.'

Melissa enters the stateroom without a backward glance.

Chapter Nineteen

THE ELDEST DAUGHTER

'Horrible place to be, huh?' Fortified by caffeine, a scalding shower and clean, resort-appropriate clothes (white shorts and a pistachio-coloured polo), Melissa greets her father in the fake-jocular way that he responds to best. Besides, he can't stand compliments from her, even when they're genuine. He says it makes him feel as though she's patronising him.

'*Bonjour* Melissa,' Sandrine says, lifting her gaze. 'So happy you made it.'

Melissa air-kisses Sandrine dutifully. She smiles more warmly at Max, who is secured in a highchair and mashing a banana in his fat little fists, his cheeks red with the effort. 'Growing so fast!' she says. It feels weird to think of this cherubic toddler as her half-brother, so she doesn't, preferring to consider him a nephew or much younger cousin.

'Good of you to join us.' Her father is joking, but she can hear the implied criticism.

'Better late than never, Dad.' Melissa peers over her sunglasses at a plate of cut fruit that has been arranged as a rainbow. Without having to be asked, one of the stews places a cup of black coffee by her side. Steam lifts lazily from the surface.

The trip had been hell: a commercial flight, Carter's iPad ran out of juice, Bailey got motion sickness, and when Melissa finally found time to go over the financials for the Rawson Project, the numbers simply didn't add up. She was forced to go back to the beginning, not letting up until the plane was about to land. She still hasn't figured it out.

When Melissa was in the delivery suite, about to give birth to Carter, she reached a point where she didn't think she could do it. She dug her nails into Angus's wrist and wailed that she simply couldn't go on any longer. She remembers him trying not to flinch at the pain, but then he fixed her with a stern gaze. 'This baby is coming tonight and you are the only one who can get him here. You don't have a choice. You *have* to keep going.'

It occurs to her that her entire life is pretty much like that these days.

She runs her fingers through her hair, regretting that she hadn't had time to get to her stylist before she left, conscious of the rapidly appearing silver threads sprinkling her parting. She is not used to being anything other than immaculate. It's bad enough that Sandrine is so effortlessly chic that Melissa always feels ungainly by comparison, a carthorse in the presence of a racehorse.

Carter is sitting next to Evan, his chair pulled in close. Both he and Bailey adore their grandfather, who is playful with them in a way Melissa doesn't remember him ever being with her or Rocco.

'Mom, these pancakes are the best,' says Bailey, who has a ring of sticky syrup around her mouth. 'How come we can't have them like this at home?' Bailey loves to push; it's the thing Melissa most loves and also finds most frustrating about her daughter.

'Are they that good?' she asks, picking up a fork. 'I'd better try some then.'

'No!!!' Bailey shrieks as Melissa pretends to swoop. The little girl doesn't like to share.

'What a *terrible* shame Angus couldn't come. Is he going to be able to join us at all?' Sandrine asks, dabbing a napkin to her perfectly made-up lips.

'I very much doubt it,' says Melissa, pretending regret. 'It's a pretty nasty injury.' *One he definitely deserves*, she thinks with more than a smidge of satisfaction.

'Poor Daddy,' says Bailey through a mouthful of food. 'He loves pancakes.'

Melissa shoots her daughter a look. 'No talking with your mouth full, remember, sweetie?' She takes a sip of coffee. 'Interesting typography,' she muses, not realising for a second that she's spoken out loud. The boat's name is inscribed in skinny curlicues across the bow, as well as embroidered on the linen napkins and towels. It's hideous: it could be the sign for a bad nightclub. Somebody's misguided idea of sophistication. She'd never let something so vulgar adorn the company's marketing collateral.

'Sandrine likes it,' Evan says. He leans back in his chair and stretches his arms over his head, showing a strip of belly beneath his aqua linen shirt.

'Well, the name is fitting.'

'I thought you'd approve.'

The children have finished their breakfast and are beginning to fidget. Melissa whips her head around to see that Carter has climbed up on the lounge cushions and is teetering precariously over the edge. Before she has a chance to rise from her seat, a quick-thinking deckhand grabs the boy by the waist and hauls him back to safety.

'Oh my god, Carter, you know better than to climb up there. What did we talk about?' She's annoyed that her son is already in trouble, though she secretly loves his adventurous spirit, doubtless partly the source of her grey hairs.

'Settle down,' Evan says. 'There are plenty of people watching out for him.'

Melissa bites back a response.

The deckhand, a pretty blonde girl, hands Carter back to her.

'Hey kids, do you wanna go for a ride on the jet skis after breakfast?' Evan asks, oblivious to her concern.

Bailey and Carter look as though he's just offered them the keys to the kingdom, their mouths forming perfect circles of delight.

'They'll need to ride with someone,' Melissa says. 'They're not old enough to go by themselves.'

'Two of the crew can take them out,' Evan reassures her. 'You and I have something urgent to discuss.'

She should be surprised, but she's not. Like her, Evan almost never switches off. His idea of a vacation is to start work an hour later and for cocktails to be served at six instead of seven.

'You're not going to give me even a morning off?' she asks, doing her best to keep her tone light. 'My brain thinks it's still the middle of the night.' If he wasn't her father and it wasn't the family business, one that she plans to head up one day, she would have walked a long time ago.

Evan is saved from replying by the arrival of Rocco and Julian. The two young men greet Melissa with polite kisses and the children with fist bumps and finger waggles. Rocco is wearing a loose T-shirt and pale pink striped linen pants.

'Are those your pyjamas, Uncle Roc?' Bailey asks, gazing at him in awe.

'You look like a gay man on vacation in Mykonos,' Melissa says drily.

'That's what I told him,' Julian says, smiling to show he's in on the joke.

'*Un petit peu* homophobic,' Sandrine mutters under her breath.

'Did I hear you want to go play on the jet skis?' Rocco asks the children, ignoring everyone else.

Bailey and Carter nod with puppyish enthusiasm. They idolise their uncle.

Melissa experiences a brief disquiet. Rocco has a cavalier approach when it comes to safety. 'No monkey business,' she warns.

'What, from us, or these two?' Rocco asks, winking at his sister.

'And make sure they apply plenty of sunscreen. We don't want to ruin their vacation before it's even begun. Where's Kitty?' Melissa asks, as it occurs to her that she hasn't seen her half-sister yet.

'Probably still asleep,' Evan says, checking his watch, a vintage titanium Breitling that he bought himself after his first major real estate deal. Melissa's heard the story of how he single-handedly proved his father wrong and pulled off the 'acquisition of the decade', shortly after the Twin Towers fell, more times than she cares to count. 'The captain would like to be away by eleven,' he says, 'so we can get to our lunchtime stop when the tide is right.'

'Eat up then, kids.' Rocco winks, reaching across to grab a pancake from the stack on the table, folding it in half and shoving it whole into his mouth.

Only Melissa notices the flicker of disapproval cross Sandrine's face.

* * *

After breakfast – she forgoes the pancakes and picks at an egg white and asparagus omelette instead, mainlining another cup of coffee – Melissa goes in search of her father.

The door to his study is closed so she knocks, entering only after hearing his barked command to do so. At the far end, two oversized upholstered tub chairs face a large glass window. Her father is seated in one, and she walks over and takes the other.

He gets straight to the point. 'I need you to keep on top of the Rawson Project. The acquisitions team has submitted their report. I emailed the info to you last night. Have you had a chance to review it?'

'I got it.' Melissa nods. 'In fact, I have a few questions—'

'I don't need to tell you how important it is that this happens without delay. I want you to oversee this, as well as finesse the plan for taking it to market. We need to be able to press the launch button the minute the approval comes through.' He doesn't have to add that he wants her to come to him with solutions, not problems – that's a given.

The Rawson Project is one part of a real estate development near Hudson Yards that they are involved in. Thyssen Properties is a multi-million-dollar company, but this deal could take them far beyond that, possibly even make them the biggest privately owned player in the business. If – and that's a very big if – the numbers stack up.

'Anything specific I should be aware of?' she asks, sighing inwardly. Between work and the kids, she is likely to get almost no break this trip. For the first time, she wishes Angus was here, if only to take the kids off her hands.

She stops herself. Takes a breath. Jesus. How can she be thinking this? Bailey and Carter deserve better than a mother who is continually distracted and too busy to hang out with them. She signed up for this, but they have no choice in the matter. She almost envies Sandrine, whose gilded, easy life she's always been dismissive of.

God knows, Angus would love a trad wife, someone waiting with a warm smile and a cold cocktail when he returned from a hard day giving seminars and grading papers. But then he does love the money she brings in; there's no way they could afford anything approaching their New York lifestyle on his professor's salary alone. Could she ever live that life: a suburban wife and mom who bakes and cleans and cooks with a permanently delighted expression on her face? Not in a million years. She might bitch about the workload, but the reality is she thrives on it.

'Everything you need is in the email,' her father says, swinging his chair towards the window.

There's never a question – on his part or hers – that she won't do it, that she might push back, that there are half a dozen just as qualified execs at Thyssen who could shepherd this through, even for a week, so that she might have some time for herself, with her children. No, she is expected to absorb it without complaint. *Pile it on*, she thinks. *Pile that shit on me. One day I'll be the one calling the shots.*

She feels suddenly shivery, a cold sweat breaking out over her. Her ears are still blocked from the flight. Is she coming down with something? She hasn't time to get sick. With a lump in her throat, she goes to stand, but Evan swings the chair back around again, as if something has only just occurred to him.

'Tell me again why Angus can't be here?'

She repeats what she has already told Sandrine. 'A bad sprain. He'll be fine, but the doctors want to see him next week, plus he needs to start physical therapy right away. It wasn't practical for him to travel. He's devastated to be missing all this.' She pastes on the appropriate downcast but stoic expression, pulling in the corners of her mouth.

'I'm sure he is.' Evan sounds far from convinced.

mamacita**: I feel sorry for the poor children. Who's going to help them now?

porkysrevenge: I don't feel sorry for the kids at all. They're probably better off after all this.

Chapter Twenty

THE DETECTIVE

The traffic on the motorway heading towards Andratx is heavy – a combination of increasing tourism and the start of the morning rush – but Luis turns on his lights and the cars ahead scramble to get out of his way, clearing a path. He's at the scene less than forty minutes later, parking on a bluff overlooking the sea. Below, a small knot of people has gathered and he can see a dark shape on the sand a few metres beyond them.

He scrambles down the path, torn between wanting to hurry and trying to look professional. It's not as though the body is going anywhere: it's a fair way up the beach, and the tide is going out.

'Can someone tell me who found her?' he asks as he reaches the group.

A white-haired man in baggy shorts and a T-shirt with more holes than fabric, raises a hand. In the other, he holds a fishing rod, and Luis notices a bucket nearby. He confirms this is the man he spoke to earlier, the one who phoned it in, and asks if the man can wait for a short while longer, so he can take a statement.

Luis walks towards the body. It appears to be a female in her early twenties, with long dark red hair, although it's obvious the colour owes more to a box dye than to nature. Her skin is tanned, though that may also be fake, and her dress is rucked up to expose her underwear, which is lacy and purple. There's a small tattoo of a butterfly on her right shoulder. Her nails are painted with dark red polish, chipped, and there is a fine gold chain around her neck. One false eyelash is still intact, the other likely lost to the water. She could almost be asleep in this pose, lying on her side, legs and arms resting on the sand, but her skin has a bluish tint and her eyes are open but unseeing. He'd say she wasn't in the water for long.

He contacted the scene-of-crime unit before leaving Palma, so they shouldn't be too far behind.

He snaps on a pair of latex gloves and kneels down to get a better look, the soles of his shoes digging into the wet sand. From what he can tell without moving her, she has few identifying features aside from the tattoo, though he'll get more of an idea later.

He stands up. There's not much to go on, but they'll circulate her description and check recent missing persons reports.

The second young woman in as many weeks. Intuition tells him there's every chance the two are linked.

Chapter Twenty-one

THE YOUNGEST DAUGHTER

By the time Kitty arrives at breakfast in knee-length khaki combat shorts and a loose long-sleeved shirt, the rest of the family has nearly finished eating. 'No chance of exposing yourself in that,' Rocco teases.

Kitty's cheeks flame. She could quite happily kill him sometimes. Instead, she adds another notch to her annual tally of times when Rocco makes her feel like an idiot. She is nearly into double figures and it's only late June.

'Don't worry, we saved you a croissant,' he adds, oblivious to her embarrassment.

She pulls up a seat as far from her brother as possible.

'Hello darling,' Evan says, joining them at the table and calling for more coffee.

'Did you sleep well?' Sandrine asks, solicitous. 'Or is the time difference still throwing you off?'

'No, I was fine,' Kitty replies, forking slices of papaya and melon onto her plate, her brain furiously calculating the approximate weight and the corresponding calories. She never did get to the bike yesterday. She'll let herself enjoy the water – the vast expanse of sapphire-blue that sparkles seductively at the edges of her vision like diamond dust – only after she's exercised, and only if no one is watching, though she realises that is practically an impossibility. Aside from her cabin, there's almost no privacy, even on a boat this size. 'It's all very comfortable,' she adds, doing her best to be the model of a younger daughter who knows her place.

'*Bon*,' says Sandrine, satisfied.

A steward places a tall glass of iced coffee, no cream, in front of Kitty without her having to ask for it. She doesn't give a second thought to the fact that they know her beverage of choice at any given time of day – it's simply what happens when she is in her father's world. It's hard to imagine Mom ever having been part of Dad's life like this. Claire is too careful, too worried about how much everything costs. She would be horrified by the waste here: the uneaten food, the sheets being laundered every second day, the fuel required to propel a boat of this size. It bothers Kitty too, obviously, but not as much as it would her mom. There are only so many things she can stress about.

At dinner the night before, the boys talked excitedly about some place on the island where you could go cliff diving, and while she thought it was all about stupid male bravado, it did sound kind of fun. Now they're talking about going scuba diving at a place called the Blue Cave.

Rocco did his scuba certification on a family vacation in the Bahamas when he was in his teens, and Kitty got her junior ticket right before lockdown. She's never dived in a cave before, though, and as she thinks about it, the documentary she saw about the Thai boys who got trapped in a cave system by monsoon rains a few years ago flashes through her mind. Despite the airy, open deck, she feels suddenly claustrophobic.

'It's supposed to be pretty cool,' Rocco says. 'How about it, Kit? You interested?'

Kitty has a mouthful of melon. She reminds herself that accidents happen and that, like lightning, they rarely strike twice. She swallows before speaking. 'Maybe?' Her earlier resolve not to talk to Rocco has vanished. She's never been able to stay mad at him for long. But she can't get the image of those Thai boys out of her head, and she also hasn't forgotten what happened the last time she went diving with her family. A shudder passes through her.

'The water's supposed to be, like, really blue,' Rocco says, still trying to convince her.

'You don't say.' Julian's tone underlines the banality of this statement but he smiles in case Rocco takes offence. It strikes Kitty how much Julian depends on Rocco's benevolence, and that it is perhaps a more delicately balanced relationship than it might seem.

'Will you join us, Dad?' Rocco asks.

Evan appears to think about it and Kitty wonders if he is calculating the hours that will have to be sacrificed, hours away from his precious, all-consuming work. 'Absolutely,' he replies.

'C'mon, Kit,' Rocco nags her. 'You can't miss out.'

She finds herself nodding. 'It could be fun, I guess,' she says, not convinced it's going to be.

* * *

After breakfast, Kitty heads to the gym and climbs onto one of the exercise bikes. She inserts her new AirPods (another recent birthday gift, undoubtedly chosen by Sandrine, who has a far better idea of what might appeal to a teenager than her father, not to mention the time to shop), turns the music up and prepares to punish herself.

As she spins her legs and begins to breathe heavily, images of their last dive flash through her mind.

They were in the Caribbean, on an island off Honduras called Roatán. There were nine of them: Dad, Rocco, Julian, Melissa and Kitty, plus two local divers and a couple of deckhands from the boat her dad had chartered for the week. It was one of Kitty's first dives with the rest of the family and she was beside herself with excitement at finally being able to join them. They paired up: she and her dad, Rocco and one of the deckhands, Melissa and the other deckhand, Julian with one of the dive boat owners.

The reef – Mary's Place – was covered in brilliant, intricate coral formations, swarming with tropical fish. Her dad stayed within arm's reach, and the first half-hour was a dream as Kitty lost herself in a kaleidoscope of colour.

She was finning across to inspect a tiny, waving sea anemone when she sensed a disturbance in the water beyond. She turned around in time to see Rocco way off in the distance, completely on his own. Eyes wide in alarm, she tapped her father on the arm to alert him. Her breathing quickened, and although she knew she was using more oxygen, she couldn't slow it down. As the two local divers and Melissa took off after Rocco, Kitty cast around for the other members of their group. Melissa's buddy appeared to have been caught by the current and was now some distance from the rest of them, moving in the opposite direction to Rocco. Everyone's attention was on her brother. Her dad had hold of her hand, pulling her towards Rocco and the others.

Never abandon your buddy.

The rule had been drilled into her while she was training, so she allowed her dad to lead her. Kitty was the only one who noticed Melissa's buddy drifting away, but she had done nothing, absolutely nothing, to try and alert anyone.

Ever since then, she has wished she could disappear.

Chapter Twenty-two

THE DECKIE

The deck and housekeeping crew don't get days off, Piper discovers, not while the family is on board, and they'll be cruising around Mallorca and Ibiza for three to four weeks, depending on the weather. 'We'll get a few days' break after that,' Johannes says as they go down to check over the jet skis. 'You're not sick of this already, are you?'

'Of course not!' she insists.

He asks Piper to have eyes on Bailey. 'The entire time she is on the swim deck, or in the water, get it? Do not take your focus off her for a second. And make sure she keeps her life jacket fastened.'

Piper doesn't need to be told why. Children, deep water and jet skis are a dangerous combination, and she's already rescued Carter from toppling off the sun lounger twice. 'Copy that.' She likes kids, and from what she's observed so far, Bailey is strong-willed and smart, but sweet. Piper steels herself against becoming fond of anyone, even the little ones. She is crew and they are family, and there's a gulf between the two.

She and one of the other deckies accompany Bailey and Carter to the swim platform. Piper checks that their life jackets are properly fastened while Johannes gives Rocco and Julian a safety briefing.

The two young men joke and muck around as though they haven't a care in the world. *What must that be like?* It occurs to her that getting one of this group on their own might prove trickier than imagined – they seem to travel as a pack, no one is ever alone for long.

She's not got long. Will she manage it?

Julian pays little attention to Johannes, more interested in the functions of the jet ski. 'What's the top speed on these things, dude?' he asks, a privileged curl to his upper lip, his voice loud enough to carry across the water.

'You heard what my sister said,' Rocco warns. 'These are little kids.'

'Oh, don't worry, grandma,' Julian replies. 'We'll go as slow as a snail, right, Carter?'

Carter looks at Julian uncertainly, his eyes big and round, the same arresting blue of the sea. 'Are there sharks in there?'

'Course not!' Julian replies.

There are sharks everywhere.

'Just pretty fish,' Piper says. She doesn't mention the fact that there are more than thirty species of shark in the Balearics, or that there was a fatal shark attack here once, though it was a century ago.

While they were having breakfast, several more yachts entered the bay, and there are at least four other jet skis already on the water. 'It's getting a little crowded out there,' Johannes says. 'Remember to stay at least two hundred metres from the shore.'

'Yeah, yeah.' Rocco climbs aboard one of the waiting jet skis, scoots back a little and motions to Bailey. 'Hop on and let's go for a spin, little buddy.'

'I want Mom to watch me,' Bailey says, casting around to see if Melissa is nearby.

'I'm sure she'll be looking out from the sundeck,' Rocco reassures her. 'You just can't see her from here.'

Appeased, Piper helps Bailey sit in front of Rocco then stands back as they set off. 'Faster,' Bailey cries. 'Faster!' and they gather speed, riding a wide loop around the yacht, leaving a rooster tail of spray in their wake.

Piper smiles. The little girl is fearless.

She helps Carter onto the other jet ski with Julian, who eases away from the swim platform at a pace more suited to a golf buggy than a sportscar. She is relieved that he is true to his word. Carter risks a look back, a delighted grin spread across his face.

'Here.' Johannes throws Piper a life jacket. 'Take one of the other jet skis. Keep your distance but don't lose sight of them.' Piper takes no notice of the other deckie's unspoken envy. It's already warm, and being out on the water, forgetting her cares for even a few minutes, just might be the best thing that happens to her this trip.

She launches a jet ski, puttering away from the yacht before opening the throttle just enough to feel the engine's leashed power beneath her. These are brand-new machines, the only electric jet skis on the market, making them super-quiet and low maintenance. Stealth machines. Until now, she's only ever ridden a five-year-old WaveRunner with a growl louder than a Harley-Davidson. It had to be babied to go anything above fifty miles an hour. This is a whole different ballgame.

Being in or on or around the water is in her blood. From the first time her dad pushed Piper and her sister off in a tiny, unstable Mirror dinghy (Lexie was skipper, Piper happy to be first mate), she had known it was where she wanted to be. The sense of freedom as they skimmed along, the wind whipping past them, sails flapping, was more addictive than sugar.

But this isn't sailing, she reminds herself. *This is yachting.*

A shout comes from *Ambition* and Piper jerks to attention, wheeling the jet ski around to face the yacht. She scans the expanse of water.

The sun disappears behind a cloud and the sea instantly darkens. A sense of foreboding descends.

One of the jet skis is a few hundred yards to her left, not far from the swim platform. It's idling, the rider and small passenger nowhere to be seen.

www.newyorktimes.com
2 July

Property Developer in Yacht Tragedy

New York–based property billionaire Evan Thyssen, 68, is at the centre of a tragic accident on the Spanish island of Mallorca.

Mr Thyssen was on board his yacht, the 250-foot M/Y *Ambition*, at the time, along with his wife, French actress Sandrine Furneaux, his four children and various other family members.

No one from the company could be reached for comment.

Chapter Twenty-three

THE TROPHY WIFE

Sandrine is lying face-down on the outdoor massage table, her cheeks pressed into the cushioned surface. The therapist is pummelling her so fiercely she worries she might end up covered in bruises, but it's good to at least be able to feel something. She moans involuntarily as the woman wrenches her arm nearly out of its socket, pressing strong thumbs into her shoulder.

The therapist eases off without saying a word.

A shout comes from below and she rolls over abruptly, clutching the towel to her chest. There's something in the tone that indicates more than just high spirits, the note of alarm ringing clean and true. 'Can you see anything?' she asks the therapist, who is now leaning over the rail.

'I think someone fell off,' she says. 'One of the children perhaps?'

More yelling is coming from the rear of the boat, and they watch as a jet ski idles in a slow circle before eventually coming to a halt and wallowing gently in the swell. There's no sign of whoever might have been riding it. Sandrine scans the water but doesn't have a clear view from this vantage point.

She quickly replaces the towel with her bikini top. 'I had better go and see.'

When she reaches the bow, one of the young female deckhands is stroking to where Bailey is bobbing in the water about thirty metres from the boat, kept afloat by her life jacket. Rocco is also swimming towards his niece. The jet ski is some distance away. Bailey is now screaming her head off.

Sandrine hurries down the stairs to the lower deck, emerging onto the swim platform in time to see Bailey being hoisted onto another jet ski and told to hang on tight. They make their way slowly back to the boat.

'Just a little spill,' the deckhand reassures them when Bailey climbs back on board, teeth chattering despite the sunshine. Her screams have, thankfully, subsided. 'You know, the same thing happened to me once and I swallowed so much water.' The deckhand makes a face, attempting to jolly Bailey out of her shock, handing her a towel and indicating that she should sit for a while. 'Everyone falls off at some point.'

'I couldn't hold on,' Bailey wails. 'It's my fault.'

'I shouldn't have been going so fast.' Rocco is back now, stepping onto the swim platform as a waiting deckhand secures the jet ski. He bends down to give his niece a hug. 'I'm sorry you got scared, bubba.'

The towel falls from Bailey's shoulders. 'I wasn't *that* scared,' she says, setting her chin and giving a slight hiccup. 'And I'm not a baby. Can we go again?'

'Maybe later, hey?' Sandrine replies, giving Rocco a sharp look.

Bailey pouts. 'I'm fine, really.' She's as stubborn as her mother. 'Did you see us? We were flying!' There's no trace of the scared little girl of a few minutes ago. 'Did Mom see? Where is she?'

'I think she had a meeting with Grandpa, sweetie,' Sandrine says.

Bailey is downcast. 'She always says she'll watch us, but she never does.' Her lower lip juts out even further.

'Come on,' says Sandrine. 'Why don't we go look for her? I bet she was watching. I bet she saw just how brave you were.'

But Melissa is nowhere to be found.

* * *

'Can I have a Coke?' Bailey asks when they return to the lounge. She glances sideways at Sandrine to see if she'll say yes, assessing how far she can push her luck.

'How about a milkshake instead?' Sandrine suggests. *Alors!* Does Melissa really let them drink those sugary, caffeinated sodas? She checks her watch. 'I think Max should be up from his nap soon – he might need a drink too,' she says.

'Can we go see him?' Bailey asks. She dotes on the baby.

'Of course. I'll ask Amber to bring him and we'll get someone to fix you a milkshake – strawberry, maybe?'

Bailey nods happily, her absent mother temporarily forgotten.

After feeding Max, Sandrine unfolds a playmat in the middle of the lounge and shows Bailey how to get Max's attention with a rattle and a soft cloth book. Eventually, Max begins to rub his eyes with his fists.

'I think he needs another sleep now.'

'Babies don't do much, do they?' Bailey says, blowing kisses to him. 'Eww! What's that smell?' she asks, screwing up her nose as a waft of something noxious reaches them.

'They certainly poop a lot,' Sandrine replies, laughing. She pulls her phone from her pocket and sends Amber a message, asking her to come and get Max.

'There you are!' Melissa appears in the lounge. She's smiling, but there's tension in her jaw, at the corners of her eyes, as though she's been squinting at a screen for too long.

'We've been here for ages, Mom. Where have *you* been?' Bailey accuses. 'We tried to find you, but you weren't in your cabin.'

'Just catching up on some emails, sweetie.'

'Rocco and I went on the jet ski. We were going so fast!'

'Did you have fun? I can't wait to have a go, you'll have to show me how it's done.'

'You weren't watching, were you?' Bailey replies. 'I fell off and swallowed almost the entire ocean.'

'Oh Bee, really?'

'She's fine, as you can see,' Sandrine says, thinking that Melissa could be more grateful that she's been minding her daughter for more than an hour.

'Course I am,' Bailey confirms. 'I wish Dad was here, though. He would have been watching.'

Sandrine blinks. Bailey certainly knows how to twist the knife.

'Will he be able to come at all?' Bailey asks.

'I don't know, honey, but we can call him tomorrow and see how he's doing.'

Bailey seems appeased, and Sandrine checks her phone to see if Amber has responded. Where is she? She locates an iPad, flicks through several screens, then presses the call button for the nanny's cabin. There's still no answer. It's infuriating. The girl is supposed to be always reachable.

'Everything okay?' Melissa asks.

Sandrine is about to reply when the wail of a siren starts up, blasting through the lounge. She snaps her head towards the glass doors, but from where she's sitting she can't see much. The volume increases. Bailey puts her hands over her ears and Max begins to grizzle, adding to the noise.

'It's probably nothing,' Melissa says, getting to her feet and taking Bailey's hand. 'But we should go anyway, yeah?'

The glass doors slide seamlessly open and Walker is there, eyebrows drawn, his jaw set. 'Everyone to the muster station,' he barks, then, as if remembering who he is speaking to, adds, 'if you please.'

Sandrine gathers Max to her chest, her hands trembling as she clasps his tiny body.

* * *

On the lower deck, several crew members, two white-jacketed chefs and the housekeeping team (a few of whom are clutching their cleaning caddies like handbags) are milling about at a short distance from the family, glancing around repeatedly as if waiting for someone to tell them it's okay to go back inside.

The alarm isn't as loud out here, but it's giving Sandrine a headache. Max has quietened, although he's restless, not to mention stinky, wriggling in her arms, and she's grateful to see Amber appear. The nanny looks slightly flustered. There are creases in her uniform, as if she's been lying on it. Sandrine will ask her later why she took so long to respond; she is not one to make a scene in front of the entire entourage.

'Did you get caught vaping in the office, sis?' Rocco teases.

Melissa scowls at him, not deigning to reply.

Carter appears with Julian and races towards his mother, flinging himself at her legs. Melissa lifts him, settling him on one hip as his mouth wobbles and he begins to cry.

The alarm has drawn the inhabitants of several yachts in the vicinity out onto their decks, some of them using binoculars to get a better look at *Ambition*. There's at least one person holding up a phone, presumably videoing on the off chance something noteworthy happens. Evan hates that kind of attention. Sandrine hopes for all their sakes that it's not something serious. They've barely been here a day. Come to think of it, where *is* Evan? Why hasn't he come out on deck? She reaches for her phone.

But before she gets the chance to call him, her husband and the captain push through the doors. Captain Bird reassures everyone that a wiring malfunction in the galley led to an overheating stove, causing an electrical short circuit. 'The engineers are dealing with it. Only minor. Apologies for the inconvenience.' She has to shout to be heard, but in the middle of her speech the noise cuts out as suddenly as it began, and her voice echoes loudly in the ensuing silence. 'Teething issues of a new vessel, that's all.'

Evan appears at Sandrine's side, places his hand on her shoulder, the pressure of his thumb warm against her skin. 'Okay?' he mouths.

'Of course.'

'You can resume your tasks,' Walker says, nodding to the housekeepers, who scuttle back inside at his signal.

'We'll be getting underway very shortly,' Captain Chrissie addresses the deck crew.

'Time for a beer?' Rocco suggests.

'Already?' Melissa asks, her light tone sheathing a razor's edge of judgement.

Sandrine says nothing – she knows better than to intervene in disputes between Evan's children. Let them squabble between themselves. She's learned it is better to keep her distance.

'We're on vacation. And I don't remember you being my mom,' Rocco fires back.

'You're right,' Melissa relents, surprising both Rocco and Sandrine.

It's not often that she backs down, if ever.

Carter pulls at Melissa. 'I'm hungry, Mommy.'

'You ready for some lunch?' Melissa asks.

'I want hot dogs,' he demands, a tiny emperor. Sandrine vows that Max will never be allowed to speak so rudely. He will have the manners of a proper French boy.

'That sounds like a good idea,' Melissa says. 'Sandrine, would it be okay if Amber watches them while they eat? I still have some work to finish up.'

'Max needs changing,' Sandrine says. 'And his nap is overdue.' Honestly, would it kill Melissa to watch her own kids, to eat a meal with them? Of course, she doesn't say any of this out loud. 'Perhaps once she's put him down?' she offers.

'I'll have lunch with them,' Kitty volunteers. 'I like hot dogs too,' she says to Carter.

'Thanks,' says Melissa, coming over to give her a hug. 'You're a lifesaver, Kit.'

'What about you, Jules?' Rocco asks. 'Hot dog with the works?'

'What's the works?' Bailey asks.

'Ketchup, mustard, onions, pickles …'

'Cheese?'

'You bet.'

'Dad?' Rocco asks.

'Well now, I think I might join you kids too,' he says with a chuckle. 'I can't remember the last time I ate a hot dog.'

Sandrine knows better than to object. Lips and assholes, that's what hot dogs are. She has never understood why Americans love them so much. 'Why don't we all have an early lunch?' she suggests. 'Though I'll skip the dog and have a crab salad.'

Bailey laughs. 'They're called *hot* dogs, Sandrine.'

'I know that,' she shoots back, irritated at being picked up on the inaccuracy.

'I'll have something sent to the study,' Melissa says, sounding envious. 'But I promise I'll join you for a swim later, okay, Bee? Carter?' A wave of barely concealed exhaustion passes across her face and Sandrine feels a little ashamed of her earlier judgement.

'Sure, Mom.' Carter's mind is on food.

'Are you okay?' Sandrine asks Melissa. 'You look very pale.'

'Probably picked up something on the flight,' she replies, waving her hands in front of her face. 'All that recycled air. But nothing that some sun and sea won't cure. I'll be fine in a day or two.'

They head to the dining deck, where a stewardess is already setting out condiments and a chef has lit the burners on the barbecue at the far end. There's the clank and rumble of the heavy anchor chain being wound back inside the yacht's hull, and then the vibration of the engines as she gets underway.

They are heading around Mallorca in a clockwise direction. The plan is to circumnavigate the entire island, drop Melissa and her children in Palma, and then continue across to Ibiza, where Rocco and Julian will leave them for a week of hedonistic partying. It suddenly occurs to Sandrine that no one has mentioned what Kitty will be doing. The girl is too often overlooked. She supposes Kitty will stay on board, but it will be rather dull for her. It's probably too late to see if she has a friend who might want to join them. Why has no one thought of this sooner?

'Where to next?' she asks Evan.

'Deia. I've asked Walker to arrange lunch for us there tomorrow. The restaurant is usually booked out months in advance, but I've no doubt Walker will work a miracle.' He leans in and kisses her on the cheek. 'I thought you might enjoy it.'

'You are thoughtful,' she replies, not telling him that she's been to Deia before, some years ago, had spent a weekend there with a former lover. Evan doesn't like to be reminded of her life before they met. She sometimes thinks he would prefer she'd been a doll in a cellophane box, untouched, before she met him.

'It's not an ideal place to anchor, particularly if there's a northerly, so we'll stay overnight somewhere on the way.'

The secluded village of Deia is a magnet for artists, musicians, poets, rock stars. Jimi Hendrix, David Bowie, The Rolling Stones and, of course, Robert Graves have all helped to make the area famous among those who know about such things. The last time Sandrine was there, she was sure she saw at least one famous face, though she can't recall who.

The beach itself is tiny, rocky and surrounded by vertiginous cliffs. Sandrine and her lover had hiked down the steep pathway (her shoes had been totally impractical) to perch on a rock, drinking cheap wine straight from the bottle, devouring bread rolls filled with prosciutto, skinny dipping after the sun set …

She barely remembers being that woman now.

redhairedrival: What's with Mallorca being so popular with the rich all of a sudden? In my day, it was full of sunburnt pond life, drinking too much beer in Magaluf and singing that stupid birdy song. *shudder*

thisshitisreal: Ha! I remember that. Times have certainly changed.

Chapter Twenty-four

THE DECKIE

Johannes summoned Piper after the jet ski accident, chewing her out for taking her eyes off Bailey, as if it was entirely her fault the little girl fell off. There was no point in explaining that she looked away for only a second, that Rocco is the one to blame, not her, nor that there wasn't much she could have done in any case, that she was too far away, keeping her distance, as ordered.

'It won't happen again,' she promised, even as the unfairness bit at her.

Piper is more worried when, an hour or so after the kerfuffle with the alarm, Walker calls her to the bridge. Surely she isn't going to be fired for the incident?

Steeling herself, she lets him know she's on her way.

'Piper?' Walker and Captain Chrissie face her.

She nods, keeping her gaze steady. *Never look guilty, never apologise before you know what it is you're apologising for*, she reminds herself.

'I understand you have experience with children?' Walker asks.

'Yes, I …' She's momentarily off balance.

'I've seen your resume,' Walker interrupts. 'We're going to add to your deckhand duties for the next ten days.'

It *is* a punishment.

'I've cleared it with Johannes. You are to be assigned to Bailey and Carter. Neither Melissa's husband, nor their nanny, could make it unfortunately, and she needs someone to watch the children when she is occupied with work.'

Weren't they supposed to be on holiday? Piper guesses some people never stop. She feels sorry for the kids. 'Of course. I'd be delighted to.' This is not an outcome she could have foreseen, but at least she's not being sacked.

'Good. The children are having lunch. When they are finished it's up to you to keep them entertained and out of everyone's way,' Walker says, his gaze boring into her as if silently telling her not to fuck up again.

'Do you think you can manage that, Piper?' Captain Bird asks. 'And remember, you are responsible for ensuring they always wear their life jackets whenever they're on deck. That's non-negotiable.'

'Copy that, Captain.'

* * *

How hard can it be to watch an eight-year-old and her six-year-old brother?

Pretty bloody hard, as it turns out. Despite the well-stocked games cupboard in the main salon, neither of the children wants to do a jigsaw puzzle, Carter is too young for Scrabble or Yahtzee, and Bailey declares Old Maid 'too babyish'. When Piper collected them after lunch, Melissa's only instruction had been not to let them on a screen. 'They get far too much of that at home,' she said. 'I'll circle back to you later this afternoon and check in to see how you're all getting on.'

Finally, Piper gets the children to agree on Hungry Hippos, which keeps them occupied for a while, by which time Bailey is yawning like a hippo herself and Carter has already curled up on the sofa, his eyelids shuttering.

Piper leans back against the cushions, wishing she could take a nap. She's been up since dawn, hasn't eaten since breakfast, nor has she had a break all day. The low-throated hum of the engines as they cruise to their next mooring is soporific.

Instead, she gets up and goes to the window, where a rugged coastline and navy-blue ocean slip past. Out of habit, she flicks her phone on, finding the local shipping and weather forecast. Plain sailing ahead: light southwest winds, no cloud and zero precipitation. Conditions don't get much better.

'Piper?' Bailey fights her drowsiness.

'Yes, Bee?' Bailey insisted she call her this, and her earnestness had made Piper's heart contract.

'Can you tell me a story?'

Piper goes over to the other sofa. 'Scoot along then.' She settles herself next to the girl. 'What would you like to hear about?'

'You pick.'

'Okay.' Piper thinks. 'Once upon a time there was a – a raven and a lion, and they wanted to see the world, so they got themselves a boat with, er, green sails.' She is shamelessly riffing on *The Owl and the Pussycat*, hoping that Bailey won't notice.

'Green?' She yawns.

'Didn't you know that all the best ships have green sails?'

'They don't.'

There's no pulling a fast one on this little girl.

'Well, in my story they do.'

Bailey seems to accept this and snuggles closer to Piper, who suppresses a pang of guilt that the girl has so readily decided she likes her.

Piper doesn't get much further with the animals' adventures before Bailey, too, is asleep.

Piper closes her eyes, telling herself it's just for a minute …

* * *

'Aww, look, they've all flaked out. Hey, isn't that one of the deckies? Wouldn't say no to a bit.'

'Slumming it, much?'

'Shut. Up,' Rocco says. 'She's got an incredible ass.'

'I love that for you,' Julian simpers. 'Peachy.'

'Shh …'

Piper doesn't stir, pretending not to hear, not in the slightest bit surprised that Rocco is so casually objectifying her, inwardly seething that he's exactly the person she'd expected him to be.

They stifle their laughter and she opens her eyes to see the pair of them leaning over the end of the sofa, squinting and red-faced from too much sun. Beery fumes waft towards her.

'Oh, hey. Sorry if we woke you.'

'Should you be in here, you know, like this?' Julian wrinkles his nose as if she is lower than low.

'Resting for a second.' She sits upright, awkward in her effort not to wake Bailey. 'I'm here to watch the kids.' *As if it's any business of yours*, she adds silently. She has pins and needles in her wrist, and she rolls it in an effort to get rid of them.

'Yeah …' Julian drawls, letting out a loud burp. 'How about that? Hey, Rocco had a question for you …' He looks meaningfully at his friend, who shuffles awkwardly, put on the spot.

'Oh yes?' Piper does her best to be polite, but really she is livid.

'No, I didn't.' Rocco frowns briefly. 'Thanks, *buddy*.'

The two boys straighten, almost colliding with each other, which only causes them to giggle again. They tiptoe theatrically out of the salon.

Entitled fuckers. Piper takes a deep breath, reminding herself to be patient. She'll get her revenge on the pair of them.

Piper has no idea how long she was asleep for, but the sun is much lower now, and the engine note has changed, their progress slowing. The yacht makes a wide turn to starboard before nosing into a narrow inlet, the captain most likely getting ready to anchor overnight.

The engines cut out and the rumble of the anchor chain confirms that she is right. She eases herself off the sofa and cranks the window open a fraction, inhaling briny air. The muted sound of soft rock and the whoops of revellers reach her ears.

She can make out one other yacht at anchor a little way from *Ambition*. She's surprised there aren't more – the Balearics aren't as choked as some other parts of the Med, but they're not far off, and it's the summer season. Perhaps the captain knows the hidden places, the secret anchorages, that others might not.

There's a pair of vintage binoculars on a shelf nearby and although she suspects they may be purely decorative, she picks them up.

As she adjusts the dials, the nearby yacht comes in to focus. It has every appearance of a party boat, strewn with bikini-clad women and older, large-bellied, generally balding men, clutching martini glasses and each other, swaying to the thump of music coming from a set of decks. The DJ has his eyes closed, headphones on, oblivious to everything but the musical trip he's taking.

The ratio of women to men seems to be at least four or five to one.

She zooms in on a couple, watching as they stumble and collapse onto a wide, cushioned daybed, legs and arms entangled. Wasted. No one around them seems to take any notice. She pans across to a dark-haired woman in a silver bikini, watching as she dives from the boat, disappearing into the water, before bobbing up like a popped champagne cork a few moments later.

She knows all about these 'yacht girls', young, glamorous, beautiful women hired to party with onboard guests. Eye-candy, women whose only currency is their physical beauty. The unspoken truth is, of course, that they are available for almost anything else, too.

They are brought in and out of the Med, often from eastern Europe or Russia, and speak very little English, not that it seems to be a handicap. Sometimes they stay only a day or two, other times they are kept on for weeks, occasionally given extravagant gifts in addition to their pay. Often aspiring actresses or models, really they are sex workers – not that she's judging. There are far less honest ways to earn a crust.

She's heard stories … of a young Croatian who managed to escape a superyacht with only the clothes she was wearing, no money, no passport, a black eye and strangulation marks circling her neck. Of a woman who discovered that her birth control had failed her. Of another who was paid with a watch: the man had taken it off his wrist and thrown it at her. Of women who are treated as sex slaves by rich men with aggressive libidos and tiny consciences. *Tiny dicks too, probably*, Piper thinks sourly.

The yachting world might look glamorous, but scratch the surface and you'll soon find the ugliness that lurks beneath.

The kids are awake now, and Bailey asks if they can play hide-and-seek. Against her better judgement – she had been told to keep eyes on them at all times – Piper agrees.

Chapter Twenty-five

THE ELDEST DAUGHTER

After Melissa has settled the kids with the deckhand she goes to her cabin and chugs down a couple of melatonin with a mouthful of Voss. She has every intention of ploughing through the remaining unanswered emails in her inbox before taking a nap. There's a small desk – an *escritoire*, Sandrine would probably call it – not really large enough for her to work from but she needs to escape her father's study, and while her laptop powers up, she runs her hands over the polished wood, lifting the lid on an enamelled jar. Her eyes light up when she sees the contents. Someone knows her all too well. She reaches in, feeling the smoothness of a sugared almond against her fingertips. Grabbing the jar with the other hand and flopping on the bed, she feeds the almonds, one by one, into her mouth, savouring the crunch and the sweetness until the jar is empty and there's nothing left but a sticky rime of sugar coating her lips and an ache in her belly.

Minutes later her phone chimes with an incoming message. She flips it over to check the screen.

Angus.

A long, carefully composed plea begging her forgiveness, promising her it will never happen again, that he's an idiot, a fool and she deserves so much better than him. Jesus, it goes on for *paragraphs*, but that's an English professor for you.

Pull the other one, she thinks, licking the remaining sugar from the corners of her mouth. A leopard never changes its spots. Once, the handwritten letters he'd left by her bedside and the emails that would arrive at random times promising any number of delicious things he wanted to do to her, making her blush with his poetic but explicit language, had thrilled her. Once, so long ago that she can barely remember it, he had lit her up with those words.

She wants to believe him now, for the sake of the children, the sake of appearances, the sake of peace … But what's the saying? Oh, yeah. *Insanity is doing the same thing over and over and expecting a different result.*

silverstar: What about the crew? I heard that a couple of them were involved in something super-dodgy. Drugs, I'd bet. Maybe it wasn't an accident after all? They weren't that far from Italy, just saying.

monetizeme: That's ridiculous. Are you really inferring that the Mafia was somehow involved? Anyway, they were miles away from Italy.

eightyplus: Not really that far away. I guess we'll never know the full truth.

Chapter Twenty-six

THE DETECTIVE

It's after ten when Luis gets back to the station. He fills his superior in on the latest development. Inspector Miguel Vidal has been on the island's force for what Luis has been told is forever, and in charge of the Palma station for the past ten years. He was all set to retire at the end of last summer but, according to office gossip, his wife ran off with her best friend and Miguel couldn't bear to sit at home both wifeless and jobless. He insists that he is staying on 'for at least another year, maybe two'.

Luis is sympathetic to the situation, but his patience, never his strong point, is wearing thin. Miguel rarely makes it to the headquarters before ten, disappears at noon only to return several hours later reeking of booze and cigarettes, and then sits in his office staring at the walls until it gets dark. Luis counts himself lucky that he's caught Miguel before lunch today.

As Luis relates the news, Miguel nods as if he's already heard it, seemingly unconcerned by the incidence of a second dead body only weeks after the first. 'It's summer. We get our share of drunk tourists who go into the water after dark.' He shrugs. 'That reminds me, the toxicology report on the previous woman is in.' Miguel squints at the screen in front of him and stabs a few keys in quick succession. 'There. I've forwarded it to you.'

'Anything useful?' Luis asks.

'Alcohol, benzodiazepine present.' It's as if he's saying *I told you so.*

'Benzos?' Luis darts a glance at him. 'You think she was sedated? Any evidence of sexual assault?'

'You mean apart from the bruising?' Miguel asks.

'Yes.' Luis struggles to keep his tone even. 'I mean apart from the bruising.' Which could have been caused by any number of things, he reminds himself.

Miguel grunts and wipes his nose with his bare hands, flicking something onto the floor. Luis manages not to flinch. 'Yes, though whether it was just rough sex or actual assault, we can't be sure.'

'I'd say the fact that she washed up on the beach would be a bit of a clue,' Luis can't help retorting.

Miguel holds up a hand. 'Let's not jump to conclusions. We still haven't been able to identify her. Missing persons has come up with nothing. Besides, plenty of girls live on the fringes; they come here for a good time, get well paid for it too.'

Luis is shocked by his boss's attitude. 'Even if she did, she was still someone's daughter, someone's sister.' Luis shouldn't have to remind Miguel of this, but he says it anyway. 'A human being. She certainly didn't come to Mallorca to die.' He changes tack. 'What about a social media blitz? Or go old school and have some posters printed?' He'll put them up himself if need be. 'Someone has to have seen her. We've already been to all the bars in the vicinity of where she was found.'

Miguel leans forward, more animated than in the entire few weeks Luis has known him. 'Are you out of your mind? In case you hadn't noticed, this is an island full of tourists in the middle of summer. Do you want to start a full-blown panic?'

Even the local newspaper knows which side its bread is buttered on. It ran a small piece on the first body low down on its website a few days ago. Blink and you'd miss it.

'But now there are two women.'

'Even more reason to keep things quiet.'

Luis has to leave before he explodes. He'll investigate on his own, starting by interviewing the crew and passengers of as many of the yachts as possible known to be in the vicinity of the Cala de Ses Ortigues in the last couple of days. Of course, that's no easy task; Mallorca sees hundreds of thousands of yachts in high season, though admittedly not all in that area, and not everyone is likely to be forthcoming. Yacht owners tend to value their privacy. Besides, he doesn't even have a photo of the woman when she was alive, and he's not about to start passing around a picture of her as they found her.

'You interested in a drink later?' Miguel asks Luis as he exits the office, oblivious to his irritation. 'Some of us are going across the road. Maria's turning twenty-three tomorrow.'

Luis shakes his head. 'Wish her happy birthday for me.' He has more important things to do.

Chapter Twenty-seven

THE ELDEST DAUGHTER

The light has faded to a soft gold and it takes a good minute for Melissa to recall where she is. She turns her head towards the window, which affords her a view of the calm, dark sea. A thumping, insistent bass reaches her.

In the bathroom, she pulls her hair into a ponytail so tight it makes her scalp ache and splashes water on her face, trying to wake herself up. Her watch tells her it has gone six. Jesus, she's been asleep for hours, time sucked away like water down a drainpipe. She returns to the cabin, spots her laptop, then thinks of Bailey and Carter. For once, it's an easy decision to ignore the work, leave her phone on the nightstand and go in search of her children.

She steps outside, the decking smooth and still warm beneath her bare feet. Shielding her eyes with her hand, she squints into the setting sun, realising that the music isn't coming from their boat but one that's moored a few hundred feet away. Flashing lights and occasional whoops and cheers emphasise the party atmosphere.

As she watches, envious of the people on board, who seem to be having such a good time – she can't remember when she last cut loose like that – she sees the *Ambition* tender pass by, all varnished wood and classic styling, something out of a 1950s movie. It looks as though Walker is being driven over to the party boat by one of the deckhands (the good-looking one she noticed at lunch – Johannes, she thinks she heard someone call him).

Is he going to ask them to tone it down? Even the formidable Walker might have a difficult time persuading them to stop a party that looks as though it's in full swing. She turns, about to make her way aft, when she's almost barrelled over. 'Oof!' She takes the full impact of Carter's blond skull directly in the solar plexus. It winds her temporarily. 'There you are,' she gasps. 'I was just coming to see you.'

Carter barely acknowledges her. 'We're playing hide-and-go-seek. Quick, Piper's right behind me. Where can I hide?'

Bailey's footsteps thud along the deck and she giggles as she gets closer.

'Bailey! You aren't supposed to follow me. Find your own spot.' Carter glares at his sister.

'That's enough now. Be nice,' Melissa warns, but they ignore her, squeezing past and along the edge of the boat.

They don't appear to have missed her at all. At least they're wearing life jackets.

She heads to the sundeck where she finds Sandrine, cocktail glass in hand.

'Melissa! Come and join me.'

God, the Frenchwoman is always so gracious, which makes Melissa feel even meaner for disliking her.

A stewardess appears and suggests a cocktail. 'Or would you like a glass of champagne?'

'Champagne – the Roederer, not the Clicquot. Thanks.'

'Certainly.'

'Come, sit.' Sandrine indicates the seat next to her. 'Evan is having a rest, or at least he was until we arrived here.' She tips her head towards the other boat. 'I doubt anyone could sleep through that.' She shifts on the banquette cushions. 'You look better. Did you manage a siesta too?'

Melissa nods, despite feeling the admission is a sign of weakness, even though it's clear her father has done the same, and even though she is supposed to be on vacation.

'The time difference, it is a killer,' Sandrine empathises.

Melissa's champagne arrives, and as she sips from the crystal flute the alcohol floods her limbs like a shot from a hypodermic needle, releasing the lingering tension from her neck and shoulders. The music has been turned down a notch, and it's pleasant to sit in the open air as the sky slowly leaches of light and a gentle breeze plays across her skin. She gazes out across the water. It's fucking idyllic here, and she refuses to feel guilty for appreciating a few minutes of it. 'Where are the boys?'

Sandrine shrugs. 'They took off on the jet skis almost as soon as the anchor was dropped. Promised to be back before dark. It must be a little dull for them, perhaps?'

'If I know my brother, he'll find plenty to amuse himself, don't worry.' Rocco has always been one for diversions wherever he goes. Melissa remembers one summer a few years ago, when Rocco was barely sixteen. He went out with two older schoolfriends who were caught with several grams of coke. Rocco protested total ignorance. Even Evan believed him, but Melissa wasn't fooled. Fortunately for him, Rocco has always managed to charm his way out of trouble.

'Is that my eldest son you're talking about?' Evan appears, leaning down to kiss Sandrine on the cheek and placing a hand on Melissa's shoulder, squeezing it tighter than she'd like. A fleeting tic of annoyance crosses Sandrine's face, so quick that Melissa thinks she must have imagined it. 'He wants to come and work for us, in September.'

Melissa is jolted out of her champagne buzz. 'He what?'

'Yes, you heard me. It seems he's decided to defer college indefinitely.'

'But he's never shown the slightest interest …' Melissa is dumbfounded, then furious. Despite having grown up a

Thyssen, Rocco doesn't know the first thing about property development. 'And anyway, isn't he enrolled at NYU in the fall? Anthropology, wasn't it?' Though she doubts he'll make it through the first semester.

'He's going to come and get a taste of the real world. I thought you might like to take him under your wing; show him the ropes. He'll do a complete internship later on, just as you did, of course, but I've got high hopes for the boy.'

Melissa nearly chokes on her drink. 'I'm not sure that would be the best use of my time,' she says, only just keeping her outrage under control. 'I didn't realise babysitting my brother was a part of my job description.' She manages to say this last sentence with a laugh, but underneath she's deadly serious. Keeping Rocco out of trouble when she is about to bring a multi-million-dollar development to market is the last thing she needs.

'Can't he join the graduate training program right away?' Sandrine asks.

Melissa musters a thin-lipped smile, surprised at Sandrine's unexpected support.

'Yes, but I do feel he might benefit from a one-on-one approach.'

It's obvious to Melissa now that Rocco has been in Evan's ear about this, using his charm to talk his father around.

Here she is, the dutiful eldest daughter, working her ass off for more than ten years, doing her time, proving her worth, while also giving birth to two children and doing her best to raise them. 'Well, it was good enough for me,' she says baldly, choking down the words she'd prefer to say.

'Come now,' Evan says, 'you know how much I've always wanted you both involved in the company.' He looks across to Sandrine. 'Max, too, if he wants.'

'He may be a little young for that,' Sandrine says drily, catching Melissa's eye.

'This isn't *Succession*, Dad.'

'You know what I mean.'

'*Chérie*, I'm sure she was only teasing,' Sandrine attempts to placate him, resting her elegant fingers on his forearm.

'And what about Kitty? Are there going to be jobs for everyone? Regardless of skills, talent or experience?' Melissa can't help it now. She's sick and tired of biting her tongue, even if it does mean causing an argument on the first day of their vacation. Jesus. The way things are going, she's in for a long ten days.

Evan ignores her, signalling for a drink, which appears within seconds. 'And a few of those jalapeño poppers, if the chef can rustle some up.'

'And some sashimi?' Melissa asks, dropping the subject for now. She hasn't the energy for a full-throttle showdown, not on such a beautiful evening, and if she's learned anything from her father, it's to pick her battles.

'Kitty-Kat, come and sit next to me.' Evan pats the cushion next to him as Kitty slouches towards them, looking pale and, even in an oversized T-shirt, painfully thin. 'Hey,' he says, as if the thought has just occurred to him, 'see that boat there?' He gestures with his glass and Kitty looks over to where he is pointing. 'Fifty bucks if you can tell me the meaning of her name. *Moirai*.' He spells it out.

'Evan!' Now Sandrine's voice has an edge to it. 'The poor girl's on vacation.'

Kitty tilts her head to one side, chews on the edge of her lip. '*Moirai*?'

'Uh-huh.' A smile twitches the corners of Evan's mouth, and Melissa isn't sure if he's trying to trip Kitty up or have her show off in front of everyone.

'*Moirai* is the Greek name for what we might know as The Fates in English,' Kitty mumbles, still looking at the other boat. 'They were three sisters, goddesses really, who presided over human life.'

'Got it in one!' Evan crows. He seems much more pleased than Kitty that she knew the answer to such an obscure question. Melissa has certainly never heard of The Fates. They don't teach that in business school.

Food arrives, including cheese, Evan's crumbed chilli peppers, a fan of tuna sashimi accompanied by a pistachio-green nub of wasabi paste, Thai-inspired betel leaves topped with shredded crab and herbs, and a shallow dish of caviar on ice surrounded by tiny mother-of-pearl spoons. Evan raises an eyebrow at Sandrine then plunges the spoon into the greyish eggs. 'You only live once, right? Anyway, you can't get the good shit in the US.' He takes a bite straight from the spoon and Melissa tries not to wince. 'Beluga. The real deal.'

'I will not nag you about your *regime* once in the next two weeks,' Sandrine promises.

Melissa notices Sandrine shudder as her father pops another loaded spoonful in his mouth. It's a source of amusement to her that Sandrine's and Evan's sensibilities are so wildly different.

'And the forfeit if you do?' Evan asks.

'I'm sure we can think of something,' Sandrine replies, lowering her eyelashes.

Melissa can't stand to see them flirt; it's nauseating. Kitty doesn't appear to have noticed, however, staring instead at the party boat. Melissa follows her gaze, holding her breath as a mahogany-tanned older man launches himself from the top deck, cigar still clamped between his lips. He's underwater for a heart-stoppingly long time. She and Kitty exchange an amused glance when he finally emerges, *sans* cigar.

A good-looking young deckhand (there's no one ugly or old on the crew, they're all straight from central casting) tops up their drinks, fetching Kitty a lemonade without her having to ask for it. She blushes as he hands it to her. Melissa wishes she could tell Kitty not to be so self-conscious, that she's got nothing to worry about.

A while later, the tender returns and then Walker appears on deck, leaning in to whisper in Evan's ear before nodding at the group and taking his leave.

Walker has been working for her father for nearly a decade, managing Evan and Sandrine's day-to-day arrangements, the other staff and the homes in New York, the Hamptons and London, as well as more recently overseeing the yacht build. There's something about his overly servile manner that has always irritated Melissa. She can't put her finger on exactly why, but she doesn't trust him, never has.

'Apparently they promised to turn the music down after nine,' Evan says. 'And they're not planning to be here overnight.'

'*Formidable*,' Sandrine says under her breath and Melissa smirks to herself. It's not the first time she's encountered sarcasm from the inscrutable Frenchwoman, but it doesn't slip out often.

Bailey and Carter burst from the boat's interior, their bare feet slapping the teak, closely followed by the red-faced deckhand who's been asked to look after them. 'Hold on you two,' Melissa says, and somewhat miraculously they come to a sudden halt. 'How about we settle down now, hey?' she pleads. 'You must both be thirsty.'

'Can we have a soda, Mom?' Bailey asks.

'Just this once,' Melissa replies. 'But no Coke.'

'How about a lemonade, like me?' Kitty suggests, grinning at them. 'Come sit over here and tell me what you've been up to.'

God love her, Kitty totally loses any self-consciousness when she is around the children.

statethebloodyobvious: I can't imagine how terrifying it must have been. All that dark water ...

Chapter Twenty-eight

THE DECKIE

Relieved of her nannying duties, Piper heads to the galley in search of something to eat, her stomach griping with hunger. She's made it as far as the port side when Johannes spots her and beckons her over. 'These windows need going over,' he says, handing her a hose and a chammy.

Piper wants to say that she's been working since first light, but she swallows her words. After the jet ski spill earlier, it's even more important that she appear willing. Besides, she reminds herself, it's not going to be forever.

Washing the windows gives her the chance to peek into the guest cabins. Helpfully, almost everyone seems to have left their lights blazing and blinds open. She reaches the windows of the owner's suite, leaning in and pretending to peer at a spot on the glass. Clothes are draped messily over a chair, and there's a wallet and a heavy signet ring beside the bed. A dress is spread out on the coverlet.

She moves on.

In Rocco's cabin there are clothes strewn everywhere, as though a tornado has swept through. It's the mess of someone who knows that invisible hands will pick up after them.

She continues to the next cabin.

It's Julian's. It is far neater than his friend's, almost militarily so. Not a thing out of place. She leans in, cupping her eyes to see better. There is a movement from the bathroom and she rears back, nearly overbalancing. Only the railings stop her from tumbling into the water, metres below.

Her breath comes fast. That was a close call.

She steps forward again, the chammy raised. As she sweeps it over the already spotless glass, she recognises Ruby, carrying a cleaning caddy. Ruby sets the caddy down and slumps onto an armchair, legs sprawled.

Nice work if you can get it.

Piper is distracted from further observation by the splash of a jet ski. Surprised that anyone is still out on the water, she turns to see Rocco and Julian, each with a young woman. She can only assume the boys must have gone over to the other yacht. Are they insane, or merely dumb? Those women are almost certainly being paid to entertain the men on board the party yacht, not to skive off with younger, better-looking guys.

Finally, when every window is sparkling, she heads to the crew mess, finding Ruby taking a meal break. 'Hey,' she says, sitting down on the bench seat, every muscle in her body aching.

'Hey yourself,' Ruby replies. 'Hard work, huh?' she says, taking a close look at Piper.

'Something like that.'

'Eat. Get your strength back. This is a marathon, darling. Take as many breaks as you can manage.'

Ruby is kind, but Piper thinks that's easier said than done when you're on deck and someone almost always has eyes on you. She loads up a slab of baguette with ham, cheese and tomato.

Johannes appears just as Piper takes her first bite. *What now?*

'You can clock off for today,' he says, to her relief. 'Be on deck at six tomorrow. We're leaving early.'

She nods and utters a muffled thank you, inadvertently spraying crumbs across the table. Reddening, she scoops them back onto her plate, but Johannes doesn't appear to notice.

Liam passes her, going to one of the refrigerators that adjoins the galley and rummaging through it. Piper glimpses a box of khaki-green crabs, an enormous whole fish and a shelf of brightly coloured tropical fruits. The other side is filled with soft drinks. He swears, picking up several cans in succession. 'Goddammit. Is it too much to ask that people restock sooner?'

'Uh, I don't think it's working,' Piper says apologetically, having taken one when she entered the mess. 'Even the ones at the back are lukewarm.'

Liam closes the fridge and presses a touch-screen on the front. It beeps several times in response. 'Perhaps if it was set to the correct fucking temperature in the first place.'

He's no different from other chefs Piper's come across over the years, with a hair-trigger temper that'll scorch anyone foolish enough to stray into the firing line. She raises her eyebrows at Ruby and takes another bite of her sandwich. Not her circus, not her monkeys, she reminds herself, washing down the remains of her sandwich with a swig of lukewarm Coke. She's dead on her feet.

She reaches her bunk, almost too tired to wriggle out of her crew shorts and polo, let alone squeeze into the tiny adjoining bathroom for a shower, but she forces herself to clean up, knowing she won't feel like it in the morning. As she dries herself, she catches sight of her face in the steamed-up mirror. Even with the limited visibility, it's obvious she is as scarlet as a lobster. Her cheeks and forehead throb. She'd applied sun cream throughout the day, but not frequently enough it seems, or maybe the sun is just stronger here, bouncing off the water.

She rummages through the drawer where she's stowed her personal bits and pieces, pushing aside tubes, jars and roll-ons before finding a squeezy bottle of aloe vera and emptying nearly half of it into her palm. She smooths it on her face and arms, wincing as it stings her burnt skin.

What the hell was she thinking, taking this job?

Chapter Twenty-nine

THE PATRIARCH

After dinner, Evan kisses Sandrine goodnight and promises to join her in their cabin 'just as soon as I've checked on a few things'. She throws him a resigned look but doesn't object.

He'll never forget the first time he set eyes on her. He hadn't even wanted to go to the damn charity drive, but his assistant signed him up, and by the time he realised what it was, it was too late to cancel. He told himself he'd stay for lunch and then leave the minute dessert was served, but then he saw Sandrine across the crowded room – such a cliché, but it was true nonetheless – and the world stopped turning. He decided to stay, determined to meet the arresting woman who looked somehow familiar.

It didn't take him long to work out that she was a well-known actress, one he'd admired from afar, though he managed to hide that fact from her, at least on that first meeting. When she revealed herself to be a speed demon, she became irresistible.

He sits at his desk, but his eyes glaze over, the spreadsheet on the screen in front of him going in and out of focus, the numbers dancing. The pain in his chest is back, and he casts around for the bottle of antacids he usually keeps to hand. Swallowing a couple with a whisky chaser, he returns his attention to the spreadsheet, as if it will miraculously show something other than the cliff that Thyssen Properties is about to metaphorically fall off.

There is, of course, another income stream, one that only a very few know about, but it's even more volatile than the property development business, though the rewards are commensurate with the risk.

His father always said that if you think you've bitten off more than you can chew, keep chewing. Trouble is, he's been doing that for months and it's giving him, quite literally, vicious indigestion.

Last fall, when the development in Midtown was threatened with delays, he took out a second mortgage on both the New York apartment and the London townhouse in an attempt to bridge the gap. Now one of his partners in the new gaming complex has gone belly up and the cost of remodelling their seventeenth-century English barn in the Hamptons has gone nuclear. The company's debts are growing by hundreds of thousands a week in interest payments alone. He refuses to believe that the tide is going out on the family fortunes, but even he has to admit that reversing the current downward spiral might be beyond him. Things are slipping from his grasp.

He's surprised he's managed to hide the true situation from Melissa. It's surely only a matter of time before she realises the extent of their difficulties. He's no fool: he knows she's waiting for him to retire and name her as his successor. Over his dead body. He might be closer to seventy than he'd like, but he has the energy of a far younger man and won't be put out to pasture anytime soon.

Even *Ambition*, his glorious new boat (which also cost twice its original estimate), is mortgaged to the hilt. The depressing thought crosses his mind that this might be their only voyage. He had been so pleased with himself when he decided on the boat's name, but lately it's begun to feel like a noose around his neck. It's no small irony that his insatiable ambition, something he has always regarded as a personal strength, might just end up being the cause of Thyssen's downfall.

His phone beeps with a message.

Bill Katz, Thyssen's SVP, Fund Management, is trying to reach him. The message was sent half an hour ago but has only just arrived thanks to the patchy onboard signal. Jesus! All the latest tech on the yacht, but no one can provide reliable internet, not even via satellite. Evan checks his watch. It's 4 pm on a Friday in New York, but it's too much to hope that Bill is simply checking in before clocking off for the weekend. With a sigh, he dials the number, but the reception is on the fritz again and he can't get through. He's not sure whether to be relieved or even more worried.

indianheadache: I knew it had to be too good to be true – their lives seemed so fake right from the get-go.

buga_lugs: That family is a complete waste of space. Eat the rich, I say. Eat. The. Rich. Just don't get indigestion!

JimminyC: Oh, I don't know, I'd rather eat *with* the rich. Everything's better in First Class.

Chapter Thirty

THE DECKIE

It's a grey half-light when Piper's eyes fly open and although her heart thumps a warning, she's got no idea what could have startled her awake. The illuminated display of her watch tells her it's 4.37 am. More alert now, she hears it again, a soft bump, more vibration than actual sound, and then she recognises the clunk of oars grating and catching against a rowlock.

Sliding carefully out of bed so as not to disturb her sleeping bunkmate, she finds her shorts and a clean polo, then drags her hair into a ponytail. She's quick, but it takes longer than she'd like.

She scurries up the stairs to the main deck. The early morning air is cool as she emerges on the port side. Although there'll be someone at the bridge on watch, she is curious to see who might be out on the water at this hour.

Wavering lights illuminate a small rowing boat in the distance, heading in the direction of the rocky shoreline. The party yacht has vanished. She squints, trying to see more, and catches a flash in the distance, near the shore. Then another flash. Someone is waiting there, guiding the little boat to a safe landing on the rocky shoreline.

Chapter Thirty-one

THE TROPHY WIFE

Ambition is already underway when Sandrine wakes early the next morning. Leaving Evan fast asleep, she slips from their bed, wraps a silk robe around herself and walks barefoot to the outdoor deck.

She's barely had time to settle herself on the lounge when a crew member appears before her, carrying a tray on which sits a small teapot and a Spode cup and saucer. She knows without having to ask that it is her favourite Mariage Frères *Thé de Lune*. Think what she might about Walker, he certainly knows how to train the staff.

The girl places the tea on the table next to Sandrine, leaving her to enjoy the sight of the sun as it peeks, rose-gold, over the horizon. If she was a more Zen kind of person, she would be sitting cross-legged on a meditation cushion, arms aloft, thumb and index finger pressed together. Instead, she suppresses the desire for a cigarette, folds her legs underneath her and sips her tea.

According to Walker, they are heading to Port de Soller, where they'll moor offshore. A car will take them south along the coast road to a late lunch in Deia, after which they will rendezvous with *Ambition*.

Sandrine remembers a day spent wandering the quaint streets of Soller, catching the cute orange tram from the port to the town, strolling hand in hand with her lover, captivated by both him and the loveliness of the town. They had eaten lunch in a little cafe off the Plaza de la Constitución before escaping the heat and admiring the paintings (and each other) in the Can Prunera. It was utterly magical.

She nurses a faint hope that Evan might drag himself away from his phone and come with her. Perhaps they can pop Max in a baby carrier and take him too? She likes the idea of her and Evan being out together with the baby – she can count on one hand the number of times they've done that, just the three of them. Evan is usually at the office all day, and although he tries to make it home in time to see Max before he goes down for the night, it's only ever for a fleeting few minutes. He's mostly home at the weekend, but he's on the phone and often distracted, and anyway, there's always staff around.

Evan joins her half an hour or so later, kissing her on the cheek and lowering himself heavily onto a chair. He's wearing gym shorts and a workout T-shirt and smells of soap and toothpaste. 'I wondered where you'd got to,' he says.

'I've still not adjusted to this time zone,' she offers.

He takes her hand, squeezing it gently, and she seizes the moment. 'Will you come with me to Soller this morning?' she asks. 'There's a museum that might be worth seeing. I thought we could bring Max with us.'

Evan wrinkles his nose. 'A baby in a gallery? Is that wise?' He leans over and begins to massage his calf. It's been giving him some trouble, cramping up on the flight over, another reminder that he's several decades older than her.

'We could always just walk if he's unsettled. He loves to be in the carrier. He'll probably sleep most of the time anyway.'

'Darling,' Evan sighs. 'That's a lovely suggestion, but I've a conference call at ten-thirty. I don't see how I can do that from a museum, or with a baby.' He sounds genuinely regretful, and for a second Sandrine almost believes him. But as he turns to accept the glass of freshly squeezed juice held out to him, she sees a barely concealed expression of relief on his face. He might love her and Max, but he loves his work, and his company, even more. 'I've cleared my schedule after that,' he says, by way of apology. 'For lunch.'

'*Bon.*' She is well practised at not letting her true feelings show, just as she effortlessly hid any expression of disapproval when Rocco and Julian brought two women on board last night, though she knew their type immediately. After all, she'd almost been one herself. Invited to a film festival by her then-agent when she was eighteen and with only a few small, obscure parts to her credit, she imagined it an opportunity to meet people who could be influential in her career. Almost as soon as she attended the first party, on a yacht moored in the Port de Cannes, her agent hissed at her to play nice with the sweating old man who was simultaneously leering at her decolletage and groping her left buttock. It was then that she realised exactly why she had been invited. She never went back.

She's relieved that the other boat has moved on. Hopefully they won't run into it again.

It's not long before Melissa, in chocolate-brown yoga pants and a cream T-shirt knotted at the waist, her hair scraped severely off her face (not a single flyaway; even Melissa's hair doesn't dare defy her), joins them. She rubs at her temples as a steward places a coffee beside her.

'*Bonjour.* Are you feeling better now?' Sandrine asks.

'Nothing that some caffeine, Tylenol and a decent sweat won't cure.' She smiles, throws back the espresso and then excuses herself, heading for the gym on the upper deck.

'Let's touch base after breakfast,' Evan calls after her.

Something is bothering Evan. It has been bothering him since before they left New York. She thought he just needed a vacation, but that doesn't seem to be the case. Sandrine wishes he would confide in her, but he never has, not really.

junkmailermom: Safety on board has to be examined – my son knows someone who is best friends with a cousin of one of the deckhands, and according to him it was completely lax. Most of the crew didn't have the first idea, they were all wasted – drunk or high. Mind you, so were the guests.

Chapter Thirty-two

THE ELDEST DAUGHTER

In the end, Melissa, Sandrine and the two older boys are the only ones who go to Soller. Evan has a teleconference and Kitty offers to stay with Carter and Bailey. 'I promised I'd play Twister with them,' she says, looking happy at the prospect. Melissa is grateful, if a little puzzled that Kitty has come all this way merely to stay inside, especially on such a beautiful day.

The tender takes them to the marina and they catch the tram to the town centre ('More fun than a limo,' Rocco insists), where they immediately separate. Melissa suppresses her guilt that she hasn't brought the children – they would love the tram ride – but strolling around the town almost certainly wouldn't be their idea of a good time.

The boys are keen to find a record store that Rocco has read about, and Sandrine is intent on visiting a gallery, but Melissa wants to wander without a particular agenda for once. It's been far too long since she had a morning entirely to herself and despite feeling like she's playing hooky from both her family and her job, she is determined to enjoy it.

After an hour or so getting lost in the town's narrow backstreets, she finds her way to the main plaza and takes a table at an outdoor cafe, ordering an iced coffee.

'Issa?' The voice behind her is deep, crisply accented, and in an instant she is cast back more than ten years. A final semester in London at University College as part of a master's in international business and a few months of madness amid the academic grind. 'Oh my god, it is you, isn't it?'

They had been inseparable. Madly in love in the way only people in their early twenties can be. Until he broke her heart.

Melissa turns slowly, thankful that she at least washed her hair after her workout this morning, and that she's wearing a new sundress that Sandrine suggested she buy. She might be highly conflicted about Sandrine, but there's no denying she's got an unerring eye for what suits people.

Her smile falters fractionally as she sees him properly. Oh god. He's so much more attractive than he appears in recent photos, the slightly awkward, rangy, raw-boned youth transmuted into something more solid, more substantial. 'Toby!' She stands and awkwardly holds out a hand, which he takes before embracing her, kissing her on both cheeks and sweeping her up in a far less formal hug. She breathes him in, nearly weakens. He still wears the same aftershave. 'What on earth?'

He stands back to look at her and she blushes under his scrutiny. 'Of all the places ...' Why does he still make her stomach flip? 'I come here every summer, but you ... Shouldn't you be in the States? Running your father's company?'

Has he been keeping tabs on her? 'Even property moguls get to take a vacation every now and then. And I don't run the company. Not yet anyway.' She stops, taking a shaky breath. 'God, it's good to see you, Toby. You look ... well.' Incredible is the word she'd prefer to use.

The same beguiling expression, as though he is quietly amused by her. 'As do you.'

It's only when the waiter brings her coffee that she realises they are grinning at each other like idiots, his hands still entwined in hers as though she might float away if he let her go.

'Do you have time for a coffee with an old friend?' she asks.

'Of course.' He releases her and they both sit down, the small table between them suddenly too much of an obstacle.

'You never married?' he asks, spotting her ringless fingers clasped around the coffee cup.

'Oh, what?' She nearly chokes on the coffee. So he hasn't been keeping *close* tabs on her. 'No. I mean yes. I did. I am. Married. I took my jewellery off as I've been in and out of the water. Actually,' she laughs, 'he's British too.' She makes a wry face. 'I must have a type. And you?' she asks, though she already knows the answer.

'Emma. Also a lawyer,' he says with a remorseful smile. 'But she gave it up when our youngest was born. He has … he has some learning difficulties. She's been amazing with him.'

'I'm sorry to hear that – about your son, I mean.'

'We can't all live gilded lives, can we?'

'I don't believe any of us do, no matter how it might appear to outsiders.'

'How about you? I can't imagine you've had time for children, not with conquering the world.'

'I made time,' she says, hating how prissy she sounds. 'Two. Bailey and Carter. Eight and six. But it hasn't been easy. Juggling.' She checks herself. She can't believe he's here in front of her, the man who once held her heart in the palm of his hand. 'Did you become the barrister you always dreamed about being?'

She already knows the answer to this, having shamefully googled him every now and then, usually when feeling low about her own life and questioning the choices she's made. Tobias McIntyre. He's done well. Of course he has. King's Counsel. A flourishing legal practice attached to a high-profile chambers in the Inns of Court, including representation of a range of worthy *pro bono* causes. Beautiful wife (she's seen pictures, black ties and ballgowns galore).

'I did.'

His coffee arrives and she uses the interruption to sneak another careful look at him, noting the neatly trimmed nails, the crinkle of skin at the corners of his eyes when he smiles, the faint lines bracketing his lips … She allows herself a brief, delicious moment to imagine what her life would have been if she hadn't had to return to the States. She stops herself. It doesn't work like that. Choices are made, paths are taken, and who can say if those not followed would have been any better. If she had stayed, Bailey and Carter wouldn't exist, and she can't imagine a world in which that could be good, or even possible.

He gives his head a little shake as if he still can't quite believe she is there in front of him. 'I'm sorry, I'm still shocked that I ran into you. It's not often I'm lost for words.' He's charming, playful, self-deprecating … all the things that made her fall in love with him in the first place.

'As a barrister, I'd hope not,' she says, before adding quietly, 'Me too.' She is unable to tear her eyes away from his, losing herself in their inky blue depths.

'Your coffee will get cold,' he says eventually, breaking their gaze.

'It's iced,' she replies, then colours, realising he is teasing.

He looks at her thoughtfully. 'It's funny how one decision can change your life forever.'

'Kind of like a kaleidoscope. One twist and the pattern is entirely different,' she says.

'But still beautiful.'

She colours, not knowing if he is referring to her or the kaleidoscope.

'You're here with your family?' he asks.

She nods. 'The whole crazy group. Dad's new wife … French, a former actress.' She mentions Sandrine's maiden name and he blinks in recognition. 'Their baby boy, Max. My younger brother Rocco, little sister Kitty, my two—'

'Wow. Where are you staying? In town?'

'Dad's got a boat' – she deliberately downplays it – 'so we're sailing around the island, or at least that's the plan.'

'Nice.'

She'd forgotten that dry response of his. She's not sure if he's impressed or not, though it doesn't matter to her one way or the other.

'Let's not do the small-talk thing, huh?' she pleads. 'It was never like that for us.'

'No, it wasn't. Issa …' He's the only person who's ever called her that, and the way he says it, he might as well be stroking her bare skin. 'Are you happy?' he asks, and she finds she can't meet his eyes, though she feels them on her, missing nothing.

There's a long silence, and she takes another sip of coffee. 'Sometimes,' she finally admits. 'Mostly, perhaps? Isn't that all any of us can hope for?'

He laughs. 'I don't remember you being quite so fatalistic.'

'We were both much younger then,' she counters.

'God, it's good to see you, Issa.' He hesitates. 'I tried to call, after you left, but the time difference always seemed to be out. I left a couple of messages, but you never replied. Once, your father picked up. He said you had decided to stay in the States, that you weren't planning to return to England, and you didn't want to speak to me. I stopped trying to contact you after that.'

'And you believed him?'

Toby spreads his hands. 'Why wouldn't I?'

'I thought *you* weren't returning *my* calls. He never said you tried to reach me.'

'Why would he do that?'

She laughs bitterly. 'You haven't met him.'

'Anyway, it was a long time ago.'

'A long time, and no time,' she says, mustering a sad smile.

All too soon their coffee is drunk. Toby waves away the offer of another. He steals a glance at his watch.

'Don't let me keep you.' She begins to gather her things, riffling through her purse. She signals to their waiter for the bill. 'Though it has been so, so wonderful to see you again, after so long.'

'Sorry. I said I'd meet Emma. She'll be wondering what's happened to me.' He reaches for his wallet and pulls out a few Euro notes. 'And yes, the feeling is mutual. I can't tell you what a lovely surprise it was to run into you.' He hands her a card. 'Stay in touch. Please.'

'Sure,' she replies, knowing that won't happen, not in this universe, not when there are ten years, an Emma and an Angus, and half a world between them.

'I mean it, Issa.'

Then, suddenly, she can't bear to let him go so easily. 'Come and meet everyone – drinks on board? Tomorrow night, if you're free. I'll text you the details of our location when I know them. Bring the whole family.'

He looks surprised at the invitation, and she wonders if he can sense her impulsiveness. He kisses her on both cheeks. 'I'll check with Em. I'm sure we'd love to.' Always so polite.

She nods – 'Of course' – and leaves before he can see how much of an effect he's had on her. It's a full thirty minutes before her legs feel anything approaching steady again.

calloutchain: Think about the pollution. The clean-up alone is going to cost millions, I heard. Who's going to foot the bill for that, huh?

Chapter Thirty-three

THE YOUNGEST DAUGHTER

'Left hand blue,' Kitty says, as the spinning indicator comes to a stop. 'That's this one, Carter.' She guides his little palm to the closest blue spot on the plastic game sheet they've laid out in the middle of the salon.

Everything straining, he reaches towards it but topples over onto Bailey, who lets out a wail of annoyance.

'Okay, I think we've had enough of that for one day,' Kitty says, lifting him off his sister. Bailey looks ready to sulk but asks if they can play hide-and-seek instead. 'We played with Piper. It was *so* fun.'

'I bet we'll never find you,' Kitty tells Bailey. 'Want me to start counting?'

'Give me till a hundred.' Bailey is already on her feet, hopping from one foot to the other in anticipation.

'You got it. Remember, the engine room and crew cabins are off limits.'

Bailey hurries off as Kitty begins to count loudly, clapping her hands on her thighs in time with the numbers.

The little girl turns out to be exceptionally good at hiding.

Kitty and Carter scour the upper deck, the gym and the spa, then descend to the main deck, checking each of the cabins, even in the en suites and the wardrobes. They ask every steward they pass, but no one claims to have seen Bailey. Her dad's office is locked, as is the master cabin, so she can't have gone in there.

They go to the lowest deck and the galley, where there is a batch of sugar cookies on a cooling rack. Kitty feels suddenly faint with hunger. She probably last ate a cookie two years ago. The chef insists they take some as they pass (Kitty strengthens her resolve and declines) and tells them Bailey hasn't been that way.

Almost out of options, they pick their way through the watersports storage area and find Johannes, the bosun, who hasn't seen her either.

Finally, Kitty and a flagging Carter walk along a narrow corridor, trying the door handles along the way but finding no sign of Bailey. The air conditioning isn't as effective down here and Carter begins to whine that he's not having fun anymore. 'We've been searching forever,' he says, his cookie long finished.

'Tell you what, we'll just look along here and if we don't find her we'll give up. Deal?'

Carter nods.

Kitty is starting to think this wasn't such a good idea after all when she opens the last door at the end of the corridor before the swim deck. It's dark, and she can't find a light switch, and for a second she thinks it's nothing but an oversized cupboard.

'Eww. It stinks,' says Carter, recoiling.

It is sour and hot, with a smell like old socks run through the dryer. Kitty takes one step inside, calling out for Bailey, but there's no one there. At first, she thinks the room is empty, but then she sees the outline of a thin mattress, one you'd use under a sleeping bag. There's a pile of boxes stacked on top of each other, a couple of empty Coke cans and a dented plastic water bottle. Perhaps the crew come here to hang out, a private space away from everyone, though she can't imagine it's especially appealing.

She's about to leave when the light from the corridor catches something on the floor and she bends down to pick it up.

'What's that?' Carter asks.

She holds it between her fingers. A gold chain with an initial – the letter K – hanging from it.

She holds it up. 'Someone must have lost it, probably one of the crew. I'll give it to Walker; I'm sure he'll be able to find its owner.' She clips it around her neck. 'To keep it safe,' she says when Carter looks at her, questioning.

'I'm bored of this game now,' Carter says.

'Alright, buddy. Let's get out of here, huh?'

Chapter Thirty-four

THE SURVIVOR

The inspector – sorry, sub-inspector – gets very little from her, his lips flattening in silent frustration when she fails to answer his questions. She has a thumping headache and wants him to leave her alone so she can go back to sleep. All he will tell her is that she's at Palma Hospital.

After a while, a nurse comes in and, to her relief, informs him that the patient needs to rest and he should return in the morning. When he's finally gone, she asks for a mirror. After a moment's hesitation, the nurse obliges. He places it in her hand and she slowly lifts it to her face.

She inhales sharply, the movement sending another wave of pain rippling through her. She doesn't recognise the face, wide-eyed with shock, staring back at her. This person has purple bruises under her swollen piggy eyes, lips that are too big for her face and a bright red welt across one cheek. Her head is so heavily bandaged she can't even tell what colour her hair is.

She lowers the mirror, catching sight of a thin gold ring on her finger. She twists it around, then pulls it off and inspects it. There's an inscription on the inside of the band. It's faint, but she can still read it.

You carry my heart.

It tells her nothing.

Chapter Thirty-five

THE TROPHY WIFE

El Olivo is fully booked and usually only open to hotel residents, but Walker has secured them a table for two for lunch. 'Just as well none of the others wanted to join us,' Evan remarks as they are shown to their seats on the outdoor terrace where ancient, gnarled trees offer dappled shade and the view extends across the valley towards the Serra de Tramuntana. This place has existed, unchanged, for decades, and is deservedly popular. Almost every table is occupied with well-heeled, elegant patrons; floaty fabrics reveal lightly tanned skin and delicate gold jewellery. Even in the heat, many of the men are wearing linen jackets; it's that kind of place. Understated, delightfully rustic, reeking of wealth and what some might still call good breeding. Sandrine would never have dreamed of coming to such a place when she was last on the island; neither she nor her lover could have afforded it.

'Walker is a miracle worker, but I doubt even he would have been able to swing a table for eight at such short notice,' she agrees.

Melissa, Kitty and the two children have gone on a picnic, accompanied by a couple of the deckhands. Rocco and Julian said they wanted to explore Deia, mentioning a bar they'd seen on TikTok, and Max is back at the boat with Amber.

'I'm pleased that we finally get some time together,' Sandrine says, leaning back as her napkin is unfolded. 'Just us.' She's drawn her hair back into a low bun beneath a wide-brimmed straw hat and is wearing a raspberry-hued Loewe trapeze mini dress that shows off her toned shoulders. A pair of Cartier gold bangles and sunglasses complete the look. She's not sure if it's simply the effect of being back in Europe again, but she feels almost like her old self.

Evan slips his phone into his jacket pocket. 'And I promise not to check it for the entire meal.'

Sandrine smiles. 'I'll hold you to that.'

'Now, what are we drinking?' he asks, flipping the pages of a wine list as thick as a novel.

Sandrine, momentarily distracted by the arrival of a noisy party of six at the table next to them, returns her attention to her husband. 'Rosé?' she suggests.

'Whatever the lady desires,' he says to a hovering waiter. 'And a bottle of your best Rioja.'

'Certainly, sir.'

'*Excusé moi?*'

One of the men from the table has come over to them. She recognises the look in his eye. She's seen it often enough. The nervous thrill of encountering someone famous combined with embarrassment at approaching them. She stops herself. Maybe he's only after the salt. The hat she's wearing could be disguise enough.

'You're Sandrine Furneaux, aren't you?' he asks, bolder now.

She gives an almost imperceptible nod.

'I knew it! My wife said it couldn't possibly be.' He flashes a triumphant grin to the others at his table. 'Would you mind?' He scoots to her side and holds out his phone in front of them, requesting a selfie. 'It's for my brother really. He'll never believe it otherwise. *Diabolique* is one of our favourite films:

you were incredible in it. Have you been in anything recently? You disappeared off the face of the earth. Poof! Tell me you haven't retired? Or aren't the roles to your taste?' He introduces himself, and his delivery is so charming that she's caught off guard. It feels entirely natural to reply in her native tongue, to be gracious, even to gently flirt. After all, it's been so long since she went anywhere she might be recognised.

'May I?'

She smiles, he snaps a couple of selfies and then, lifting her hand to his lips in farewell, he retreats.

Evan is simmering with fury. 'Did you have to let him touch you like that?'

'I was being polite to a well-mannered gentleman,' she insists. 'What would you have me do?' The truth is, she is never recognised in New York and had forgotten that it's not always a chore, that sometimes, in fact, like today, it can be quite delightful.

'You were flirting with him.'

'Nonsense. He was just being … French.' She shrugs, although even to her the explanation sounds weak.

'Exactly!' Evan thuds his palm on the table, making the cutlery jump. A couple of women sitting at a table next to them pause in their conversation. 'And you lapped it up.'

'For goodness sake, he was with his wife, didn't you hear him say?'

Evan pauses. 'Am I not enough for you, is that it?'

'Now you're being ridiculous.' Sandrine fidgets with the heavily starched napkin on her lap. There's no appeasing Evan when he gets like this. Sometimes she deals with it by dissociating, her body still present but her mind somewhere else entirely. Other times, she pretends she's playing a role: the compliant, meek *petite femme*, but it doesn't suit her today. 'Please don't make a scene.'

'Have you come to a decision?'

She's never been more relieved at the arrival of a waiter. They both order the sea bass, with sides of green beans and new potatoes, and Sandrine does her best to change the subject.

The sommelier brings a glass of rosé for her and presents the Rioja for Evan to taste.

Sandrine's uncle was a négociant, and although her family was far from wealthy, she grew up with an appreciation of some of the finest wines in Europe. Evan really doesn't know as much as he pretends to about wine, but she's never felt it appropriate to comment. He swirls it briefly around his mouth and pronounces it good.

At least Evan's mood is improved by the arrival of the food – *vraiment superbe*, she thinks as she spears a bean on her fork and dips it into the spinach and pine nut sauce. 'Are you happy with the way *Ambition* is performing?' she asks in an effort to further distract him.

She succeeds, and the rest of the meal passes pleasantly enough, though she finds it hard to concentrate on what Evan is telling her, thinking back to the pleasant morning spent in Soller, the delight of the cobbled streets and ancient buildings, the slower pace of life. She feels far more at home here than she ever has in the States, but perhaps she shouldn't be surprised.

They are finishing their dessert – exceptional liqueur-poached peaches and a tangy yoghurt ice-cream – when Rocco, Julian and Kitty join them.

'Who let you in?' Evan teases as extra chairs appear and they squeeze around the table.

More drinks are ordered, beers for Rocco and Julian and a Diet Coke for Kitty. 'Did you hear, Dad?' Rocco asks, alert to the promise of a juicy tidbit of news. 'They found a body on the beach yesterday morning. Further around the island. A dead woman.'

'What?' Evan replies, licking the final traces of ice cream from his spoon.

'A cove southwest of here.'

'It's really sad,' Kitty says, playing with a straw.

'Was she a local?' Evan asks.

'Apparently the police haven't identified her yet,' Julian says. 'We heard it from an English couple in the bar we stopped at earlier. That's all they knew.'

'*Quelle tragédie*,' Sandrine murmurs. There's something unsettling about the news, and she shivers despite the warm afternoon.

'How was your lunch?' Rocco asks.

'Lovely,' Sandrine replies, pleased that he has changed the subject.

'Where's Melissa?' Evan asks. 'Why didn't she and the kids come with you?'

'Bailey and Carter wanted to swim after our picnic, so she went to the beach with them,' Kitty explains.

'God help her,' says Sandrine, remembering the narrow winding path that leads from the town down to the beach.

Evan looks up sharply. 'Why do you say that?'

'I believe it is quite a walk to get there, especially for Carter and Bailey,' she says quickly. Evan's always taken such delight in showing her the world and all the experiences in it; it would be awkward – possibly worse, given his volatile mood today – if he were to discover that she's been to Mallorca before and hasn't mentioned it.

'Don't worry, I'm sure she'll cope,' Rocco says, plucking the untouched bread from Sandrine's side plate and dipping a piece of the crust in a nearby dish of olive oil.

'Do you want to order something to eat?' Sandrine asks, affronted but not entirely surprised by his lack of courtesy. The terrace has emptied out and nearly all of the other tables have been cleared. The sun is much lower in the sky, and the waiters look like they're counting down until the end of their shift, folding napkins and polishing glasses.

'We got something at the bar,' says Julian. 'Rocco's just being a pig.'

'Thanks for that,' Rocco says, annoyed.

'Take a joke, buddy,' Julian teases, ruffling his friend's hair.

'Don't. Touch. The. Hair.' Rocco scowls.

Evan signals to the waiter. 'Let's get back to the boat.'

The waiter brings the bill almost instantly and Evan gives it a cursory glance. Walker will have arranged to settle the bill later.

As they gather their things, Sandrine is relieved to note that the Frenchman who spotted her is long gone. It was a pleasant encounter, but she has no desire to provoke Evan's temper.

Deia's little beach is further than she remembers, and once again Sandrine wishes she had chosen different shoes. The woven sandals pinch her toes. Though it's late afternoon, the sun still has some bite to it, and Evan pulls out an oversized handkerchief and begins to mop the back of his neck and forehead. 'They will have towels for us on board,' she reassures him.

'I'm fine,' he says, though he is clearly uncomfortable, sweat running down his cheeks and into his collar.

The boys and Kitty have scampered on ahead, nimble as mountain goats on the rough track.

'It's not far now, anyway.' The words are out before she can take them back and she catches her breath, waiting to see if Evan has noticed.

He lurches to one side, one of his knees buckling beneath him, and she reaches for his arm to steady him. 'I'm fine.' He shakes off her hand and keeps walking, if anything quickening his pace.

The little cove is thronged with tourists. The memory of her last visit surfaces, bright and fragile, spun glass in the golden light of the afternoon. The noise of the crowds, even of her own breathing, fades to the background and she could almost be there again, the warmth of her lover's hand in hers, the feeling of drowning in the beguiling blue-green of his eyes. How little she knew then, how full the world was, such possibilities … She shakes her head, as if trying to dispel the memory. This is her life now. She has nothing to be sad about. Nostalgia does her no favours.

Ambition is waiting offshore and the tender is tied up at a small dock. When they are almost upon it, Bailey races up to greet them. She's damp and salty, her hair hanging in wet tendrils, an enormous grin on her face.

'Grandad, guess who's here?' She beams at him.

Evan takes the opportunity to lean against a rock wall. 'What's that, Bee?'

'I said, guess who's here?'

'How can I possibly do that? I have no idea. Santa Claus? The Easter Bunny?' He enjoys playing with her.

'No, silly.' She giggles, her hand over her mouth. 'Daddy!'

'Daddy?'

'Yes!' She dances around him in glee. 'He's got to wear a special boot for his sore ankle, but the doctor said he shouldn't have to miss his vacation.'

Sandrine wonders if Melissa is as happy about the surprise appearance of her husband as Bailey is. She's picked up on a strained vibe the last few times she's seen them together.

'Well, that's wonderful, Beebee. Where is he?'

'He and Mommy went for a walk. Johannes and Piper have been swimming with us. I saw a starfish.' With that, Bailey skips away.

'Let's get back on board,' Evan says. His handkerchief is now so wet you could wring it out, and his face has turned an alarming shade of reddish purple. 'I need a shower.' He strides off towards the dock, not bothering to see if his wife is following. 'Too fuckin' hot.'

Sandrine scans the cove for the children and is relieved to see them frolicking at the water's edge with Kitty and the boys, two uniformed deckhands nearby collecting a beach bag and shaking off towels. There's no sign of Melissa and Angus and, save for the path out, the narrow inlet doesn't offer many walking opportunities. If she had to guess, she'd bet they've gone for a drink at Patro March, the picturesque restaurant perched near the base of the cliff.

She bends over to remove her shoes, which are gritty with tiny rocks, and hurries after Evan.

At the dock, Walker is on board the tender, his face inscrutable behind glasses that reflect the water. He rises as they approach, sitting hurriedly back down as the boat begins to rock beneath him.

'You could have sent someone else to meet us.' Evan is jocular now, his relief at having reached the tender evident.

'Really, it is no bother,' Walker replies.

They climb aboard, aided by a deckhand, and press cold face towels to the back of their necks. Walker hands them each a bottle of icy mineral water and they set off, the breeze whipping past them, forcing Sandrine to clap a hand onto the crown of her hat as they zip across the short stretch of water to where *Ambition* is moored.

Walker shouts something to Evan, but their voices are snatched away on the wind. Even if Sandrine had any interest in what they're saying, she couldn't read their lips – Walker has his hands to his mouth as he leans in towards Evan. She closes her eyes, tired – not so much from the heat of the day, but more from the stress of worrying if Evan was going to completely lose his temper during lunch.

She's only witnessed Evan lose it a handful of times in their marriage, and each time she's been able to get away until he's calmed down. She wasn't sure she could have done that in the restaurant.

She's looking forward to a few hours with Max, and she gingerly cups her breast with her free hand. It's full and heavy to the point of soreness: he's overdue a feed. She wonders if it might be a good idea to stop soon. Evan flicks a glance in her direction and she drops her arm to her lap. He misses nothing.

It's not until they slow on approach to the swimming platform that Sandrine catches the tail end of his conversation with Walker. The words send a chill through her.

uppercasetwit: The captain should take the blame. He should have seen the weather forecast and found a safe harbour.

bombasticfantastic: They were in a supposedly sheltered harbour. And the captain was female, get your facts straight.

uppercasetwit: There you go. What more do I need to say?

bombasticfantastic: Are you kidding? I've never heard anything so sexist – this is the twenty-first century, dude.

Chapter Thirty-six

THE ELDEST DAUGHTER

'No swimming for you, then.'

'I suppose not.'

Melissa regards Angus's left leg, encased from knee to toes in a large, supremely ugly orthotic boot. Above it, his leg is white, hairy and skinny. He is wearing what he sarcastically calls his 'vaycay' attire: shorts that he's had almost since they first met and an old band T-shirt, both of which only appear when she hasn't had the chance to vet his clothing.

Bailey saw him first, letting out a squeal of joy when *Ambition*'s tender reached the shallows and Angus was carried ashore. When the kids had finished dancing around him, peppering him with questions (yes, he's doing okay; yes, isn't it cool that he's made it; and yes, he can stay for the entire vacation), she scoots them back to the water and the deckhands, telling them this is their chance for one last swim before it's time to go.

Angus leans over and gives her a sexless peck on the cheek and she tries not to flinch. At least his arrival has taken her mind off the shock of running into Toby and discovering her father's interference.

'You could have called.'

'I did. You weren't picking up. Besides, I thought it would be a nice surprise.'

Melissa hates surprises. 'We can't talk here. Think you can make it over there?' She gestures to the restaurant. 'I don't know about you, but I need a drink.'

He looks doubtfully at the expanse of shale and rocks. 'I'll give it a try,' he says, adopting a resolute but slightly pained expression, as if he is making the effort purely to please her.

She offers her arm as he limps towards the restaurant. It is clearing out after lunch and she manages to persuade the waiter to give them a table. 'A quick drink, that's all,' she promises.

'I think they took pity on me,' Angus says as they reach their seats.

'I was under the impression you weren't able to travel,' she says, signalling to a waiter and ordering sangria for both of them.

'I got a second opinion.' He shrugs. 'Dr Greenberg is too conservative.'

She nods, accepting his point. After all, what choice does she have? 'And you still thought it was a good idea to just turn up?'

He pours them both a drink when the pitcher arrives. 'I wanted the chance to apologise,' he says, pushing a glass towards her.

Melissa sits back in her chair, arms crossed, and considers this. She's nowhere near ready to forgive him, not this time, but she can hardly send him straight home again without raising suspicion, especially not now that the children have seen him. There's no way she's going to be the bad guy in this shitshow of a marriage. 'Go on then.' She takes a long slug from her glass.

'Go on then what?'

She rolls her eyes. 'Apologise.'

'You want me to bleed?' He spreads his hands in surrender. 'Because I will.'

Melissa has always excelled – at school, university and graduate school. She was top or near top of the class at all of them, even as the pond got bigger and bigger. She is used to winning, has never learned how to lose. But it is safe to say her marriage is not a triumph.

'Disembowelling would not be enough.' Goddammit. He looks so pathetic that she doesn't have the heart to draw this out. Besides, she's sick of listening to his excuses, she's heard them before. 'Okay. You can stay, but don't think for a second that it's for any other reason than the children's happiness.'

Relief spreads across his face and he raises his glass to her. 'Darling, I really don't deserve you.'

'Damn straight.' She throws back the rest of her drink and gestures for him to refill it. 'Would have been nice if you'd remembered that a few weeks ago,' she adds under her breath.

* * *

After several glasses of sangria, Melissa is feeling a little more mellow, the day's heat and rough edges wearing off. When the pitcher is empty, they pick their way across the beach to the jetty, where the tender is waiting. A thought occurs to her. 'How did you know where to find us?' she asks.

'Evan arranged it.'

The revelation that her husband has been in touch with her father pulls her up short. 'Did you call him?' she asks, suspicious.

'He rang me, as it happens. Wanted to know how bad my ankle was and said he'd got me in to see another specialist.'

Melissa sighs. She might have known her father would have had a hand in the situation. He thinks he's helping, but sometimes he really isn't. He's always been controlling. She wonders if he somehow got wind of the trouble in her marriage. Evan Thyssen might be on his third wife, but that doesn't mean he wants any of his children or grandchildren to experience a break-up. More cynically, nor would he want the family wealth to be diluted, prenups notwithstanding.

The alcohol and the sun have given her a headache. All she wants now is a cool shower, a nap and to avoid thinking about what to do about her feckless, cheating husband.

Seeing Toby earlier has galvanised her. He's reminded her of a time when she was someone who laughed easily and lived more lightly. Somewhere in the course of her career, her increasingly shitty marriage and the relentlessness of motherhood, she has hardened into an entirely different person. Well, she's no longer willing to accept the status quo. She deserves better.

askmeanything: All the money in the world won't protect you from tragedy, that's for sure.

Chapter Thirty-seven

THE TROPHY WIFE

Angus Silk isn't the only unexpected arrival.

The next morning, as Sandrine, Evan, Melissa, Angus and the children are having breakfast, a boat from the Spanish Guardia Civil pulls alongside.

Sandrine calls for Amber to take the children.

'But I want to see the policemen,' Bailey says, her chin set.

'Sorry, sweetie, but they need to talk to the grown-ups,' Melissa says.

'Are we in trouble?' she asks, her lower lip trembling.

'Not at all, darling. Everything's fine, they're just visiting.'

'Then why can't I stay?'

The children are persuaded to leave with the promise of jet ski time later, but only if they brush their teeth.

Walker and the captain go to meet the boat, returning with two officers wearing serious expressions and pistols in leather holsters at their hips, in case anyone is under any illusions about their capabilities. Walker converses with them in fluent Spanish, showing them their entry documentation and passenger manifest. He then explains to the group that the police are investigating the death of a woman, as yet unidentified, whose body was discovered on a beach to the southwest of the island.

'We heard about it,' Evan says.

Sandrine thinks back to the conversation between Walker and her husband on their return from Deia the previous day. She heard the words 'Belarus' and 'Beluga' and assumed they must have been talking about caviar, which, given Evan's obsession with it, isn't surprising. But that wasn't what had chilled her. That came later, as the tender approached *Ambition*.

Evan is capable of many things, and she wouldn't be surprised if he sometimes sails close to the wind, but he'd never be involved in anything that would result in a dead woman, surely?

'I understand you were anchored in the vicinity of Cala de Ses Ortigues the night before last, the twenty-eighth?' the one with the silky moustache asks, speaking in English now.

Evan nods. 'We were.'

'We're making general enquiries at this stage. Checking on a number of vessels along this part of the coast. Did you see any other yachts in the area?' the officer asks.

'There was one other. I remember the name: *Moirai*. I had a conversation with my daughter about it, so it's stuck in my memory.'

The officer looks around at the rest of the group. 'Your daughter?'

'Katherine. Kitty. She's not up yet, but I can't see any reason to wake her. Unless of course you would like me to.'

The other officer takes notes.

'That would be helpful, thank you. Can you tell us anything else about the yacht? Did you see anyone on board?'

Evan signals to Walker, who speaks into the microphone clipped to the collar of his shirt.

'There were a large number of people on board and they were noisy. Some sort of onboard party, I think. Walker went over to ask if they could keep the volume down.' Evan points to Max, who is sitting in his highchair mashing bananas between his chubby fingers. 'We have young children aboard and it was early evening. Everyone is entitled to their fun, but we didn't want them to spoil our peace for too long.'

'I see. And what was the result of this request?' The officer addresses Walker now.

'They claimed that they would be moving on within a few hours,' Walker replies. 'They were perfectly gracious.'

'Do you remember seeing a woman with dark red hair? A tattoo on her shoulder?'

Walker shakes his head. 'As I said, there were a large number of people on board and I was only there for a short time.'

No one says anything about the two women who Rocco and Julian brought over to *Ambition* later that same night, and Sandrine is not about to bring it up. She shares Evan's philosophy: never give anyone more information than they directly ask for.

Kitty emerges, blinking in the bright sunlight. The two officers ask her if she remembers anything more about the yacht, but she only gives monosyllabic responses and their questions soon come to an end.

A burst of static and some garbled Spanish comes from the police radio. The officers seem suddenly keen to leave. '*Gracias*,' the moustachioed one says. 'We have your details if we should need anything further, but you have been very helpful.'

'Not at all,' Evan says smoothly.

Walker ushers them to the deck below.

'Do you think the dead woman was from that party boat?' Melissa asks when they're out of earshot. 'It seems odd that they'd come and ask us about it.'

'Possibly,' Evan replies, watching the police cruiser motor away. 'And it's not that odd – they said they're talking to all the boats that were in the area. Let's not let it spoil our vacation, hey?'

'Just as well Rocco and Julian aren't up yet,' Melissa mutters, not looking at all convinced by Evan's brush-off. That's the thing about Melissa, Sandrine thinks, not for the first time. She's sharp as a kitchen knife, runs rings around most people, nearly all of whom underestimate her. Sometimes she thinks even Evan underestimates his daughter and what she's capable of.

Amber returns with Bailey and Carter, now dressed in bathing suits, faces white with sun cream.

'What are the plans for today?' Evan asks.

'You tell us, darling,' Sandrine says, spearing a piece of pineapple and smiling in his direction.

Evan suggests that they might motor on to Bahía de Alcudia. 'Max should visit the beach at least once this trip,' he says. 'And I bet Bailey and Carter would love a sandcastle competition.'

Sandrine is surprised that he would want to go to such a popular beach – he usually shies away from anywhere too crowded, not wanting to mingle with 'the great unwashed', as he puts it.

Melissa blows out a puff of air through her lips. 'Can't say I ever remember you having time to make sandcastles with Rocco and me,' she says. 'I don't see why we can't at least go to a beach club. Gran Folies or Nikki Beach are supposed to be good.' (Her assistant had given her a dossier on all the best places to go on the island. Had Melissa had the time to read it closely, she would have seen that Nikki Beach is strictly for over eighteens.) 'I could handle a few cocktails while lounging on the daybeds at some point.'

'I do believe we've passed both of those. Besides, who said I'd be the one building sandcastles? You and I have a submission to wrestle.'

So he doesn't even intend on coming. Sandrine doesn't relish the prospect of sitting on the beach with a million other tourists, with sand getting in places she'd rather it didn't, but Max will almost certainly love it – he's at the age where everything is to be explored. She swallows her disappointment. 'That sounds lovely, darling, but what a shame that you will miss out. You couldn't spare even an hour?'

She scans his face for a reaction and he eventually smiles regretfully. 'It really depends how much progress we make this morning.' He finishes his coffee and rises. 'I'll be in the study in half an hour, Melissa.'

'Let's see if we can wrap it up quickly then,' Melissa replies, her gaze flicking to her children. '*I'd* like to build a sandcastle with my children.'

Angus isn't paying any attention to his wife; he's absorbed in something on his phone. Sandrine glances sideways. He's playing some kind of video game with the sound turned off. Clearly the ultra-smart professor isn't as rarefied as he'd like everyone to think.

Evan holds up his hands in submission. 'Outnumbered by my wife and daughter. I know when I'm beaten, god help me.'

Sandrine chooses to believe that he is trying to make up for his overbearing behaviour at the restaurant the day before.

'Can Piper come with us, Mom?' Bailey asks. She has been listening in to the adults' conversation.

'Who?' Melissa looks puzzled.

'Piper. She's really good at lots of games.'

'I don't see why not. We'll need some help carrying everything.'

Bailey gives her mother a gap-toothed grin.

'What's that, Bee?' Angus asks, finally giving them some attention.

Sandrine looks across at Angus again, just as his phone lights up with a notification. He covers it quickly, but not before she sees a photo of a smiling young blonde.

* * *

They make quite a spectacle, nearly a dozen of them walking along the long strip of golden sand towards a grid of palm-fringed umbrellas. Some are in uniform, toting bags, sand toys, coolers with snacks and drinks, or loaded up with towels, spare clothes, a stroller and everything else needed for a family trip. The others, who walk slightly ahead, are unencumbered, clad in pastel-hued resort wear, straw hats and reflective sunglasses. Angus lags a little behind the first group, limping, one leg encased in the cumbersome orthotic boot. Melissa has joined them and Evan claimed he would follow, but Sandrine is not holding her breath.

As they park themselves on a stretch of sunbeds, two of the deckhands chase after Bailey and Carter, who are already halfway towards the water.

'We're going to go check out the other end of the beach,' Julian says.

'Heading to a bar, more like,' Melissa says. 'Don't let us cramp your style.' She grins.

Angus seems as though he wants to go with the two boys but instead sinks heavily onto a lounger with a small groan.

'Kitty, you wanna come?' Rocco asks and she nods in response.

Sandrine unclips Max from his stroller and lifts him out, lowering him until his toes rest on the sand. He instinctively curls them and leans forward, trying to bend over to investigate this strange new thing. Laughing at him as his hat slips over his eyes, Sandrine sets him on all fours and he immediately grabs a handful of sand and puts it in his mouth, gumming at it. '*Non, ma chérie*.' She wipes his mouth, which is now smeared with sand and saliva, but he is undeterred, lunging forward again, eager to explore. Sandrine thinks of her mother with a pang of sadness, wishing she could have seen her with Max; she would have doted on her grandson.

'I remember when Carter did exactly the same thing on his first visit to the beach,' Melissa says fondly. The two women share a rare moment of connection.

'I might take him down to the water,' Sandrine says after a while. 'It won't be too cold for him?' A shadow falls across her.

'There's only one way to find out.'

She looks up to see her husband standing over them. 'Evan! You made it after all.'

'I thought you hated the *hoi polloi*,' Melissa mutters.

'I couldn't miss my son's first swim in the sea, could I?'

'Well then,' says Sandrine, lifting Max up and offering him to Evan. 'Let's all go in.'

silentpartner: It's just the annual billionaire sacrifice – god knows we can spare them.

tictactoe99: You crack me up. I needed a laugh today.

flex8760: Hey, they're real people, have some respect.

silentpartner: No chance.

flex8760: And there were crew on board, just trying to do their job.

Chapter Thirty-eight

THE ELDEST DAUGHTER

Melissa watches from behind her sunglasses as the trio trot towards the shore. Her dad looks like Max's grandfather rather than his father, but then people become parents at all ages these days, and he at least appears to be doing a better job of it than he did with her and Rocco, or even with Kitty, for that matter. *Fourth time's the charm*, she thinks sourly.

Almost without warning, a lump rises in her throat and a tear tracks its way down her cheek. Christ. It can't be Angus's infidelity; she should be used to that by now. Perhaps it's the shock of seeing Toby again, or perhaps she's just exhausted, her Teflon facade finally cracking. Maybe it's all become too much now she's finally got a moment to relax. She looks around self-consciously, but no one has noticed. Angus, on the lounger next to her, has his nose in a book and his hand around the neck of a beer. It's just the two of them here now. She sniffs and dashes the tear away.

Angus puts the book down. 'Are you getting sick?' he asks, taking a pull of the beer.

'Sun lotion in my eye,' she lies.

Seeming satisfied by this, he frowns at the ocean as though it has done him some kind of injustice. 'Do you think we should talk?' he asks, turning his attention back to her.

'Probably.' She swallows. 'But not now. Can we leave it until we get home? I've got a lot on my plate right now.' She would like to be able to tell him about the Rawson Project, how she's convinced the numbers are cooked, but he switches off when she talks about work and she's learned to solve such problems on her own.

'When? We hardly see each other on our own these days. You're either at the office or with the children.' He sounds like a sulky child himself.

'That's the world of working moms, Angus,' she replies heavily. She will *not* accept responsibility for his inability to keep his pants zipped.

He continues to frown at the water, letting out a faint belch.

She sighs and tries for appeasement, not that he deserves it, but if he thinks she's come around it'll make the next few weeks run smoother. 'I'll schedule dinner. DeStefano's.' He loves red meat.

'Sure.'

She won't let herself think any more about Toby. It won't solve anything. She's already regretting having invited him to drinks. 'I'm going to go hang with Carter.'

'What's that?' he asks. 'Did you say we should go and get a drink? Is there a bar near here?'

'Angus!' She gets to her feet and scans the ocean. 'They won't be little forever. Before you know it, they'll be off to college and that'll be it.' As she says the words, it occurs to her that this could well be their last vacation together as a family. The future is going to look very different for all of them. She won't be persuaded to change her mind this time, no matter what Angus might say.

She walks down to the water's edge, where a couple of the deckhands are helping Carter build a castle and a moat with a channel out to sea. A fine layer of sand coats his legs and she realises that they've lost their former toddler chunkiness without her even noticing.

Evan, Sandrine and Max are knee-deep in the gentle waves, swinging Max between them. Just like she and Angus used to do. In happier times.

Bailey is nowhere to be seen.

'Hey, honey, that's so good. Where's your sister?'

Carter doesn't look up from his task. 'I dunno,' he shrugs.

'I think she's with Piper,' the deckhand says, pointing to the sea. 'They're out there somewhere …' There's a swarm of people in the water and it's hard to recognise individuals among the bobbing heads.

'Thanks.' She turns to the other deckhand. 'Do you think you could go in and have a look for them while I stay with Carter?'

'Of course.'

'You can make the wall bigger, Mom – the waves keep melting it.' Carter is a busy little worker and it occurs to Melissa how much he is like her, industriously trying to keep the structure of his reality intact, even when outside forces threaten to overwhelm it.

She's just patted a section into place when a rogue wave washes towards them and the walls of the moat disintegrate into a soft puddle.

'Oh Mom!' Carter cries.

'Oh Carter!' she replies, falling dramatically back on her heels, not caring as another wave heads towards them and her hair tangles in the wet sand.

For a second Carter looks as though he might cry, but then he sets his chin and begins to shore up the walls again.

So much like her.

'I can't see them anywhere,' the deckhand says when he returns a minute or so later, puffing as though he's run the length of the beach. There's a barely concealed note of panic in his voice.

Squeezing the salt water from her gritty hair, Melissa asks. 'Where have you looked?'

He spreads his arms wide, 'Just about the entire beach.'

'Did you go in?'

'Up to my waist.'

'Oh, for Christ's sake,' she mutters, pushing past him and breaking into a sprint.

onthedownlow: At the end of the day, this is a family that has experienced a tragic loss, regardless of their privilege, wealth and extravagant lifestyle. They are human beings. My heart breaks for the little ones.

Chapter Thirty-nine

THE DECKIE

Two wrongs don't make a right.

Piper has never understood that phrase. Sometimes the only way to make things right is to do something wrong. She prefers 'an eye for an eye'. Let the family know something of the fear of losing a loved one …

July the eleventh. Three years ago. An ordinary Sunday. She was about to finish up after a squally afternoon rescuing kids from capsized dinghies, helping to haul the little boats out of the water, when the call came.

'It's Lexie,' her dad said, his voice cracking on his daughter's name.

She and her sister had video called a few days earlier. Lexie confided that she'd met someone. 'He's amazing, Pip,' she said, practically sparkling through the screen. 'I can't wait for you to meet him. He works on the boat too – he's a massage therapist, can you believe it? As soon as the season's finished, we're going to come over. It's been so crazy, I can't remember what eight hours' sleep feels like. It's gorgeous here, of course. The water is nothing like the grey old Solent. And you should see the ports – how the other half live!' She'd signed off as she always did, with a mock-salute and a wink that scrunched up the whole right side of her face.

She had sounded so happy.

'There's been an accident.' Her father's voice broke into her thoughts.

'What?' In an instant Piper forgot how filthy she was, how bone-tired. Every muscle tensed against what she was about to hear.

'She's in a local hospital, but they're talking about flying her to England when they've stabilised her.'

'What happened?'

'I don't have any more details.'

As soon as Piper heard those words she knew that everything had changed. 'But she's going to be okay, right?'

Her father's voice cracked again, and she could have sworn he was crying, though she'd never seen him do so. 'We don't know yet, darling.'

'Is there a number we can call? Which hospital, where? We need to go to her. We need to find out.'

'The man who rang me said he'd be in touch again as soon as he had more news.'

'I'll be home as soon as I can,' she promised. 'We'll figure this out.'

Lexie had saved her once when they were out sailing. A storm was brewing, and they'd been trying to outrun it and get back to shore. Piper was only eleven but over-confident, cocky about her ability to go about, steering the dinghy into the wind. She forgot to duck as the boom swung towards her and it threw her sideways out of the boat. Lexie reacted in an instant, throwing her a lifebuoy and then yelling to her when she was too stunned to reach for it. The sound of Lexie's voice was almost drowned out by the wind, but something got through to Piper and she grabbed the orange ring and held on. Somehow Lexie had the strength to haul her back into the boat and they made it home safely.

Lexie never said a word about the incident to their parents, who would almost certainly have stopped her going out on the water again. Piper owes her sister not only for that, but also probably for her life.

'Piper, can we go deeper?' Bailey asks, bringing her back to the present. They've walked about a hundred yards further down the beach, to a spot where the waves look a little calmer.

'Sure, sweetie, pop your goggles on and hold on to my hand.'

Together they swim into the sea until Piper can no longer feel the sand beneath her feet, until they are both out of their depth.

Chapter Forty

THE PATRIARCH

'Evan Thyssen, is that really you? Son of a gun, it is! *Hola señor!*'

The last thing Evan expects is to find himself accosted on a public beach while bending over to scoop up his crawling son and simultaneously sucking in his gut.

He straightens and thrusts a wriggling Max at Sandrine. Wiping sandy hands on his shorts, he curses the fact that he discarded his shirt earlier. He hates being caught out, especially by people he's known forever. 'Jim Murray, what the hell?' He extends his hand, torn between a handshake and a friendly clap on the shoulder, but the man pulls him into a sweaty bear hug.

'Whaddya know? Babe!' Jim shouts to the woman right next to him, drawing the attention of almost everyone in the vicinity. 'I told you it was him!' Jim releases Evan and lowers his sunglasses, looking him in the eye. 'We were talking about you at dinner just last night, weren't we, doll?'

'We were, he's right – but then he's always right, at least that's what he tells me.' The woman dazzles him with her veneers and Evan can't for the life of him remember her name. Jim's first wife was Betsy, quiet and dark-haired, but he's no idea what this woman with the leopard-print bikini, streaky extensions, fake boobs and over-inflated lips is called.

'Virginia,' she says, reminding him.

'Of course, I knew that, Virginia,' he says, recovering himself. 'What a surprise! How good to see you both. What brings you here?'

'Haven't you heard?' she replies coyly. 'Anyone who's anyone is on Mallorca this summer.' She thrusts out her chest and wraps a gold-braceleted arm possessively around Jim. 'Finally persuaded this guy to come and see what all the fuss is about.'

'Hi Sandrine.'

'*Bonjour*,' Sandrine says, focused on dealing with Max, who is grizzling about being taken away from the sand. 'Nice to see you. It's been a long time.'

They'd last run into Jim and Virginia at a benefit the winter before. Sandrine never warmed to Virginia, commenting that she wears too much make-up, not to mention a cloying perfume that lingers like the proverbial bad smell.

'Ha, I know, it's been crazy, huh? Nothing new about that, though. We're just up the hill there,' Jim says, turning and waving vaguely in the direction of the buildings that line the beach. 'How about you?'

'Not too far from here.'

Jim's eyes light up. 'I heard you got yourself a flashy new toy,' he says, digging Evan playfully in the ribs. 'Don't be shy about it.'

'Well, you know ...' An idea occurs to him. Jim might just be the answer to his current problems. He can't believe he hasn't thought of him before, and now here he is, served up on a platter. Really, it's remarkable how the world turns. 'You should come and take a look. Join us for a drink. Tonight, if you like.' Jim is richer than Croesus and, even better, hates to miss out on what he thinks is a good deal.

Sandrine shoots him a look, but he ignores it. He's still a little pissed at that sleazeball fawning all over her at lunch yesterday.

'That would be wonderful!' Virginia gushes. 'We're free, aren't we, honey?'

'Sure are.'

'Okay then,' Evan replies. 'We're planning to relocate a little further along the coast this afternoon, so I'll text you our new location as soon as we drop anchor. We can send the tender to pick you up from the closest beach to bring you on board *Ambition.*'

'Say what?' Virginia asks.

'*Ambition*,' repeats Evan. 'That's the boat's name.'

'Of course it is.' Jim slaps him on the back. 'Of course it is.'

Max begins to wail, an ear-splitting sound that causes the people around them to stop what they are doing and sets Evan's teeth on edge.

'I think that's our cue to leave,' he adds with a mock grimace.

princeamongthieves: They should have all gone down. Would have served them right.

abbeyhatesbananas: Ooof. Harsh much?

boybait: I heard he was in trouble, over-leveraged. Who knows – maybe it wasn't an accident at all?

princeamongthieves: Stranger things have happened at sea.

abbeyhatesbananas: That's a cliché if ever I heard one.

Chapter Forty-one

THE DETECTIVE

After a fruitless day spent checking yachts that had been in the vicinity of Cala de Ses Ortigues, Luis is sweaty, frustrated and queasy. He is not a good sailor. The swell has flipped his stomach and despite being back on land, the world still hasn't stopped sloshing. He can't understand how some people choose to spend their holidays on a boat, much less live on one. Everything about the idea – the smell, the unknowable depths, the constant movement, being confined to a tiny vessel or even a large one – ugh. Another wave of nausea washes over him as he returns to the station and flops down at his desk, tossing his sunglasses, keys and wallet on top of a pile of unfinished paperwork.

Maria approaches him. 'I got hold of the Port Authority. The M/Y *Moirai* you radioed about?'

'That was fast. What did you find out?' Tracking the arrival and departure of watercraft in the Med has become much easier since regulations were reintroduced in response to the huge numbers of economic migrants flooding the area, but it's still not a given.

'She left Mallorcan waters yesterday, bound for Ibiza.' Maria stops and looks closer at him. 'Are you okay? Your face is paler than milk.'

He waves off her concern. 'The sea and I don't get along. Oh, and sorry I missed your birthday drinks.'

She barely acknowledges the belated apology. 'The manifest shows a crew of twenty-eight, plus ten passengers. All males.'

The people on that superyacht, *Ambition*, said they witnessed a party on board the *Moirai*, with several women present. The women clearly weren't passengers or crew, so had to have come from somewhere on the island. *Ambition*'s captain answered his questions with alacrity and a suitable level of deference. But the man he'd spoken to … Luis looks back at his notes … Walker. He had been less cooperative.

Maria leaves, returning a short while later with a small tin. She offers it to him.

'What?'

'Ginger. For nausea.'

He flashes her a brilliant smile. 'You are kind.'

'It's nothing.' She goes back to her desk.

He sucks on one of the pieces of hard candy and almost immediately begins to feel better. There had been something off about Walker. He was dismissive, as if Luis wasn't even worthy of being on board, as if it was beneath him to answer Luis's questions, as if he couldn't wait to be rid of him.

He looks up the number for the Ibizan port authority, picturing Walker's haughty expression, as though Luis was as mildly irritating as a stain on his shirt. When Luis asked Walker if anyone else on the boat had any contact with the *Moirai*, the man denied it, but his gaze shifted sideways, perhaps distracted by something.

Luis crunches down hard on the remainder of the candy, feeling it grip his molars. It's not the first time someone has lied to him, and it probably won't be the last. The question is, was it a lie of any consequence? He doesn't have an answer to that.

Yet.

Chapter Forty-two

THE ELDEST DAUGHTER

'Mom!' Bailey races across the sand towards Melissa, arms open, pure excitement spread all over her face. 'We saw so many fish! It was amazing!'

'Did you? How wonderful!' Melissa's voice is only slightly shaky. She's had a good ten minutes to imagine the worst, but her daughter is here, living and breathing and so full of delight and joy that she can't be mad. She takes a deep breath and gathers her scattered nerves. 'I've been looking for you.'

'Sorry about that, Mrs Silk. I didn't realise how far we got swept along the beach.'

The young deckhand probably has no idea how a mother can worry, but Melissa nevertheless eyes her suspiciously, attempting to gauge her remorse. She *seems* genuine. 'No problem. I've got this now, thanks.' She's terse to the point of rudeness, her earlier panic not entirely dispersed by Bailey's safe return.

The girl – Piper, she suddenly remembers – smiles guilelessly. 'Of course, enjoy your swim. You've got a terrific little girl there.'

Bailey pulls Melissa into the water, 'Come on, Mom, you gotta see this.'

'Okay, okay,' Melissa replies. 'But we can't be too long. Your dad was worried about where you were and he won't know that I've found you.'

She has no compunction about letting Angus wait a few minutes more.

* * *

Irritatingly, he is behind his book again by the time they return. 'I saw you together,' he says by way of explanation. 'See, I told you there was nothing to worry about.'

He had done no such thing, but she lets it slide.

There's a plate of food on a small table next to him that's spoiling in the heat, jamon curling up and darkening, cheese sweating. He's drinking another beer, his second? Third? One thing is for certain; his injury doesn't seem to be bothering him. He's taken the boot off, and although his ankle is a riotous shade of purple, it doesn't appear to be too swollen.

A cry from Max interrupts her thoughts. 'Looks like someone's hungry,' she says to Sandrine, who is walking towards them with her squirming baby.

'Or tired,' she replies, jiggling him gently up and down and patting his bottom in an effort to quieten him.

'You.' Melissa addresses Piper now. 'I wonder if you might find a drug store and get me some drops. The water's blocked my ear.'

'Of course, but we do have a fully stocked first-aid kit and other medications on board. There may well be some there.'

'I'd rather not take that chance.' She wiggles the tip of her pinky in her ear. 'Goddamn. I can't clear it.'

Angus grabs one of the beach umbrellas for balance as he attempts to stand, yelping as his injured leg smacks the side of the lounger. 'Christ!'

Melissa hides a smile. Serves him right.

Chapter Forty-three

THE DECKIE

Obviously Piper would never harm Bailey. She'd never harm any child: she's not a monster. If anything, she's already far too fond of the little girl. No, she was merely giving them a taste of what it feels like. Powerless. Imagining the worst. Terrified for the safety of someone they love. Irritatingly, Melissa didn't seem the slightest bit bothered by the fact that Bailey was swimming out of her depth.

She's hot and thirsty by the time she reaches the main strip of bars and restaurants. She has no idea where to find a chemist in this town and her Spanish is almost non-existent. She's thinking about asking at one of the bars when someone calls out to her.

'Hey! You!'

Rocco waves to her from his seat at a high table on the other side of the bar.

She can hardly ignore him.

'Hey,' she says when she reaches their table, where Julian and Kitty (wearing her hair in French braids that make her look even younger than she usually does) are fighting over a basket of shoestring fries. There are several empty beer bottles littering the table but Piper is focused on the fries, her mouth watering. It's been hours since she last ate.

'You want some?' Julian notices, pushing the basket towards her. 'Go on, we won't tell on you.'

Rule number twenty-seven in Walker's handbook states that there is to be strictly no fraternising with the family.

Sod that.

'Thanks.' She helps herself to a handful. They're good – hot, salty and crisp. Her stomach growls.

Kitty offers her a shy smile.

'What are you doing all the way over here?' Rocco asks. 'Please don't tell me the others are right behind you?'

'No, they're headed back to the boat,' she replies. 'I'm looking for a chemist. Your sister needs some ear drops. I don't suppose you've seen one?'

'A what?' Julian asks.

'A drug store,' she says, remembering what Melissa called it.

Rocco summons a waitress and asks in broken Spanish if she knows of a *farmacia* nearby.

'*Si.*' She gestures further along the street and smiles prettily at him, nodding to their drinks. '*Mas cerveza*?'

'Si,' he replies with a wink and indicates Piper too.

'No, no. I really, absolutely, cannot drink while I'm on duty,' she protests.

'We think you really can,' he says, gripping her elbow so she can't get away. 'Isn't that right, Julian?'

'Not a problem for me,' he replies, though he doesn't sound exactly pleased about it.

Rocco gives her no choice but to join them. She's halfway through her second beer when she manages to steer the conversation around to another topic. She's primed them by asking about *Ambition*, and then, 'So is this your family's first yachting experience?' she casually asks, knowing full well it isn't.

Rocco and Julian exchange glances. Kitty, meanwhile, stares down at her glass, twirling the straw in it and making the ice chime.

'Not really,' Kitty says. 'But it's been a few years.'

'Oh, really?' Piper sits very still, pretending that this information means little to her. *What will they say?*

'There was an accident on our last trip, so, well, we haven't all been away together on the water for a few years,' Rocco says.

Kitty shoots him a warning glance.

'An accident?' Piper asks. 'That doesn't sound … good.'

'One of the deckhands was messing about on a dive,' Julian chips in.

Piper is frozen in place. That's not right. She knows exactly who he is referring to, but Lexie would never 'mess about', not when she was at work, and certainly not when she was diving. She took her responsibilities seriously and she was an experienced diver. The sour taste of beer rises in her throat; Piper is suddenly nauseous. 'What happened?' It's a miracle she can keep her voice steady.

'The stupid girl swam off, leaving Melissa, her buddy, and must have got caught in the current. By the time anyone realised what had happened, she had gone to the surface,' Julian says in a bored tone. 'She was lucky one of the dive masters noticed and went after her.'

'She got carbon dioxide poisoning,' Kitty says quietly, chewing the end of her braid. 'And lost consciousness. It was awful.'

'Oh god.' Piper acts as if she's never heard the story before. 'How did that happen? I mean, I'm not a diver, but …'

'I don't know. It's possible her equipment was faulty,' Rocco says. 'But if it was, the dive company covered it up.'

Piper can't believe the lies she is hearing.

'The service log for the scuba equipment was incomplete,' Kitty adds. 'Though that might have just been a coincidence.'

'Why are you so interested?' Julian looks at her, suddenly suspicious.

'Just curious,' Piper says. 'That's really awful. For you all, I mean.' She rises from her stool. 'Anyway, I'd better …' She can barely keep the choking rage from her voice, but Rocco and Julian are too drunk to notice, though Kitty shoots her a confused look. 'I'd better get to the chemist, er, you know, drug store,' she says.

She leaves them in the bar, fuming that this is the story they've told themselves, that none of them has accepted any of the blame. Of course, no one would admit responsibility, certainly not wrongdoing, but even so …

She's so incensed that she almost misses the sign for the chemist, the green cross suspended high on the wall. She is about to step inside, the air conditioning luring her in, when someone in the alley up ahead snags her attention.

Walker.

Even from behind she recognises him, his baggy shorts and chicken legs, ridiculous lace-up brown leather shoes and straw Panama hat. He's about ten feet ahead of her, a holdall slung over one shoulder. He's not alone.

A woman in a short, figure-hugging sundress and sandals, her face obscured by a fall of bleached blonde hair, stands in front of him. They seem oblivious to their surroundings. She can't hear what they're saying, but their gestures escalate and they appear to be having an argument. Piper doesn't dare get any closer. After a few minutes they turn and begin to walk away, and before she realises what she's doing, she is following them, keeping her distance. They round a corner, and when she reaches it they have vanished. She scours the street, but it's deserted.

A number of shops front the narrow street, and about halfway along is a bar. She crosses to the other side and, doing her best to appear casual, turns to glance through the window as she passes.

The interior is dark and cluttered with wine bottles. She strolls past and when she reaches a cross street a little further on, slows and pretends to be interested in a shop window. The bar is the only place they could conceivably have gone; all of the shops are shut for the afternoon siesta. She loiters, wondering if they might reappear.

She can't afford to hang around for long, but as luck would have it, she doesn't have to. Less than five minutes later, Walker emerges. It's a moment before she realises what is different.

He's no longer carrying the holdall.

And there's no sign of the woman who was with him.

Piper ducks around the corner to avoid being seen, her breath catching at the subterfuge. She counts to fifty before returning to the main street, by which time he is a small figure in the distance.

She follows quite some way behind, for he is headed towards the marina now. She waits until there is no possibility of running into him, and it is only later, as she boards the tender to return to the yacht, that she realises she's forgotten all about the ear drops.

Chapter Forty-four

THE TROPHY WIFE

By the time they gather their things to leave, Max is on the verge of a full-blown tantrum. His eyes squeeze shut and two tears appear at the outer edges. His mouth opens so wide that Sandrine can see his tonsils, his little face puce, enraged that he is no longer allowed to crawl on the sand. For a small person, he is capable of making a great deal of noise.

'I've let Rocco know that we're aiming to be away by four,' Evan says.

'Rocco and Julian have gone to meet some girls they've been talking to on Tinder,' Bailey pipes up.

'How do you even know about Tinder?' Melissa asks.

'Mom, come *on*,' Bailey says. 'Everyone knows about Tinder.'

'Well, anyway, he's got the message.' Evan is griping to get going, his patience for the crowded beach exhausted.

Leaving the deckhands to pack up the beach toys and damp, sandy towels, Sandrine persuades Evan to wear Max in the baby carrier as she strolls beside him, hands free for once. He usually hates the papoose-like thing, claiming it makes him look as though he's a grandfather on daycare duty but, distracted now, he doesn't complain. It helps that Max falls asleep the instant he's secured.

They're passing a beach bar, skirting the outdoor umbrellas, when someone calls out to Sandrine in French. The voice is deep, accented.

It takes her a second to work out where the person is sitting, but then he calls her name again and she sees him. Thinking it could be another fan, or even someone from the paparazzi, she instinctively ducks, pulling on the brim of her straw hat to hide her face.

He calls to her again. 'Sandrine! Sandrine!' He is standing now.

She stops short. It's Pierre Foulard, the director of *L'Assassin*, the movie she made in France right before she moved to the US.

She ignores the expletive from Evan and hurries to the bar, making a beeline for Pierre's table.

She greets him amid a flurry of kisses, thrilled to see a familiar face from her former life. They spend a few minutes catching up, Pierre complaining about delays on his current project and the lead actor who has been foisted on him. He always did like to gossip. It's as though she is right back in that world again, of impossibly long days on location, weather challenges, co-workers whom she either fell in love with or despised, the thrill when she nailed a scene *just so*. How alive it had made her feel.

Time stands still.

Sandrine suddenly becomes aware of Evan next to her, and switches to talking in English. 'Oh! Darling, there you are.' She makes the introductions, explaining that she once worked with Pierre – 'years ago now!'

'Christ, is the entire world vacationing in Mallorca this summer?' Evan mutters, extending his hand to Pierre.

Max lolls sideways in the baby carrier, sunhat tipped drunkenly over one eye. Pierre congratulates Sandrine on her son. 'You'll be ready to go back to work soon, no?'

Sandrine shrugs. 'I haven't really given it much thought,' she lies. Only a few months ago she'd been so desperate she'd even considered putting herself forward for *Real Housewives of New York*. 'Motherhood is a big gig, you know? And I love it.' She is deliberately evasive, aware of Evan listening to her.

Pierre lifts his shoulders and spreads his hands in the air, as if he doesn't completely agree. 'Of course.'

As they are leaving, Sandrine invites Pierre for drinks that evening.

When they are out of earshot and before Evan has a chance to grumble, she suggests they make it a party. 'You said we should entertain at some point,' she says, intent on making him think it's his idea.

'Why go on vacation only to see all the same faces in a different setting?' he grumbles.

'Come on, you old grouch. You just invited Jim and Virginia. It seemed to be the perfect opportunity.' At least there will be one friend of hers there. 'What is the expression? The more the merrier?' She smiles sweetly, daring him to object.

It occurs to her that running into Pierre is a sign. A sign that it's perhaps time for more than just the role of wife and mother that she's been playing for the last couple of years.

jajajones: I've never understood what all the fuss is about caviar anyway. Stinky fish eggs.

freethewaffle: Yeah, you know people serve it on Pringles and even corn dogs now. It's the ultimate flex.

redondo23: I wouldn't mind it if it wasn't so damn fishy. Hehehe.

Chapter Forty-five

THE SURVIVOR

The sub-inspector – 'Please, call me Luis,' he says, perhaps trying to ingratiate himself – returns the following morning. He is freshly shaven and his shirt is crease-free. She wonders idly if he has a girlfriend or a wife, or perhaps both. He seems the type.

'How are you feeling?'

'Better. I think.' She is hesitant. He is going to ask her again if she remembers anything, if she knows who she is. She still doesn't have the answers, but she is strangely unconcerned. It's as if she's in a bubble, isolated in this cool, sterile hospital room. Perhaps if she knew more she'd be worried, but right now, ignorance is bliss.

The doctor, who swept through earlier with his coterie of eager interns, tells her that memory loss is common after such an injury, that the swelling must go down before a full assessment can be made, that rest and minimal disturbance are what's required. 'It is better if we allow your memories to come back naturally. That way we will learn what is genuine.'

She sleeps. A lot.

This morning, Luis brings photographs. He shows them to her one at a time. First, a hawkish older man with greying temples, next a beautiful dark-haired, elegantly dressed woman with a seductive look about her. Then a man in his forties wearing round, wire-framed spectacles and a tweed sportscoat.

She shakes her head.

'Nothing?'

'Sorry.' She wants to help, but the photographs don't tell her anything. 'Wait.' She reaches for the picture of the woman. 'Is she someone famous?'

'Yes, yes, she is.' He is excited by this, perhaps seeing it as a breakthrough. 'Do you recognise her?'

'Sorry. I thought I did, but I'm afraid I have no idea who she is.'

Chapter Forty-six

THE YOUNGEST DAUGHTER

Kitty is acutely aware of Julian's tanned, muscular forearm resting on the table beside hers. She plucks another French fry from the haystack in front of them, unable to stop herself accidentally-on-purpose brushing against his arm as she does so. In her clumsiness, she dislodges the stack and the fries scatter like spillikins.

'Careful!' Rocco says, annoyed. Some of the fries have landed in the pooled condensation from their beers.

'Sorry, sorry.' God, she can't do anything without screwing it up. She attempts to collect them.

'Don't sweat it, darling,' Julian drawls, lighting a cigarette. 'We've had enough anyway, haven't we, Roc?'

'I guess,' Rocco replies, motioning to Julian to give him a cigarette too.

'Kitty?'

She looks up to see Julian offering her the packet, and blushes. Has he realised how interested she is, that she can't prevent her gaze from fastening on him whenever they are in the same room? 'Er, no, no thanks.' It would be too embarrassing to cough and splutter in front of them. She's never even had a drag, has no idea how it's done. Until now she'd always thought it a ridiculous habit, but Julian makes it look cool.

She is surprised when Rocco asks the deckhand, Piper, to join them. He is a cat toying with a mouse, only really interested because it's obvious that the girl can't or won't say no. Kitty loves her brother, but sometimes he can be cruel and thoughtless, particularly when it comes to girls. To him, they're disposable, forgettable, not people with feelings who can be hurt. She remembers a girlfriend of his, Jenna, who had lasted longer than most, sobbing in the downstairs bathroom at the New York apartment, then wailing as Walker escorted her off the premises while Rocco hid in his room. She never did find out exactly what had happened, but the girl didn't visit again.

This girl even looks a little like Jenna, though that's not altogether surprising. Rocco definitely has a type – wasp-y, delicate-looking blondes who seem as though they might snap after a heavy frost.

Kitty grows restless as Rocco tries to impress the deckhand, make her laugh with his outrageous statements. It's as though they've all forgotten she's there.

Minutes after Piper leaves them, Kitty drains the last of her drink and gets to her feet. 'I'm going for a walk,' she announces. 'I'll see you back at the boat.' She doesn't give her brother the chance to object, not that he would. After all, she gets around the city at home by herself often enough.

'Don't get lost,' Julian calls after her.

'I've got maps,' she says, waving her cell phone in the air, oblivious to the fact that her battery is at fifteen per cent.

Chapter Forty-seven

THE DECKIE

'Did you find some?' Melissa is alone on the aft deck, legs tucked underneath her, peering over her sunglasses at something on her laptop.

Piper pastes a rueful expression on her face. 'Siesta time. Every single pharmacy I found was shut. I'm so sorry.' The lie comes effortlessly.

Melissa sighs heavily. She's obviously unused to her needs not being met. 'Not your fault, I suppose,' she says ungraciously. 'God, this place is so backward. Haven't they heard of twenty-four-hour trading?'

'They reopen in about an hour, so I can pop back as soon as they do,' Piper says. 'There's one not far from the marina.'

'I thought we were departing any minute?' Melissa addresses Walker, who has appeared from starboard.

'Change of plan,' Walker says. 'Julian, Rocco and Kitty haven't returned yet. I've tried calling Rocco's cell, but he's not responding. Did they say anything to you about where they might be?'

Piper hovers, not sure if she should wait for instructions.

'No, he didn't.' Melissa doesn't appear to care. 'I need ear drops. She couldn't find any.'

'I'll check our first-aid supplies and someone will meet us with medication if we have nothing suitable on board,' Walker says smoothly. 'Should I arrange for a doctor to check you over?'

Melissa refocuses on her laptop. 'Thank you, Walker, but that won't be necessary.'

Relieved of her assignment, Piper steps away, hoping for a few minutes in her cabin, but Walker's voice sounds in her ear. God, she hasn't even had time to pee. She confirms she's on her way, then stows her shoes in her cabin and shuts herself in the head, sitting on the loo with her elbows on her knees, resting her forehead against her palms, going over her conversation with Rocco, Julian and Kitty, still incensed by their lies.

* * *

'You should have come to me as soon as you were unable to fulfil Mrs Silk's request.' Walker stands over Piper, crowding her in the confined space of the passageway. She flinches, both at his tone and his unexpected closeness, shrinking back against the panelled wall. 'I would have handled it.'

There's no point in telling him that Melissa was the first person Piper saw when she returned to the yacht. 'Yes. Of course. I'm very sorry. It won't happen again.' *Is it really such a big deal?*

'It's essential that the family and their guests are never inconvenienced. My job – our job – is to ensure that they want for nothing, that their every desire is anticipated.'

Walker is about to say more when Julian and Rocco appear. She turns sideways to let them pass and Rocco raises his hand, out of Walker's line of sight, miming drinking a beer and grinning. 'Piper. Walker.'

Julian simply ignores them both.

When they've disappeared, Walker adds, 'I shouldn't have to remind you that there is no fraternising with any members of the family. You might be of a similar age, but you have absolutely nothing in common. You are an employee, and an expendable one at that. Understand?'

Oh yes, she understood, but how did he know what she'd been up to? Was it a lucky guess, something in Rocco's tone tipping him off, or had Walker seen them at the bar?

'You are fortunate that Mr and Mrs Silk's children have taken a liking to you, and that they need a nanny for the next week. If that were not the case, I wouldn't hesitate to put you on the next flight to whatever backwater you came from.'

He is really pissed off.

'Yes, sir.'

'I shall be watching you carefully,' he warns. 'One more step out of line and you'll be off this boat faster than you can say man overboard.'

* * *

'Everything okay?' Liam asks when he sees Piper's expression. He's in the galley rolling out pastry and notices her reddened cheeks, which have flamed with frustration. 'Did you get too much sun out there? It's stronger than you realise.'

'Yeah, I must have.' No point in explaining, or complaining.

The usually immaculate galley is awash with dirty pots, pans, utensils and food scraps. He raises his eyes skywards. 'Cocktail party for forty in three hours' time. Be a yacht chef,' he says flatly. 'Work in exotic locations under impossible conditions. Have the time of your life … Nah, it's nothing I can't handle.' He goes to the cool room and returns with a pot of Greek yoghurt and a spoon. She is surprised when he hands them to her. 'Smear some of this on your skin; it'll take the sting out.'

Tears well up. The dressing-down from Walker affected her more than she'd expected, and this small kindness touches her. It seems a crazy suggestion, but she takes the yoghurt from him and dabs a teaspoonful onto her fingertips.

'Thanks.' She dots yoghurt onto her cheeks, patting it in gently so as not to inflame her skin further. 'It's a beautiful island, isn't it?' she says, making conversation.

He shrugs. 'I've seen my share of pretty places. The Caribbean is more my style.'

'Yeah, well, I've never been further than Europe.'

'You'd like it.'

'I'm sure I would. Anywhere with warmth and water sounds good to me.' She goes to the large steel fridge and opens it, but jumps back as she sees a box of live lobsters eyeing her, their pincers secured with elastic bands.

Liam barks with sudden laughter. 'Careful, they might bite.'

Chapter Forty-eight

THE ELDEST DAUGHTER

'You want the shower?' Angus asks when they reach their cabin.

'It's fine, you go,' Melissa replies, shutting the door behind them. 'I need to check my emails before dinner.' She shakes her head to one side, still struggling with her waterlogged ears.

She can't ignore the growing feeling that her father is keeping something from her. She wants to speak to Bill Katz to find out what he knows, but it's not strictly her purview; she'll need to be subtle. Bill has been with the company for more than three decades and he and Evan have always been pretty tight. The last thing she wants is Bill telling her dad that she's been asking questions about matters that don't strictly concern her.

Angus collapses on the bed and begins to unstrap the boot from his leg. Melissa winces at the rip of Velcro as she checks a message on her phone. Honestly, she can hardly remember what she once saw in him. Everything he does sets her on edge right now, and although she's doing her best to ignore him, he's making it a challenge.

'Did my stuff get pressed?' he asks.

'I expect so – check the closet.'

He looks helplessly at her.

'What?' She's annoyed at being distracted.

'It's all the way over there.' He points beyond her to the other side of the room.

She stifles a sigh, then feels mean. The cabin isn't huge, but she *is* closer, and he *is* incapacitated. She takes three steps and slides back the door. 'See?' His clothes are hanging neatly, lined up in colour order, shirts, then pants. T-shirts and underwear are folded and stowed on a set of built-in shelves. 'What would you like?'

'Whatever.'

Oh god, does he actually sound sorry for himself?

She picks out a linen shirt, one of five that she had handmade for him in London only a few months ago, and a pair of pants and a brown leather belt, then hangs them all on the back of the bathroom door.

'Thanks.'

'No problem.' They are coldly polite with each other.

He hops to the bathroom and as soon as she hears the shower run she flops back against the pillows, worn out by the effort of being civil to a man she can no longer stand to be in the same room with.

Her eyes are closing when she hears a beep. She checks her phone, hoping it's the message from her assistant that she's been waiting on, but there are no new notifications. Then she hears another beep and realises it's coming from Angus's phone. He's left it on the nightstand on the other side of the bed. Curious, she reaches for it and catches the name before the screen blacks out.

Amelia.

Immediately, another message pops up, a photo notification this time.

She unlocks his phone – the security number, Carter's date of birth, was a no-brainer – and is confronted by a selfie of their former nanny in a low-cut T-shirt smiling like a goddamn

Cheshire cat, the distinctive gothic facade of Gaudi's Sagrada Família in the background.

Barcelona is only a short ferry or plane ride from Palma.

The absolute fucking idiot.

It was only a matter of time until her humiliation hardened into hatred, then calcified into rage. Nevertheless, she is surprised it has taken her so long to get there. What started out as love has now irrefutably curdled to something darker than contempt.

He has brought Amelia with him. Stashed her in Barcelona, no doubt with the intention of hooking up with her once he's done his family duty. She can just imagine Angus sweet-talking her into the plan, promising her that he just has to see his kids, spend a week with the family, and then they can be together …

She scrolls back through their messages, until she sees one sent that morning.

Don't worry. I'll fix everything. She'll be out of the picture soon, I promise. And then we can be together, every day, for the rest of our lives. Are you ready for that?

Her blood runs cold. *Out of the picture?* The last time she brought up the subject of divorce was several years ago, but his words are still crystal-clear in her mind. 'Till death do us part,' he'd repeated, glacially calm.

Now those words seem like a threat, not a promise.

He wouldn't … would he?

She throws the phone on the bed, dismissing the thought, telling herself not to be paranoid, then has second thoughts, returning his phone to its original spot. The last thing she wants is for him to know that she's seen the message.

She picks up her phone now, logging in to the fake Instagram account she set up a few years ago: *Becky J – 'Don't count days: make days count.'* A twenty-something New Yorker who posts pictures of streetscapes and cute brownstone stoops, Central Park, doughnuts and coffee … the usual inoffensive, banal but pretty stuff that Gen Z loves to scroll through.

Becky J followed Amelia's account when Amelia first started working for them and Amelia followed her back almost immediately. Melissa doesn't consider it an invasion of privacy: it's important that she knows what's going on with the person who cares for her children. She's kept tabs on all their nannies in this way.

She checks Amelia's account. Photos of Barcelona, the markets, a huge dish of paella, the Sagrada fucking Família …

Melissa is done.

Done pretending everything in her life is okay.

Done giving in.

Done trying to make everything right.

Angus doesn't deserve her pity for a minute longer, and certainly not her forgiveness.

There's a feeling of inevitability as she flicks through the evidence on the screen and accepts what must be.

flybuoy: Fun fact. I live nearby and saw the rescue helicopter. That boat sank like a stone.

Chapter Forty-nine

THE PATRIARCH

When they finally arrive back on board, Evan hands Max off to the nanny, kisses his wife and retreats to his study, claiming he needs to catch up on emails. In reality, he's stewing, has been the entire way back from the beach.

It had been a mistake to bring the boat to Europe. They should have gone to the Caribbean, where there was no chance of Sandrine bumping into anyone from her former life.

He couldn't miss her animation when Pierre accosted them; there'd been a spark in her he's not seen for months. And now she is behaving as if nothing untoward has occurred, chattering away about which of their friends and acquaintances might be in the area, who else they should get Walker to invite to the boat that evening.

He closes the study door and brings up a contact on his phone. As it connects, he sits down at the eighteenth-century walnut inlaid desk and opens his twenty-first-century laptop. He clicks on the spreadsheet, hoping that this time it might tell him something different, that he might have misread the figures, but they're exactly the same as when he first saw them.

The call connects and he barks at the person on the other end. 'Bill … Yes, I'm looking at it now … I appreciate that we're running out of time. Is there anyone else we can go to?

We've got to fucking fix this before the month's end … yeah, Melissa's aware something's up. Don't worry about her, I'll deal with that … What do you mean? Of course it's not too late.'

He ends the call and leans back in his chair, the acid burn and tightness in his chest making an unwelcome return. Thinking it's indigestion, he picks up a nearby iPad and keys in an order for peppermint tea, pronto.

He should really take a shower; sand still clings to his calves and the sweat on his forehead and scalp has cooled and dried in the air conditioning, leaving a grainy film of salt. Everything feels sour and slightly off, his mouth, his gut, his skin … as though he's at the tail-end of an all-nighter, instead of relaxed and expansive as he should be on vacation. This trip, anticipated for so long, isn't turning out as he expected.

A few minutes later, there's a discreet knock on the door and a steward enters with a tray, placing a china teapot and cups on a sideboard before pouring the steaming liquid from a theatrical height and placing it in front of him. There's also a plate with *langue de chat* biscuits on it, Sandrine's favourites and a delicacy she introduced him to on their honeymoon in the South Pacific. He had persuaded her to go there despite her expressing a desire to visit France, and he'd been right in his assumption that she would love it.

'Will there be anything else, sir?' The steward stands at a respectful distance.

'No, thank you.' He dismisses the young man, whose healthy, athletic presence makes him feel suddenly geriatric.

He can no longer ignore what's staring him in the face. With Thyssen on the brink of collapse, he wonders if he will lose Sandrine too. She will fly away and, as with so many caged things, will be unlikely to return.

Sick with frustration, he picks up a bottle of antacids on his desk and swallows two with a mouthful of tea. He thumps his chest in an effort to dislodge the pain, but that only serves to make it burn more fiercely.

eleanorRigby: Did you see that recent photo of them all that he posted on Insta? The stress was showing even then.

luisegrimer: It's a classic story of fake it till you make it. No one is who they are pretending to be anymore.

drinkmesober: Yeah. Grifters, the lot of 'em.

Chapter Fifty

THE DETECTIVE

Luis waits on hold with the Ibizan port authority, eventually getting through to a message bank and leaving instructions for someone to return his call. Then he sends a preliminary report to Interpol, picks up his keys and wallet and prepares to leave the office. He decides to stop by the forensic pathologist to see if she can share her initial findings.

While Luis has been on the water all day, two hikers have gone missing in the mountains and a middle-aged woman has suffered a fatal accident at her apartment in Magaluf. Three migrants have been rescued after being found clinging to a life raft several nautical miles off the southeast coast, and a British man has fallen to his death from a sixth-floor window. The department is stretched, and it seems that he's the only one with any interest in these two anonymous women, neither of whom seem to be missed by anyone, at least not anyone on Mallorca.

* * *

'Bruising around her neck, on her thighs, and here' – the pathologist points to the woman's breasts – 'bite marks. Almost certainly human. Made prior to death.'

Luis suppresses a shudder. He's seen the worst kind of indignities inflicted on a body, particularly women's bodies, but it never gets any easier. In a way, he's glad about this. If he ever becomes numb to it, he knows it will be time to do something else. 'Cause of death?'

'By the condition of her lungs, I'd say drowning. But drugs could be a contributing factor. We'll know more when the tox report's back.' She goes to her laptop, clicks on something. 'Oh, and her dental work was rudimentary. There were cavities in her back molars. No evidence of orthodontics. She didn't – or wasn't able to – look after herself very well. It might indicate that she was raised in poor circumstances.'

'Got it.' Luis nods and turns away, finding it hard to look at the woman for much longer.

'Any idea who she might be?'

'At this stage, no one matching her description has been reported missing.'

'Just like the first one, huh?'

'Seems so.' Luis isn't the only person to have made the connection.

The pathologist is keen to finish up – it's after five – so Luis takes his leave, heading out of the building and into the still-bright afternoon sunshine. He's just wondering if he has time for a late swim when his phone rings.

'Sir?' It's Maria. 'Sorry to bother you, but I thought you might want to know right away. Interpol has identified the first woman – her fingerprints were in the system.'

His pulse skips a beat. 'Go on.'

'Krystina Hana Svoboda. A Czech citizen, last known address in Brno, South Moravia. She was twenty-three years old. There's no record of her entering Spain either on Mallorca or the mainland. I'm going to send through the photo now.'

He waits, and then his phone pings with an attachment. The photograph shows a pretty, dark-haired girl with high cheekbones, her eyes heavily ringed with kohl. Better lighting and she would likely have been a stunner.

'She was arrested at the age of nineteen for breaking and entering, but released on a good behaviour bond. Did you get the photo?'

'I did, thank you, Maria.' He looks at the photo again.

What happened to you, Krystina, that saw you end up with lungs full of sea water on a Spanish beach?

She is wearing a light-coloured T-shirt and her hair is tucked behind her ears, large hoop earrings and a thin gold chain her only jewellery. He pinches his thumb and forefinger and zooms in on the woman's neck.

He stops as he realises that she is wearing an almost identical necklace to the one found on the second woman – but instead of the letter A, Krystina's bears the letter K. The pixels are grainy, but he'd swear it. It's the same flowing script.

Then he remembers where he's seen yet another, similar necklace.

The necklace that the young girl on the yacht was wearing, the gold glinting in the sun. He looks back at his notes … her name is Kitty, the yacht owner's teenage daughter. He could have sworn she was wearing a similar necklace with the initial K.

Chapter Fifty-one

THE TROPHY WIFE

Sandrine stands in front of the full-length mirror in her cabin, fastening a pair of art deco diamond earrings, a gift from Evan after she had Max. She isn't entirely sure how she feels about being given a gift for giving birth, but she is never going to turn down jewellery, that would be stupid. When she's done, she stands back, her gold bangles chiming as she lowers her arms, and takes in the one-shoulder blue ombre silk sheath, appreciating the contrast with her blood-red lipstick. She shakes out her hair so that it tumbles in loose waves down her back and checks her Cartier wristwatch.

Five minutes past seven.

She peers out of the cabin window, noting that the sun is lower, the hem of her dress an exact match for the sky's royal blue hue. A chime comes from the iPad and she sees a message saying that the first guests have arrived. Evan went up on deck ten minutes ago. She goes back to the bathroom and checks her make-up again, fixing a smudge of lipstick and staring at the lines around her eyes in the magnifying mirror. Should she look into surgery? Get her eyelids done, tighten a sagging jawline? Everyone is doing it these days. She pulls a face, thrusting her chin forward to see what it might look like.

She goes back to her stateroom and the iPad buzzes again. More arrivals expected in five minutes. The tender must be flitting back and forth from the marina like a pond skater.

She hurries up to the main deck where the cocktail party is to be held. She can hear the distant beat of the music.

'You found us!' She greets Jim and Virginia, who already have a drink in their hands. Stewards balancing trays of champagne are stationed at the entrance to the deck and others are on hand to help guests onto the yacht.

'Hard not to.' Jim raises one eyebrow. 'It's the biggest in the bay. Quite the statement. What's the LOA?'

'The LOA?' Sandrine is puzzled.

'Length overall.'

Oh, it's a dick-measuring contest. Why is she not surprised? 'A little over two-fifty feet, I believe,' she says. 'Evan would be able to tell you exactly. I don't take much notice of such things.'

'Well, regardless, she's a beauty.'

'We like it,' Sandrine says airily, pretending not to notice the envy in his words. She kisses Virginia on both cheeks. 'Welcome. Now, who chose this music?' She raises her eyebrows at the thumping beat. 'Rocco, no doubt.' She casts around, spotting her stepson and his friend near the bar with a young woman she doesn't recognise. They're about to do shots of some vile-looking bright yellow drink. That won't end well.

She flits from one group to another, making small talk with Evan's friends, all the while keeping a watchful eye on Angus, who is standing in a far corner, gazing into his glass as if he'd rather be anywhere else. Sandrine excuses herself and makes her way over to him. Tonight, she is required to play the role of hostess, and she is determined to do it well.

But before she reaches Angus, she is almost run down by Carter. He and Bailey are the only kids on board and they weave between the guests, involved in some kind of game of chase. She hopes they won't be kept up at the party for too long. There is a time and a place. Isn't there supposed to be a deckhand or stewardess or someone looking after them? And aren't they supposed to be wearing life jackets?

More guests arrive, and for the next half-hour or so she is occupied with greeting them and ensuring the drinks and food keep coming. She catches sight of Evan from time to time, noticing him deep in conversation with Jim Murray more than once. Nearly all of the guests are friends of Evan's, in the area for the summer ('We heard you were throwing a party, got our driver to bring us over from Palma'), and most of whom appear to know each other already, if not personally then by reputation. It at least makes her job a little easier, and before long the roar of conversation is vying with the music. She's still hoping that Pierre will make it, but time-keeping has never been his strong point.

It is gone nine o'clock by the time Sandrine realises she hasn't seen Kitty all evening. She hurries over to the bar, where Julian is showing one of the stews how to mix a Manhattan, though there is every chance she already knows.

'Boys. Have you seen Kitty?' She swallows. 'Rocco? Your sister?'

The two young men exchange a glance. 'She left us at the beach bar, what …' Rocco glances at his watch. 'Late this afternoon, say at about four?'

Concern snakes its way down Sandrine's spine. She feels responsible for the girl: no one else is looking out for her, and certainly her father appears to have more pressing matters on his mind. 'You haven't seen her since?'

'She said she wanted to explore.' Rocco gets his phone out. 'Shall I call her? She's probably holed up in her cabin with that lesbian book she was reading.' The pair dissolve into childish laughter and it takes all of Sandrine's self-control not to shout at them.

'No. Don't worry. I'll go and see for myself.'

Chapter Fifty-two

THE DECKIE

'Watch out for those prawns,' Liam growls as Piper picks up a platter and prepares to ferry them from the galley to the main deck. There's already a stain on her formal uniform shirt and she clamps her elbow to her side to hide it. Walker expects nothing short of perfection, and she can just imagine what a bollocking he will give her if he sees it, but she hasn't had a second to go and change. She doesn't bother to reply to Liam, who looks to be one step away from a full-blown tantrum. The galley ovens are playing up again and they've already turned an entire tray of tartlet shells to charcoal. Liam vented his frustration by screaming at an unfortunate deckie who happened to be in the vicinity.

Piper steadies the tray with both hands and forces herself to smile as she edges around the tight knots of guests, hovering until they notice her. Or rather, until they notice the fat prawns, arranged in concentric circles, pink commas around a lime-chipotle-spiked mayonnaise strewn with gold leaf.

Gold leaf. Jesus, people actually put that in their mouths? The rich really aren't just like the rest of us, no matter who might try and argue otherwise.

Somehow she also manages to juggle a stack of snow-white linen cocktail napkins, each one bearing a gold-embroidered

Ambition insignia. 'Tacky?' Tamara had asked, holding them up earlier. 'Or chic?'

Piper had shrugged, not wanting to be drawn in to the discussion. They're definitely tacky.

She finds herself in front of Rocco and Julian and the smile she's pasted on falters. She hurriedly covers it up with an even broader one. 'Canapé?' she asks, thrusting the platter under their noses.

'Thanks, sweetheart.' Julian helps himself to a giant prawn.

'I'm okay,' Rocco says.

She turns, readying herself to plunge into the crowd, then jumps in shock as a hand wraps around her waist, squeezing so hard it hurts, then abruptly lets go. She yelps, but no one hears over the music and the roar of conversation. The tray of prawns wobbles dangerously as she scoots out of the way. She stalks off.

It had to have been Rocco.

* * *

She returns to the galley with an empty platter, collapsing for a moment on a seat in the crew mess. Liam is the only other crew member there, standing at the galley counter, attempting to open more caviar with a little metal key attached to the tin's lid. 'You know you can't get this from BFG,' he says.

'Sorry, what?'

'BFG, the provisioning company we use.' He waves the tin in the air. 'They think I don't know, but this stuff is wild, not farmed, and there would be a huge stink if anyone found out we were serving it on board. It's completely illegal to import wild caviar.'

'Oh, okay,' Piper replies, not really sure why he's sharing this with her. 'Where did it come from then?'

He shrugs. 'The captain told me the Thyssens wanted it served, and to fetch a carton from the laz.'

So that's why he had been down there. It's an odd place to store food.

'Dammit!' He flings the tin onto the counter in frustration. 'These things are so badly made.' He rummages for a can opener and begins to work it around the edge. 'What the fuck?' he says, peering inside. He digs the point of a knife into the tin and puts it to his tongue.

His eyes widen.

'Everything okay?' she asks.

He looks up, hurriedly replacing the lid. 'Yeah, just not what I was expecting.'

Liam grabs a half-full bottle of champagne and pours them both a glass. 'Go on, it's okay.' His mood seems to have improved, perhaps because most of the food has been served.

'I thought this was strictly against the rules?' She takes the glass anyway and puts it to her lips.

'I won't tell if you won't,' he says, draining the glass.

'Thanks.'

He heads to the galley again, turning his back to her and pulling an enormous sheet of boat-shaped tartlets from one of the ovens, dropping it on the counter and flicking his hand away at the heat of the tray.

She takes advantage of the lull to escape. If anyone asks, she'll say she is going to change, but instead of heading to her cabin, she continues along the passageway.

Of course, it's no accident that she got the job on board *Ambition*.

As she reaches a series of unfamiliar doors, she wonders briefly how Penny is getting on. Penny is the girl who is supposed to be here, the bona fide deckhand, the one with far more experience than Piper.

She should be fully recovered by now, probably even has a job on another boat.

Piper spotted her within an hour of arriving at the hostel in Palma. Loud, confident, pretty. The kind of girl who loves to draw attention to herself, flicking her long hair over her shoulders and batting her eyelashes at the two boys sitting across from her. She was holding court in the small cafe adjoining the pool area and as Piper stopped to order an iced coffee, she listened to Penny boasting about the fabulous job she had just landed on the newest yacht in the marina, an eye-wateringly expensive vessel that only the rich, beautiful, famous, or those whose lot in life is to serve them, could hope to gain access to.

As soon as Piper heard the word *Ambition* fall from Penny's lips, she did a mental fist pump. This was the opportunity she'd been looking for, and here it was, right in her lap. She could hardly believe her luck.

Piper befriended her over drinks that night, pretending a lack of experience (true) and knowledge (not true) when it came to getting a job on one of the yachts lined up in the marina.

Penny had been astonishingly generous, telling Piper what to look out for, what documentation she would need and the name of the agency that she was contracted to. 'Too many people have seen *Below Deck*, think they can try their luck by walking up and down the dock. But you'll get to work on a far better class of yacht if you go through the agency,' she said, hiccupping.

'Do you think they need anyone else?' Piper asked, playing with the straw from her drink. 'I mean, wouldn't it be cool if we ended up working together?'

Penny gave her a hard look and Piper thought she might have pushed too far, too fast, but then Penny crinkled up her face into a sloppy attempt at a smile, slinging her arm around Piper's shoulder. 'Yeah, it's a shame they've got a full crew. I was the last person hired.' She leaned in and Piper felt her new friend's hot, sticky-sweet breath in her ear. 'But let's stay in touch, yeah? See if we can meet up during the season?'

Piper didn't have a chance to answer, as Penny knocked back the rest of her drink and stood up. 'Le's go get some food before I throw up,' she slurred, belching loudly.

It took Piper until the next morning to work out what to do.

As soon as she was awake, she set herself up in the cafe at a table with a direct view of reception. Two hours later, Penny still hadn't emerged and Piper began to think she'd missed her chance. She was about to give up and send Penny a message asking if she wanted to meet later, when she appeared, dishevelled and obviously hungover. 'Hey!' Piper called out. Penny heard and headed towards her, slumping down in the chair opposite, just as Piper had hoped she would.

'Big night?' Piper asked, already knowing the answer. She had tagged along with the group, only leaving after they went to a nightclub after dinner and she was sure Penny had had a skinful.

Penny groaned. 'Gotta have a good blowout before going aboard, right?' Her eyes were bloodshot and she looked terrible.

Piper smiled and pushed a smoothie towards Penny. 'Go on. I think you need this more than me. It'll make you feel better.'

It would in fact make her feel worse – Piper had surreptitiously added a hefty dose of laxative to the drink, hoping for this exact opportunity.

Penny gave her a weak grin. 'Cheers.'

Piper watched as she sucked down the drink, downing it in almost a single swallow.

'Thanks, mate. Fuck, I feel like shit.' Penny wobbled as she tried to stand up, grabbing the table and nearly pulling it over. 'I think I'm going to have to have another little lie down.'

'Let me help you, hey?' Piper offered, taking her by the waist and leading her back to her room.

Piper thinks now how one slip can mean the end of a job, the end of your dreams. Tragic, really. How one careless, hungover stumble when rushing to the bathroom can cause a person to break a finger, making their summer season a total washout. But then one person's misfortune is another's open door, and if she'd helped the situation along a little, she wasn't going to lose any sleep over it.

Chapter Fifty-three

THE YOUNGEST DAUGHTER

Kitty's heard of a second-hand bookshop in Bahía de Alcudia, seen photos on Instagram of shelves crammed with a mix of Spanish and English volumes, their cloth-bound, foil-stamped spines in faded colours of sage, terracotta and pink, and she is determined to track it down.

After a few wrong turns (the maps app on her phone lagged badly), she at last finds the shop and heads inside. It appears to be deserted, save for a fluffy tabby cat curled up on the windowsill. Almost immediately, she spots an old edition of *Jamaica Inn*. It is falling apart at the seams and according to the flyleaf had once belonged to someone called Annabel Collins. She has to have it. As she goes up to the counter to pay, an old dude with wild salt-and-pepper hair and a scraggly beard appears from the back of the shop. He motions for her to sit and so she does, settling into a cosy armchair.

It honestly feels like a religious experience, to be surrounded by old books in the world's most comfortable chair. If she could have stayed longer she would have, but after half a dozen or so chapters she starts to feel thirsty, plus she gets the sense that the owner might be keen to close up (rattling the pens on the counter and lowering the window shades are obvious hints).

It is only once she leaves the bookshop and checks her phone that she realises it won't turn on. Black screen. Completely dead. She must have drained the battery by using the maps app for so long. It's an old phone; her mom wouldn't, or couldn't, buy her a newer one.

The town isn't big, but Kitty's sense of direction is terrible. At one point, after turning down a narrow alley, she is hopelessly lost, unable to locate the shoreline and find her way back to the marina. Trying not to freak out, she turns left, then right, and all at once pops out in a narrow, cobbled street, a tantalising sliver of deep-blue ocean visible at the end of it.

Thank fuck for that.

Half an hour or so later, she reaches the marina. Of course, without her phone, she has no idea how she's going to contact anyone to come and pick her up.

Eventually, she manages to persuade a water taxi to take her across to *Ambition*, using sign language and elementary-level Spanish to explain that she will pay when she gets there.

When she gets to the boat, there's a party in full swing on the deck above. She's pleased that no one appears to have noticed her arrival, save for a deckhand standing watch at the transom. He greets her and, when she explains the situation, is only too willing to fix up the water taxi fare. 'Don't worry,' he says, when she asks if it's okay, 'Walker will reimburse me tomorrow. I'm just about to go off-shift.'

She doesn't want to join the party and remembers from her games with Bailey and Carter that there is one empty cabin, at the stern, almost directly above her. There is little likelihood of her being discovered there, and even less chance of running into anyone on the way. She hurries up the stairs from the swim deck and enters the unoccupied cabin, where she strips off her sweaty, salty clothes and hits the shower. She stays under the water for a long time, and when she emerges, pink and damp as a freshly boiled shrimp, the thunder of music pulses above her. Wrapping herself in a towel, she flicks on a lamp, lies on the bed and picks up her book again.

The real world disappears and she has only an appetite for a distant Cornish landscape, a bitter November day and the sinister *Jamaica Inn*.

Chapter Fifty-four

THE ELDEST DAUGHTER

Before joining the party, Melissa finds Walker, pulls him aside and asks him to arrange for a car to be waiting at the dock first thing the next morning, before the kids will be awake, before anyone else in the family will be up.

She then slips into her father's study, where she is certain not to be disturbed, and opens up her fake Becky J Instagram account. Thank god she posted a photo of the sunset from the boat two days earlier, captioning it #mallorcansunsets. She checks it again – twelve likes (she doesn't have many followers) and sees that Amelia is one of those who has liked it. Becky J hearts several of Amelia's photos from Barcelona and then she fires off a quick DM, exclaiming at the coincidence that they are both in the same part of the world at the same time, what are the chances? She says she's travelling alone and will be in Barcelona tomorrow, and would love to meet up. Becky J is online and replies almost immediately, suggesting lunch the next day. She names a popular cafe in the centre of the city (number three on TripAdvisor, she adds, with what Melissa hopes is an ironic exclamation mark). After signing off with emojis of the sun and a cocktail glass, Melissa closes the app. She'll delete the account later.

A surge of pure pleasure courses through her body as she thinks of Amelia waiting there, all on her own, hopefully for hours. She's not proud of such pettiness, but sometimes she just can't help herself.

Arriving on the fringe of the gathering, she gratefully accepts a glass of champagne and is pleased to note that only her pinky finger is trembling. She has it all under control.

Angus won't know what's hit him. Walker assured her he would make reservations on the first flight out of Palma that morning, that he would also arrange for the locks on their brownstone to be changed and for Angus's personal effects to be packed up and transferred to a downtown studio, the rent on which will be paid for three months. After that, her feckless husband is on his own.

You fuck around, you find out just how bad it can get, she thinks, holding tightly to her fury like a lifeline, pretending she's not bothered by what he might have been planning to do to her.

As soon as she returns Stateside, she will contact the family lawyer and set the wheels for divorce in motion, common sense overcoming Catholicism. Only then will she let her father in on her plans. Breaking the news to him will be even harder than telling the children. She'll have to deal with his disappointment in her. But then she remembers what Toby shared with her and she cares a little less.

Parking those unpleasant tasks for her future self, she turns her attention to the present. One of her talents is being able to compartmentalise. 'What did I miss?' she asks, pasting a bright smile on her face. Her voice is thick with unsaid words, accusations she'd love to hurl at Angus, but instead she greets him with a brief kiss on his smooth cheek as if all she has on her mind is the party ahead of them. Sandrine isn't the only actress in the family.

'I don't know a soul here,' Angus begins. 'Who are all these people? And how come they're all in Mallorca? Did we really come all this way to be surrounded by Americans?' He says it with amused distaste, but he looks at her with disdain, as if she is somehow to blame.

'Haven't you heard? It's *the* place to be in Europe this summer,' she says lightly.

'I thought that was Ibiza?'

'Keep up, honey,' she says, unable to temper the slight edge from her tone. 'Ibiza is *so* last decade.' She swerves out of the way as Bailey careens towards them. 'Hold up, kiddo!' she calls, but Bailey employs selective hearing and dashes on. For once, Melissa can't be bothered to reprimand her.

No one else seems to have noticed. The small crowd are busy knocking back their drinks, checking out the other guests as they gossip about mutual friends and local scandals. 'Did you hear? It's the second woman in as many weeks.' … 'They think it's something in the water.' … 'What, like poison? That's frightening.' … 'For all of us.'

She spots her father and he beckons her over. She raises her glass to acknowledge him. 'Shall we?' she asks Angus, but he is already reaching into his pocket for his cell phone, the screen lit up with a call.

'Sorry, sorry.' The corners of his mouth turn down in a way she once found charming. 'I really need to get this.'

She swallows her usual objections. 'Of course, come and join us when you're done.' She smiles graciously and sweeps towards Evan, leaving Angus staring after her, no doubt confused that for once she hasn't bawled him out about his preoccupation with his phone. It'll take a while before he realises that she's simply stopped caring.

'Melissa.' Evan places a fatherly arm around her shoulders, full of bonhomie, but it sounds a false note to her.

What is he up to?

'You remember Jim. He's just been trying to convince me that the melting polar ice caps are an opportunity – that they're opening up lucrative new shipping routes.' Evan laughs as though it's the funniest thing he's heard all day and Melissa feels nauseous at the thought. Is this really what her father is like now? How has she never seen it before?

She turns to the tall, heavily built stranger helping himself to an oyster from a passing tray. Her body is alert to an electricity in the air, the hairs on her arms standing on end, a tightness threatening to close her throat. 'Mr Murray, of course.' She extends a hand, but he leans in for a kiss, grabbing her elbow with his free hand, and it's all she can do not to recoil. His rumpled pink linen shirt is open to the waist, exposing a thatch of greying chest fuzz. She catches a whiff of his aftershave. It is repellent, and horrifyingly familiar.

'Come now, surely after all these years you can call me Jim?' he replies, the teasing note in his voice failing to reassure her.

Jim and her father used to play golf at Oak Hill on the weekends when Melissa was much younger. He'd often come over afterwards and hang out at their townhouse, though Melissa made herself scarce, her intuition telling her even then that he was a creep. Jim was once a promising pro golfer, but had to give it up after a badly torn rotator cuff. He still clings to his glory days, always keen to talk about his past achievements while demonstrating his swing in front of anyone who'll watch.

Only once had she made the mistake of being alone in the kitchen with him. That was when he'd switched from being merely a bore to someone far more sinister.

She was getting herself a soda when Jim sauntered in from the living room and began talking to her, his gaze roaming her body like he had a right to it. She was fourteen, the same age as Kitty is now, and had thought there was no one else in the house at the time. She can't remember what they discussed, only that she had frozen when he placed a hand on her waist, broken out in a cold sweat when he'd leisurely stroked the curve of her ass, trailing a finger up the crease. She knew it was wrong, so wrong, but was unable to utter a sound, unable to move.

The spell was only broken when her father appeared, and she will never know what might have happened if she'd been left alone with Jim a minute longer. She has always hated herself for clamming up, for never saying anything to stop him. The worst of it is, he probably doesn't even remember.

'Jim, of course.' She musters a corporate smile. She'll be damned if she gives him the satisfaction of showing the effect he has on her.

'Evan was just telling me how invaluable you are to the company, that you've got some pretty interesting projects about to launch, including the one in Hudson Yards,' Jim says. 'Goddamn, it's something when you can be proud of your kids.' He adopts a putting stance and pretends to sink a ball in the hole.

'There's still a few things to finalise,' she says, prevaricating. 'But we're happy with the way things are progressing.' The lies come easily, but then the property development business has always been about smoke and mirrors, pretending everything is wonderful even when it isn't.

'My cautious daughter,' Evan says, patting her on the shoulder. 'It's the deal of the century. That's why the smart money's getting in on the ground floor, so to speak.'

Melissa gives her father a sharp look, but knows better than to say anything. From her understanding of the figures, confirmed by her conversation with Bill Katz, the project is a turkey, and no amount of investment can save it. The numbers just don't add up. She's not surprised, however, that her father is talking it up to an old friend. He'd sell sand in the Sahara if he thought it could make him a buck.

The music booming from the sound system cranks up even louder, no doubt at the request of Rocco, who appears to have invited a posse of young women aboard. He and Julian are dancing with them at the far end of the deck. At first glance the girls seem harmless enough, and they have at least removed their shoes. Bailey has joined them and is watching with open-mouthed fascination as one of them grinds her rear against Julian.

'Excuse me,' Melissa says, seizing the chance to get away. 'I think it's time I put my children to bed.' She strides towards her daughter, nearly colliding with a deckhand carrying a tray of glasses.

'Sorry,' he says, pivoting neatly out of her way.

When she looks to where Bailey had been, she's disappeared. 'Rocco?' The music is even louder here; they must be right under a speaker. She taps her brother on the shoulder and shouts in his ear, 'Have you seen Bailey?'

'What?'

'Never mind.' She hurries through the motion-sensor doors into the main salon, where a group of people are gathered at the bar and another around the baby grand. She doesn't recognise any of them and marches on, scanning the area for an eight-year-old girl with braids and a cheeky laugh. There are too many hiding places on a vessel this size, and once again she curses her husband for screwing the nanny, who should be here to do her job and keep an eye on the children.

When she eventually reaches the kids' cabin, she peeks inside to find her daughter lying fully dressed on top of the covers, thumb plugged into her mouth, fast asleep. Or at least pretending to be.

Melissa's head thumps from the champagne and the sun and the music, and she wonders if she can risk lying down next to Bailey, just for a minute, surrendering to exhaustion with the same abandon as a child. But then she sees the empty bed beside Bailey's and knows that she must also find her son and settle him for the night, for Angus sure as shit won't think to do it.

britpapa: I hope they have at least learned something from such a tragic event. What a shitshow.

gobbledegook52: It's just like that accident a couple of years ago when the yacht with the insanely tall mast sank in that freak storm – the tech guy from the court case. He and his daughter were trapped in their cabins. It happened in an instant. A matter of seconds. Such a tragedy.

Chapter Fifty-five

THE DECKIE

It's silent in the bowels of the yacht, the state-of-the-art design and insulation ensuring that the noise from the party doesn't penetrate the interior. Piper is banking on the assumption that she'll be alone: the captain and the engineers will have clocked off for the night by now and the rest of the crew are occupied with serving the party guests. She hopes to override the temperature settings for one particular cabin, to literally make the occupant sweat. It's part of a series of escalating events she has planned. This is going to be one vacation the group – Rocco, Julian and Melissa in particular – never forget.

'Piper?'

He rolls the *r* of her name and she freezes at the sound, slowly turning around. 'Liam. I … I …' *Not again.* The chef is carrying a large rectangular box, the size of a case of wine, but flatter. He must have come from somewhere up ahead. Her brain turns to mush. She can't think of a good reason for why she is down here, at least not one that he will believe.

'Walker sent me,' she says finally. Somehow her subconscious has taken over and come up with the only excuse that is likely to fly. 'They're running low on Patrón.'

'Listen.' He's standing over her now and she flattens herself against the wall. 'This isn't the first time I've found you somewhere you shouldn't be. The liquor stores are at the fore, not aft.'

She shakes her head. 'I swear he said it was back here.'

'I wasn't born yesterday.' She can feel his breath on her cheek now. He leans closer, and she is aware of his five o'clock shadow, the sweat beading his upper lip. She swallows, and for the first time the extent of her vulnerability is clear. They are the only people in this section of the yacht. He could do anything to her and no one would be any the wiser.

She says nothing. Holds his gaze. If she shows weakness, she'll be lost.

'You'd be wise not to mess with things that don't concern you,' he says in a low voice. 'I'm sure you're a nice girl, but you could wind up in a lot of trouble if you're not careful. Curiosity killed the cat, don't forget.' It sounds to Piper like a coded warning, but he can have no idea what she's looking for.

He stares at her.

Sudden comprehension flashes across his face. 'Oh my god, now I know why you seem so familiar. You have a sister, yeah? Alexandra – Lexie. We worked on a boat together about three years ago. In the Caribbean.' He is incredulous. 'I *knew* it. Oh god, are you totally off your rocker? This family will eat you alive when they figure out who you are. Look how they behaved when Lexie was hurt.'

Piper sets her jaw but doesn't bother denying it. 'You know, my dad tried to find out what really happened. He went out to the site, spoke to the dive operators, tried to contact the family, but he was completely stonewalled. The whole thing stinks of a cover-up.' She's not about to tell him everything she knows.

Liam regards her pitilessly. 'You won't get the answers you want from anyone on board. Families like the Thyssens and their associates don't give a shit about the "little people". To them, people like Lexie, like you, like me, are interchangeable.

No matter how friendly they might be on the surface, no matter how much they might praise your work and your talents, the truth is they'll burn you as soon as look at you.' He sighs. 'I'm afraid I will have to report you to Walker. There is zero tolerance for deckies being down near the engines.'

'Please,' she begs. 'Please don't. I promise, I won't do anything out of line. I just wanted to see them up close, to see what kind of people they are.'

Liam's expression softens. 'How is she? Lexie, I mean.'

A lump rises in Piper's throat and she can hardly speak. 'I'd better get back,' she says in a strangled voice, turning to flee, then quickly turning back to Liam and adding, 'But please, please don't tell Walker.' She has no idea if he will listen to her plea, but she has to hope.

She takes the stairs to the main deck two at a time, willing herself not to cry.

Chapter Fifty-six

THE TROPHY WIFE

Sandrine goes to Kitty's cabin, but she's not there. The only sign anyone has been there recently is a small pile of paperbacks and an abandoned swimsuit on the floor.

She steps into the en suite bathroom, but the shower is dry and the towels neatly folded on the brass rail. The bed isn't turned down, so housekeeping hasn't been in to tidy up yet. That means Kitty almost certainly hasn't come back from Bahía de Alcudia. '*Merde!*' She leaves the cabin, hurrying back to the party in search of Evan.

She heads up to the top deck and passes the hot tub, where several people she's never seen before have stripped down to their underwear and jumped in, holding their champagne glasses clear of the frothing water. She sees a flash of nipple. The music cranks up so loud she can barely hear herself think, and the hot tubbers whoop in appreciation.

One of the chefs is working the outdoor kitchen – it's much too grand to be called a barbecue – flipping burgers for the now-ravenous guests. Concern and the smell of grilling meat turns her stomach.

She eventually locates Evan on the other side of the pool, in a tête-à-tête with Jim. His nostrils flare with annoyance when she interrupts them by tapping on his forearm. 'It's Kitty,' she whispers urgently. 'No one's seen her since this afternoon. Rocco says she decided to explore the town by herself.'

'You mean she's not back on the boat yet?' Sandrine doesn't think he appreciates the seriousness of the situation, but there is a muscle ticking in his jaw and he beckons to Walker, repeating what Sandrine has just told him.

Walker taps his earpiece and has a discussion with the bosun, then turns back to them. 'It's confirmed: she hasn't returned to the boat on the tender,' he says.

Sandrine is about to insist that they send a search party, that someone should contact the local police, when a Guardia Civil boat pulls up alongside *Ambition*. She doesn't see it until it's nearly upon them, but she recognises the paintwork as someone shines a light down on the boat.

The three of them hurry down to the swim deck at the stern. She hopes it's not too much to ask that the police might be arriving with the missing girl. Evan is going to be furious with Kitty for staying out so late, but in Sandrine's opinion it's Rocco who should be held responsible. He was supposed to be looking out for his sister; he should never have let her go off on her own.

The two policemen come aboard – not the same ones who came before, Sandrine thinks, though she can't be sure – but it soon transpires that they are there because of a noise complaint. Walker signals to a deckhand to go and speak to the DJ. 'It's probably time we started ferrying guests back in any case,' he adds.

He explains to the officers that they have just discovered that Kitty is missing. 'She's only fourteen and should have been back before now.'

'Is it normal for her to be out by herself, after dark?' The officer's voice is flat, but Sandrine can sense his underlying judgement. He asks for a description and Sandrine shows him a photo she has on her phone, taken only that morning. Kitty is sitting between Carter and Bailey and all three of them are laughing. She looks so young. She *is* so young.

One of the officers radios back to the town's police station, the static making it impossible to hear the response. He gives Sandrine a number to send the photo to and then presents Evan with a card. 'Someone will be in touch.'

'Hardly reassuring,' Sandrine says when the officers have left.

'Don't worry,' Walker reassures them. 'I'll get Johannes to drop a few of the deckhands at the marina and they'll check the bars and restaurants. I promise, we won't stop until we've found her.'

Evan's phone rings and he checks the caller ID. 'Sorry,' he shrugs, 'I really have to take this.'

What can be more important than your missing daughter? 'I'm going to search the cabins again,' Sandrine says to Walker. 'Just in case.'

yourworstnightmare: I heard it wasn't an accident at all – just made to look that way so they could claim it on insurance.

sUpri*me: but then it all went horribly wrong?

Chapter Fifty-seven

THE DETECTIVE

All thoughts of a swim are forgotten as Luis hurries towards his car. According to his notes, *Ambition*'s captain had mentioned they were planning to move on to Bahía de Alcudia and then, depending on the weather and the forecast wind direction, anchor overnight somewhere near Cala Mesquida, about an hour's drive from Palma, on the island's northeast tip. He tosses a mental coin as to which way to go.

Checking the map on his phone, he sees that there is a road that connects the two. He plumps for Cala Mesquida, figuring that if the yacht is not there, he can always head back to Alcudia, which is about forty minutes away. He contacts water police HQ and is pleased to learn that there's a vessel in the vicinity. He lets them know he'll be in touch once he's located the yacht.

He sets off, ignoring the flickering of a dashboard warning light.

He wants to talk to the owner's daughter, to find out just how she came by her necklace. He also wants to see the reaction of the others on board when he asks about the necklace. The more he thinks about it, the more he suspects that there might be a connection between this yacht and the dead women.

He's halfway across the island when his phone rings. Not having a hands-free set-up, he pulls over to a side road to take it. The warning light on the dashboard flashes an ominous orange at him again. He should have taken one of the other pool vehicles and left this one at the station.

'Sir? It's Maria. I thought you might want to know that some more information came in about Krystina Svoboda. It turns out she was living in Slovenia until a month ago.'

'Slovenia?'

'Yes, sir.'

'Any other intel?'

'That's all I've been able to come up with so far.'

'Thanks, Maria, speak to you tomorrow.'

He turns the key in the ignition, still thinking about what Maria told him. It could mean that the island has a bigger problem than anyone realises.

The engine coughs but fails to turn over. 'Fuck it!' He slams his palm against the steering wheel.

He waits a few minutes and tries to start it again, but there's no response bar a cough that would make a pack-a-day smoker proud. Furious with himself, he arranges for a tow truck to come and retrieve the car. He swears again when he learns that there will be a delay of several hours.

With nothing to do but cool his heels and wait, he finds a protein bar stashed in the glove box, grabs it along with a bottle of lukewarm water and climbs a rise at the side of the road. Sitting on a patch of scrubby, dry grass in the shade, he unwraps the bar. Now there's no way he'll get to Cala Mesquida before it's far too late to call on the yacht. He calls Maria to let her know what's happened. 'I think it's the battery,' he says. Then he leans back against a tree and passes the time listening to the police radio.

Below him, the traffic becomes increasingly intermittent.

Slovenia. He turns the name of the country over in his mind, unable to work out why it tugs at him.

More than an hour and a half later, no one has arrived. He is about to call the towing company for an updated ETA when his radio emits another burst of static, followed by a report of a missing young woman from the yacht *Ambition*. He jerks upright, listening carefully.

Chapter Fifty-eight

THE YOUNGEST DAUGHTER

Kitty has no idea what time it is when she's disturbed by a sharp rap on the door. Startled, she hugs the towel to her, aware now that her hair has dried while she's been reading. She glances at the small window but can't see anything but her own reflection staring back at her. It has become night without her really being aware of it.

The handle turns and the door opens a fraction. 'Anyone there?'

'Just a sec,' she says, searching for the robe she had seen in the closet. She locates it and wraps the silky fabric around her.

'Kit-Kat!' Julian looks her up and down and Kitty hastily crosses her arms over the robe. He grins at her wolfishly. 'There's a search party out looking for you in town. No one knew where you were.'

'Well, I'm fine,' she replies. 'Thank you.'

He steps inside, closing the door behind him, and is suddenly uncomfortably close. He has the distant, glazed demeanour of someone who's been drinking heavily.

This is what she's wanted, isn't it? Just the two of them, with no one else around? So why does she feel like a rabbit in the spotlight?

She backs away, stumbling over the corner of a rug, and is about to fall when he grabs her under her arms and pulls her upright. Her robe slips, and she's uncomfortably aware that she's completely naked underneath.

'Take it easy now,' he murmurs in her ear, one hand now caressing her wrist, the other pressing her to him.

Kitty swallows. She doesn't want to be here with him, not like this. She tries to push past him, desperate to get away.

'Not so fast, little kitten.' He tightens his grip on her wrist, wrenching it painfully, and pushes her down on the bed.

Her knees buckle and then her head slams against the hard cover of the book she had been reading.

'Don't!' she cries, struggling against him. 'You're hurting me.' He takes absolutely no notice.

He's all over her, his lips smeared against her cheek, his stubble grazing her mouth, his hips clashing painfully with hers, pinning her wrists above her head with one hand, pulling her robe open with the other.

It's *nothing* like her fantasies.

'C'mon, Kitty-Kat, you know you've thought about this,' he says, his breath ragged. 'Don't think I haven't noticed.'

All she can smell is the noxious combination of cigarette smoke and alcohol on his breath. A wave of nausea rolls up from her stomach. She twists away from him, retching, heaving. Through streaming eyes she sees a chunk of partly digested bread land on the sheets, another flecking the expensive rug. Vomit everywhere.

Julian recoils and she rolls away from him, landing heavily on the floor, her ankle twisting beneath her. Dry heaves wrack her body.

Julian's expression is one of utter revulsion.

Kitty burns with shame. She stumbles but finds her feet, limps the few steps to the door, her hand closing around the handle. As she wrenches it open, she hears a snigger behind her.

'You're still just a kid, Kitty-Kat,' he taunts. 'Not yet ready to play with the grown-ups.'

* * *

She runs towards her cabin, reliving the terrifying experience: his hand bruising her wrist, the paralysing fear and then being horribly, shamefully, sick to her stomach. Her breath comes in halting gasps and she ricochets off the walls of the corridor, disorientated. The lights flicker and dim. She's scared he might be following her.

The lights come on again and she sees her door. Stumbling towards it, her fingers close around the handle and she throws herself into the room, slamming the door shut behind her and burying herself under the bedcovers. Tears slide hot and fast down her cheeks and she bites her lip to stifle the sobs. How is she ever going to face them all?

She vaguely hears the door open and ice-cold fear slides down her spine. After what happened, she really didn't think he would follow her, but maybe that was naïve.

She freezes, feeling her heart beat throughout her body, every muscle tensed to fight.

'Oh, thank god. Kitty, *chérie*, are you awake?'

She doesn't move, can't face Sandrine right now.

The door closes and Kitty forces her muscles to unclench.

Everyone loves Julian. God, even she thought she was in love with him. He's been part of their family since he became Rocco's best friend in kindergarten – people sometimes joke that he and Rocco are conjoined twins. She hates him now, can't believe how stupid she's been.

A steely resolve takes the place of her fear.

She will find a way to get back at him.

Chapter Fifty-nine

THE TROPHY WIFE

Sandrine goes to her cabin and touches up her make-up, reapplying lipstick and spraying her hair in an attempt to revive it. The damp night air has flattened the cascading waves she had less than an hour ago.

She'd been so frightened that something dreadful had happened to Kitty, could have sworn the girl wasn't in her cabin the first time she checked, but when she went back a second time, there she was, huddled under the covers, only the top of her head showing, fast asleep. Sandrine will get the blame for raising the alarm for no reason; Evan will be furious.

When she returns to the party, Pierre has finally arrived. '*Salut*!' she says, hugging him fondly and forgetting all about finding Evan for the moment.

He cranes his head to take in the enormity of the vessel. 'This is quite the set-up.'

She shrugs, mockingly humble, and repeats the response she'd given Jim and Virginia earlier. 'We like it.'

'I bet you do.' He laughs, introducing her to his partner. 'Lucie Allard, Sandrine Furneaux. Lucie and I are working on a new project together.'

'Very good,' says Sandrine. She recognises the name: Lucie is one of Europe's up-and-coming producers. 'How exciting.'

She almost doesn't want to ask but can't help herself. 'Who is attached?'

Pierre and Lucie exchange a glance. 'We have cast most of the parts,' he says, 'but we haven't found our lead. We're looking for someone who can play the jaded former showgirl down on her luck.' He grins widely. 'Perhaps you might know someone ...?'

Is she hearing correctly? Is he suggesting they might consider *her* for the part?

Her hand flutters self-consciously to her throat before she sees an infinitesimal shake of his head.

'Of course, it is such a shame you are no longer working, otherwise we would have been in touch at once ...'

Is he going to make her beg? Please, no. She's never had to do that. 'Well, is it not true that actresses never properly retire?' She arches her eyebrow at them both.

'On the contrary, Sandrine. It is obvious how truly content you are with your new life, with your divine baby, with all this ...' Lucie says as Pierre wraps an arm around Sandrine's shoulders.

'Well ...' she begins, inadvertently catching Evan's eye. He is standing a few feet away, next to Jim. His expression is thunderous. She remembers that he doesn't know about Kitty yet. '*Merde! Excusez-moi*, I must speak to my husband.'

Chapter Sixty

THE PATRIARCH

Evan can't stand to watch another man fawn over his wife. It was bad enough when he first met Sandrine and she was away working for weeks on end, leaving him to imagine the worst.

'*Chérie*, I found her!' Sandrine says, delighted.

'You what?' he asks.

'Kitty. She was asleep, in her cabin. Though I swear she was not there earlier. Anyway,' she adds, 'she is safe. Thank goodness.'

'Perhaps you might also let Walker know,' Evan says coldly. 'We've got half the crew out looking for her.' He turns back to Jim, annoyance compounding his fury at seeing his wife flirt with another man. Sandrine obviously didn't bother to check properly for Kitty before raising the alarm. It makes him look stupid, and if there is anything Evan hates, it's being made to seem a fool. 'I'll get my team to send a prospectus over to you in the morning,' he says, beckoning Rocco over as he speaks. 'You remember my son?'

'Of course I do. How are you, Rocco?'

'Good, thank you, sir.'

'We were just talking about the Rawson Project,' says Evan. 'I took Rocco over there a week ago, didn't I, son?'

'Sure did.' Rocco sways slightly, though the yacht is hardly moving. 'It's a huge site – so much potential. I can't wait to see it come to life. It's the opportunity of a lifetime.'

'Don't you two ever stop?' Jim jokes. 'Some of us are on vacation.'

'People like us never completely switch off, do we?' Evan replies, sneaking another glance at Sandrine. She has rejoined the couple she was with earlier, leaning into them now, her hand resting on Pierre's arm. He turns away but struggles to regain his focus. 'Besides, I know what an appetite you have for a good deal. You won't want to miss this one, believe me.'

Jim holds up his hands in submission. 'I'll find the time to look it over.'

'Promise?' Evan knows he should let it drop – there's nothing more off-putting than the smell of desperation – but he needs this, and he can't afford to delay.

Virginia sashays over. 'You two had better not be talking business again,' she says, pouting her over-inflated lips at Evan. 'Besides, we really should be going, isn't that right, honey? Evan, your boat is faaa-bulous,' she says, air-kissing him before dragging her husband towards the stern where the tender is waiting.

Evan looks over to Sandrine again, failing to catch her eye. She is deliberately ignoring him now. He turns back to find Melissa standing in front of him.

'What's going on?' she asks, glancing in the direction of Jim and Virginia. 'And why is Rocco in the loop and not me?'

Evan spreads his hands wide. 'Sweetheart, you're being paranoid …'

Rocco, rightly sensing a storm brewing, heads after a passing waiter holding a tray of food. 'Later, yeah?' Rocco says.

Evan can't admit just how badly things are going. This is a hiccup in the process; he's been here before and things have righted themselves. It's his responsibility to handle it. The trouble is, he's only got a week left before the interest is due on the loan, no way of making the payment without an injection of cash and he's fresh out of assets to leverage.

Melissa fixes him with a stare. Not much gets past her.

'It's a cash flow issue, Melissa. It's only temporary.'

'You can talk to me about this, Dad,' she says. 'If I'm to step up, then I need to know everything—'

'Let's enjoy the party, shall we?' he interrupts. 'We're on vacation, after all.' Only he and Bill Katz know just how precarious the situation is, and as far as he's concerned, they're the only two people who need to.

'You're never going to trust me, are you? No matter how hard I work, even though I show up every single fucking day, give my all to the business, it's never going to be enough, is it?' She stops, her face hardening. 'Oh, and there's something else. I ran into Toby McIntyre when I was in Soller.'

Evan frowns. 'McIntyre?' The name doesn't ring a bell.

'Yes, Toby McIntyre. Remember him? From my year in London? He told me that you told him some cock and bull story about me having no plans to return to England, that I didn't want to speak to him. Care to explain that to me?' She shows him none of her usual deference.

Evan raises a warning hand. 'Calm down, honey. Let's not make a scene. We can discuss this in the morning.' Pain flares in his chest, making him regret that last canapé.

'I don't know, it seems pretty simple to me.' She thrusts her empty glass at a passing deckhand. 'I need to find my son, but don't think I'm going to let this slide.'

That's his eldest daughter's biggest problem – forgiveness is not in her vocabulary.

untiltomorrowcomes: It's a bonfire of the fuckin' vanities.

Chapter Sixty-one

THE TROPHY WIFE

Sandrine hurries towards her husband and places a hand on his arm. 'Is everything okay?' He is red in the face, sweat beading on his forehead, darkening the hair at his temples.

He shakes her off. 'Abso-fucking-lutely,' he says under his breath. 'Do you think I enjoy watching my wife being fawned over by other men? Even someone as obviously beta as that stupid Frenchman.'

He's drunk. Evan is impossible when he's drunk.

'Pierre is one of my oldest friends and he is here with his girlfriend,' she says.

Evan pulls out a handkerchief and wipes it across the back of his neck. 'Goddamn it's hot.' He is even redder in the face now, almost purple. He pulls her to him and whispers in her ear. 'You really expect me to believe that? He couldn't keep his hands off you, the fuckin' greasy frog. Stupid woman for encouraging him.'

'*Pardon?*' Sandrine can't believe what she just heard. Evan might have been jealous in the past, but he's never put her down like this before.

He grunts and grabs a drink from a passing deckhand, tossing it back, then grabs her wrist, squeezing it hard.

Her eyes water at the pain but she refuses to let him see how much it hurts. She grits her teeth, counting silently in her head until he lets go.

She's mortified at the way he has treated her, embarrassed that Melissa might have overheard, might have seen him squeeze her wrist so hard it nearly made her cry out.

If she's honest with herself, they're all awful: bastard Evan, spoilt Rocco, overbearing Melissa, even thoughtless Kitty. Why did she ever think she wanted to be a part of this rotten family? Max is the only good thing to have come from it. She decides that she won't stay and let her son become infected by their self-centred, narcissistic ways.

'*Excusez-moi.*' She flees without another word.

When she reaches the master cabin she locks the door. She won't deal with Evan again tonight. She opens the wardrobe and begins flinging her clothes into her suitcase. She'll pack her own goddamn bags and get out of there at first light, taking Max and the nanny with her. He's pushed her to the limit, making the pull of Paris and the siren call of her former career impossible to resist.

Chapter Sixty-two

THE ELDEST DAUGHTER

Melissa finally tracks down Carter, who is with one of the deckhands on the yacht's port side, and gets him into bed before returning to the party. She hasn't forgotten that she invited Toby and his family this evening, but figures if they were going to show up they would surely have done so by now. She had texted him with the boat's new location, apologising and saying it was probably too far for them to drive, but she'd held out a faint hope nonetheless. Disappointment stabs at her even as she thinks it is probably for the best. She might have guessed he was only being polite – and so very British – when he said he'd come.

She finds Angus at the bar, pouring whisky into a tumbler. The bottle chinks against the glass and he spills some, amber drops beading on the white marble.

He's also making eyes at a pretty, very young deckhand, attempting to cajole her into trying some of the twenty-one-year-old single malt. 'Just think, this was distilled before you were even born,' she hears him saying.

'I'm really not supposed to, and anyway, I'm more of a tequila drinker,' the deckhand simpers.

'Angus.'

He looks up, seemingly surprised to see his wife. 'I thought you'd be outside with the great and the good.' He winks slyly at the deckhand, who, correctly assessing the temperature of the situation, murmurs an excuse and leaves.

Melissa can't help it. Three glasses of champagne have gone straight to her head, and the alcohol and the terse exchange with her dad have made her punchy. 'Should we go somewhere more private?' They're alone in the salon now, but she doesn't want to risk being interrupted, or overheard.

He raises an eyebrow. 'Whatever you say, darling.' He moves away from the bar, bringing the glass and bottle with him, limping as he follows her.

When they get to their cabin, he collapses on the bed, holding his glass aloft to avoid spilling it and then hauling his boot-encased leg up after him. Melissa closes the door behind her and leans against it.

Angus gestures for her to join him on the bed.

She shakes her head. 'Not yet. I need to freshen up. Pour me one, will you?' She points to an empty glass on the bedside table before going to the bathroom. Splashing her face and then drying it, she returns to the cabin, carrying a couple of sleeping tablets and a glass of water.

Angus is on his phone but hastily puts it face-down on the nightstand as she reappears.

She pastes on a smile and takes a sip of the whisky he has poured for her. It's smoky and rich, but it burns the back of her throat. She's never been a big fan of hard liquor.

'You don't like it?' he asks, seeing her expression falter.

'I think perhaps I've had enough for one night,' she says. He grimaces as he moves over to make room for her on the bed.

'How is the ankle holding up?' she asks, pretending sympathy. 'I've brought you some more painkillers.' She holds out the glass of water and the tablets. Fortunately, they are exactly the same shape and colour as Tylenol, but in fact are benzos, the strongest sleeping tablets Melissa's doctor would prescribe her.

'Thanks.' He looks at her suspiciously, clearly not used to her being so thoughtful, then takes them, swallowing down the entire glass of water. He falls back against the pillows. 'God, I'm exhausted. It's been a lot this past week, you know?'

'Hasn't it?' she agrees.

The drugs are quick-acting, and combined with the alcohol, should work even faster. She's careful not to give him too strong a dose – she doesn't want to kill him, not literally anyway, not even when she thinks he might want her dead.

She twists the gold ring on her finger. 'I saw the messages, Angus. Between you and Amelia. What exactly did you mean by "*I'll fix everything. She'll be out of the picture soon, I promise.*"'

'You've got it all wrong,' he mumbles, struggling to sit upright. 'It's not what you think.'

'Honestly, exactly how stupid do you think I am?'

He doesn't reply, his eyes glazing over.

'So listen.' She stands facing him, cupping her chin in one hand, mocking the way he likes to talk, doing her best to feign a complete absence of emotion. 'Here's what's going to happen. You are going to be leaving the boat tomorrow. You will be taken straight to the airport, where you will board a plane back to New York.' She doesn't tell him he'll be flying coach; let him find that out all by himself. 'A driver will meet you and take you to Brooklyn, where I've arranged for an apartment for you. The rent is paid for three months. After that, you are on your own. We'll discuss visitation with the children at a later date.' She's relying on him being too sedated to argue, but nevertheless, she deliberately doesn't bring up the words 'divorce proceedings'.

'If harm comes to me, to so much as a hair on my head, my lawyers have screenshots of the text messages, evidence of you plotting against me and they will not hesitate to act.' Her legs are shaking as she says this, but her voice remains calm.

Angus flutters his eyelids, then they are stilled. The sleeping pills have done their job.

She retrieves his phone and goes to his messages. As she suspected, he has been in touch with Amelia throughout the evening. She scrolls back, her hands shaking as she sees another message, from two weeks ago:

> It's all under control. Melissa won't be around for much longer and then I'll be free, we'll be free to be together. A little patience, darling, is all I ask.

Jesus. A tiny part of her hadn't wanted to believe him capable of it, but this is irrefutable proof that she was right to have been alarmed.

She takes a breath, then begins to type a message from Angus to Amelia, explaining that he's sorry, he won't be able to make it after all, that for the sake of his children, he can't be with her, that it is over between them, that she deserves so much better. He is sorry he has misled her but his children must come first, and he has been reminded that marriage can only be dissolved by God. She reads the message through, presses send, and then pockets the phone before letting herself out of the cabin.

Angus, mouth agape, snores on, oblivious.

100Worrier: Why were some of them able to get out, but others weren't? It all smells fishy to me.

Thatmakesnosense: It was the middle of the night, dumbass. I'd say they were asleep, and wouldn't have known what was going on.

Chapter Sixty-three

THE DECKIE

For four days, Piper and her father took it in turns to keep vigil in Lexie's hospital room.

No one could tell them when – or even if – she would wake up.

On the morning of the fifth day, as Piper dozed on a reclining chair, she felt a tap on her arm, and opened her eyes to see a nurse beckoning her over. Her sister had turned her head and was staring, bewildered, at them.

At first she had no memory of what had happened to her. 'I was diving,' she whispered. 'I was excited to see the fish and the reef … then, it's all black. Nothing.'

'It's normal in the case of brain swelling for there to be some memory loss,' the doctor explained later. 'Especially in the short term.'

No one from the Thyssen family bothered to get in touch. 'They sent a pathetic bunch of flowers,' Piper fumed before thrusting them at the nurses, claiming that her sister was allergic to pollen. 'As if that will absolve them from responsibility.'

'At least their insurance was up to date,' her father replied, doing his best to see the positive in the situation. Lexie had been medevaced back to England within a few days of the accident, all costs covered by the Thyssens.

* * *

After about a fortnight, when Lexie came home, her memory started to return. As well as being physically weak, she was also suffering from migraines and severe dizziness. Piper had begun sleeping in the same room as her sister, in case Lexie needed her during the night.

One night, Piper had only been asleep for what felt like a minute when she was woken by Lexie groaning and thrashing in the bed across from her.

'It's okay, it's okay,' Piper said. 'Here, let me in.' She lifted the sheet and climbed into her sister's bed, wrapping her arms around her the way their mother had once done. 'You're safe.'

'I can't breathe,' Lexie gasped, sitting bolt upright in bed.

'What? What is it?' Piper put her arm around her sister.

'I remember now. My regulator failed. It just stopped working halfway through the dive. No air was coming through, though my tank was more than half full – I remember checking it. I tried to get my buddy's attention but she had swum off, too far away to see me. I had to do an emergency ascent, but when I got to the boat I pretty much passed out. If they'd been able to get me on oxygen, things would have been okay. I don't know why they didn't. It's all blank after that.'

'Who was your dive buddy?' Piper asked.

'Melissa – the adult daughter. She never should have left me. But that's not what's important. I remember now, Julian swapped gear with me at the last minute, said he didn't like the feel of the regulator, that Rocco suggested trying the one I'd been given. I couldn't say no. He was a guest and I was crew.'

'But wouldn't the dive company have checked everything beforehand?'

'I think maybe Rocco messed with the equipment without anyone noticing. I saw him and Julian over by the gear as we suited up. And then later, just before we got in the water something felt off, but I didn't know at the time what it was.'

Piper was horrified. 'Would he really be that stupid? You could have died out there, Lex.'

'I can't prove either of them did anything, but I believe now that he wanted to get back at me.'

'What? Why?'

'Rocco tried it on with me a couple of times earlier in the trip, "accidentally" touching me, leaning in for a kiss when no one else was around. Low-key stuff, mostly. That's how it is on yachts sometimes; you have to learn to deal with the harassment without making a fuss. I didn't take it that seriously. I tried to brush it off, but he still wouldn't leave me alone. I told him I'd go to the captain if he ever touched me again. I thought it had worked, that he got the message. But now I'm not so sure. Maybe he saw me with Erik and got jealous. Rocco and Julian were tight: I think they could have cooked up the plan between them. I don't think they realised just how dangerous it could be. At least, I hope they didn't, because otherwise that's pretty fucking awful.'

Piper ground her teeth in fury. 'It's criminal, Lex. We have to tell someone about this, we *have* to.'

'It won't do any good, Pip. I can't prove anything. They probably only meant to scare me. And anyway, people like that always get away with it. I'm lucky to be alive and out of there. I hope I never see that family again as long as I live. They're toxic, the lot of them.'

* * *

Three weeks later, Lexie was dead.

Piper woke up one morning and instinctively knew something was different. She rolled over, seeing her sister's head on the pillow in the bed across from her, her lips parted, her eyes glassy. Piper shook her, but she didn't respond. Lexie's skin was cool against her fingers.

A scream brought their father into the room, but nothing could wake her.

The post-mortem found that Lexie had suffered a sudden, silent cardiac arrest in her sleep. Piper had been right beside her and yet completely unaware of it. There was no warning, and nothing about Lexie's heart that could explain it. 'A tragic occurrence, especially after everything she had been through, but there is no evidence to show that it was in any way related to her earlier accident,' the report concluded.

Total bullshit. It had everything to do with the dive incident, and Piper was going to make sure those who were responsible paid for it.

Chapter Sixty-four

THE ELDEST DAUGHTER

Melissa leaves the cabin and goes out onto the main deck, where deckhands are clearing up after the party, pulling down fairy lights and retrieving abandoned glasses. The DJ has packed up and left and the remaining guests have been taken ashore.

There's a faintly deflated feeling about the scene, as if the energy has been drained from it, and she's suddenly exhausted too. She hears the rumble of the anchor chain at the bow and then the boat gets underway, sailing out to sea. She doesn't stop to question why they're leaving the anchorage this late at night: there are far more pressing things to concern herself with.

She rolls her shoulders, attempting to ease the tension in her traps. Perhaps tomorrow she'll be able to get off the boat and go for a long run – running has always been her way to destress, to forget about everything, and she craves the release, the endorphins.

She'll be glad when tomorrow is over and Angus has been dispatched. At least one issue on her long to-do list will have been crossed off.

She finds her father in his study. He has his head in his hands and for a second, as she enters, he doesn't appear to notice her at all. She clears her throat and he looks up, his eyes bloodshot, ringed with tiredness.

'I have concerns. There's something about the Rawson Project financials that's been bugging me.' She won't tell him yet about Angus, about the end of her marriage: business is a far easier subject to broach.

'Can we do this tomorrow?'

Melissa blinks. Her father is always available to discuss work, no matter what time of day or night. His reluctance sounds a tiny note of alarm.

'I don't think so.' She sits back in the small sofa, sinking into its feather cushions. 'In fact, it's my belief that we've got bigger problems than the Rawson Project.'

The first generation makes the money, the second spends it and the third blows it, or so the saying goes. Her father has always impressed upon her the story of Cornelius Vanderbilt, who left a billion-dollar inheritance (in today's money) when he died in 1877. Fifty years later, his fortune had dwindled to almost nothing. As the eldest child, third-generation Thyssen Properties executive and its eventual CEO, god willing, there's no way Melissa is going to fulfil that particular prophecy. Spot the opportunities early, diversify to spread risk, don't be afraid to aggressively reinvest, and sweat the small stuff; that's her business philosophy. Her father is more of a maverick, with a cast-iron stomach for risk, 'betting the farm' on more than one occasion. Fortune has favoured the bold, so far at least, but a lucky streak never lasts forever.

He sighs. 'What is it?'

She opens her laptop, clicking on a window, then leans forward and swivels it around so he can see the screen. 'When I realised that the Rawson projections didn't make sense, I took a closer look at the entire company's financials.'

Her father looks about to protest, but she silences him.

'Bill Katz gave me what I needed. Not without me leaning on him heavily, I might add. He's loyal to you, but even he can read a balance sheet. He's worried too.'

Evan pulls his glasses off and tosses them on the desk. He looks decades older.

'Unless there's something I'm missing?' She knows she isn't; she's been over it too many times. 'With the level of funding available to us at present, I don't see how we can continue to operate much longer.'

'Nothing gets past you, does it?'

Melissa ignores the compliment, rare though it is. There is a stone in the pit of her stomach. She had been hoping against hope that her father would tell her she's wrong, that somehow she's overlooked something crucial, that there is something in the works to get the company out of this jam.

'You always were the smart one. What can I say? You're right. I put so much pressure on you about the Rawson Project because I thought if anyone could make the numbers work, suggest a way to find the extra funds we need, you could.' He rubs a hand across his eyes. 'But without a miracle, the company is – we are – screwed. Even if I manage to get Jim Murray on board, it's only going to buy us a little extra time.'

He is tugging at a piece of loose skin on his thumb, biting down on it, drawing blood. 'We're too far in to get out. I've leveraged everything, given personal guarantees, but it's still not enough to make up the shortfall. And the first loan repayment is due next week. I don't need to spell out what will happen if we don't meet it.'

'Have you lost your fucking mind?' Even though she's staring right at him, Melissa forgets she's talking to her father. 'How could you not share this with me sooner?' *When there might have been a chance of minimising the damage*, she adds silently. *When we weren't a week away from foreclosure.*

'I should have,' he says. 'It was a mistake not to.'

He never admits he's wrong. This alarms Melissa even more, if that were possible. She's trying to get a handle on things, frantically computing the scale of the problem. 'What precisely do you mean, you've leveraged everything? The Hamptons house? The apartments? This?' She sweeps her gaze around the study.

Evan nods slowly. 'That's about the size of it.'

'Jesus Christ. Do you realise what you've done? You've put our entire family in jeopardy, not to mention everyone who works for us, people whose livelihood depends on us.'

'I know, I know. Look, I thought some of the other income streams would help, but there have been a few hiccups there.'

'Other income streams?' She has no clue what he's talking about. 'What do you mean?'

Evan doesn't answer and Melissa flops back against the cushions and closes her eyes, feeling the blood pulse at her temples. 'What are we going to do?' she asks.

'I have no idea.'

'Who else knows?'

Evan shakes his head, staring at his reflection in the window. She's never seen him out of answers before. 'Only Katz, and even he doesn't know all of it.'

Despite their occasional differences, her father has always been a giant, a scale by which to measure herself, a standard she's tried so hard to reach. 'I could remortgage the Brooklyn house – god, I'll put it on the market if I have to,' she says, doing some furious mental calculations.

'It wouldn't touch the sides.' He rubs a hand down his face, dragging at the skin and giving himself jowls. 'You never give up, do you? Even when there's not the slightest shred of hope.'

He has no idea what she's given up on in the last few hours.

'And I was never really serious about Rocco joining Thyssen in any meaningful way – just thought you could stand a little competition, keep you hungry.'

She looks at him in utter disbelief. 'Yeah, that was just about the worst idea I've ever heard. He's only keen because he thinks it will please you. It's not what he really wants.

Anyway, there might not be a company for him to join unless there's some kind of miracle.'

'If anyone can conjure one up, it's you.'

'Really? So now it's *my* job to get us out of this hole? A hole, I might add, that I had little part in digging?' She can't believe what's unfolded this evening.

Only one thing is certain: it really can't get any worse.

MartinB: What about the crew? Don't forget they were affected as well, they've lost their jobs, some of them might not work again. No one ever thinks of the little people, the do-ers.

Chapter Sixty-five

THE HANGER-ON

'Are you going to explain yourself?'

Julian has never seen his friend so glacially calm. The easygoing, lovable charmer has been transformed into someone he doesn't recognise. Someone who is looking at him now as if he's no better than the dirt on his shoe.

'I saw my little sister running out of a cabin in tears and then a minute later you followed her. What the fuck did you do to her?'

'You know what girls are like, they always exaggerate.' Julian desperately scrambles to redeem himself but Rocco, if anything, is even icier.

In the past when they've disagreed, he's always been able to win his friend over, but he feels a prickle of alarm that it won't work now. He tries a different tack. 'Come on, bro, you know I'd *never* do anything to hurt Kitty. God, she's like a sister to me.' He swallows, feeling his Adam's apple almost block his throat. 'She must have got the wrong end of the stick. You've seen how she looks at me. If anything, I was the one trying to fight her off.' He claps a hand on Rocco's shoulder in an attempt at reassurance.

Rocco flinches. 'Don't touch me.'

'She pulled *me* into that cabin,' Julian lies. 'She's got this enormous crush on me and somehow imagined that I felt the same way about her, but honestly, I would *never* … she's family. I tried to let her down gently, I really did, but she took it the wrong way.'

'If you've done anything to her …'

'Dude!' Julian splutters. 'No way! Come on.' He spreads his hands, appealing. He has to make Rocco believe him. 'I promise.'

'It would be better if you left us for a while, yeah?' Rocco suggests coldly. 'I think perhaps tomorrow you should get off the boat and head to Ibiza a few days early. I'll get Walker to arrange it in the morning.'

Julian tastes the bitterness of Rocco's rejection. 'You'll still come, right? You can't miss out. Ibiza's insane, man. You should see the chicks …' He gives a low whistle, but even to his ears it sounds fake, as though he's grasping at the broken straws of their friendship.

Rocco shakes his head. 'I don't think so. We need to give each other a little space.'

'Really?'

Rocco, for once, is immoveable.

Julian recalibrates. 'But we'll be cool, yeah? When we get back to the city?'

'I don't know, man,' Rocco replies. 'It might be best for us both if we take a break, focus on our own stuff.'

'You can't mean that. We've been best friends, like, forever.' Julian doesn't know who he is without Rocco as his wing man. 'We've always been there for each other.' He's frantic, feeling Rocco slipping away from him. 'Besides, I know all your secrets,' he says in a last desperate bid to keep him close. 'Even on this trip, there are things I'm sure your father wouldn't want to hear about …' He is, of course, referring to the hook-up with the two women from *Moirai*, not to mention Rocco's fondness for nose candy.

'Are you *seriously* threatening me?' Rocco asks, disgust lacing his words. 'Start packing.' He turns on his heel, heading down the stairs to the main deck.

Julian is stunned. Rocco can't mean it. He's never been one to hold a grudge. The Rocco he knows is easygoing, forgiving. He must know Julian would *never* betray him, certainly not to his father. The two of them are a team; they're inseparable. It's always been that way.

Chapter Sixty-six

THE DETECTIVE

Three hours pass before anyone comes to Luis's aid. He's almost resigned himself to spending the night by the side of the road when an approaching vehicle flashes its lights and slows. He stands and waves, nearly tumbling down the embankment with relief.

Maria climbs out of her car.

'They sent you?'

'You have a problem with that, sir?'

She's polite, but he can see he's annoyed her and is immediately sorry. 'No, no, not at all. Really, I'm grateful. Just surprised no one else was available.'

She shrugs. 'It's been busy,' she says, going towards his car. 'Pop the hood for me, will you?' He hesitates, and she gives him a stern look. 'What?'

'Nothing. I shouldn't have ignored the warning lights. More fool me.' He does as she asks and she attaches a pair of charging leads to the battery, running them between the two cars.

'Try starting it now.'

He turns the key in the ignition and holds his breath. The car stutters into life and a grin spreads across his face.

'You could continue on,' Maria says, 'but that battery looks original and if this happens again out there in the middle of nowhere …'

He considers her advice. He should keep going, but her note of caution persuades him. 'Fair point.'

She smiles again, her cheeks dimpling, and attraction curls unexpectedly in his belly.

Decision made.

'I'm going to follow you back to Palma,' she says, 'and we'll drop it at the mechanic. Don't run the air conditioning or the radio – we've no idea how much juice is getting to the battery. It could be a faulty alternator.'

'Maria, you're a lifesaver, really. I'll cancel the tow truck, if they're even on their way yet.' He claps his head to his forehead. 'Oh god. It's your birthday, isn't it? You probably had plans tonight. I'm an idiot. Let me at least buy you dinner when we get back to town.' He tries to sound casual, like it's no big deal.

Someone else is responding to the report of the missing girl. He's not abandoning his duty, not really. Besides, he's way over his shift hours.

* * *

After they've left his ailing car in the forecourt of an auto place and dropped the keys in the letterbox, Maria drives them to a nearby restaurant. 'It doesn't look like much, but the food's good. The chef is a friend of my brother's.'

The restaurant is busy, but the waiter greets Maria fondly and they are immediately ushered to a small table at the back. There are no tablecloths, no menus and simple glassware, but within minutes bread, wine and a small plate of meatballs appears in front of them, followed by a stream of dishes at regular intervals. The food is fresh, hot and delicious and they both dive in.

While they eat, they talk. Luis learns that Maria is a third-generation cop who grew up in Palma. 'I went to the mainland for a few months, but I missed home too much,' she adds. As she speaks about her family, her eyes light up and Luis realises he is enjoying himself. This – friendship, warmth, and the beginning of something else perhaps – is what he's been missing since arriving on the island, though he'd not been aware of the lack of it until now.

'So, why were you heading to Cala Mesquida?' she asks, spearing a chunk of potato with her fork.

He explains that he had seen the young girl on the yacht *Ambition* wearing a similar necklace to the ones found on the bodies of the two women washed up on the beach. 'You know, the kind with a small initial on a gold chain.' As he says it out loud, he realises how little proof he has of any connection between the two. 'Though I guess those kinds of necklaces aren't that unusual.'

She looks at him thoughtfully. 'My father always says that honouring your instincts is what makes the difference between a good cop and a great one.'

He smiles and signals for the bill, feeling slightly less foolish. 'And then someone from the yacht went missing tonight. From *Ambition*.'

'Oh, she's been found – nothing more than a misunderstanding apparently. The report came in while we were dropping your car off.'

A fraction of his certainty deflates, like a balloon gradually losing air. 'Well …'

'Don't ignore your intuition,' she insists, a hint of flirtation in her tone.

His intuition is saying he should lean across the table and kiss Maria right now, but the waiter arrives with the bill and the moment is gone.

Chapter Sixty-seven

THE PATRIARCH

A hot knife of pain jerks Evan back to consciousness. 'Fucking heartburn,' he grunts, heaving himself to his feet and attempting to swallow the acid rising in his throat. Despite the frigid air conditioning, sweat gathers at his collar and runs down his neck, dampening his shirt.

He grabs a bottle of whisky and goes out on deck, heading towards the stern.

It's late now and the boat has reached its new mooring. Earlier, he'd seen a message from Captain Bird saying that she was concerned about an incoming storm, and thought it wise to relocate to a position that would afford more shelter. He has no idea where exactly they are, not that it matters greatly.

There's only one deckhand still working, hosing down the teak. He leaves as soon as he sees Evan, giving him privacy. As the captain predicted, the wind has picked up, little waves slapping at the hull, and it blows Evan's hair across his forehead.

He leans against the guardrails, breathing heavily. On a shorter man, the rails would hit at mid-thigh, but in his case, his knees meet the metal. If he's not careful, he could be in danger of losing his balance. It is dark as pitch and he faces out to sea, staring into the void.

The pain in his chest intensifies, causing him to stagger and he stumbles, falling awkwardly against a steel stanchion, grabbing the guardrail with one hand. The wire bites into his palm.

Righting himself, his heart thunders at the near miss, sending a jolt down his arm and making him breathless. He'll be damned if he is going to fall overboard. Everyone would think he'd done it on purpose, and he can't stand the idea of being remembered as a quitter.

A shadow snuffs out the light behind him and he turns to see a slight, indistinguishable figure silhouetted against its glow.

'Mr Thyssen, we need to talk.'

Forsakeme: They're saying that the bilge pump wasn't working, that the vessel would have gone down in mere minutes. It was lucky more people didn't die.

Chapter Sixty-eight

THE ELDEST DAUGHTER

Melissa can't face returning to her cabin, even if she knows Angus will be asleep. Instead, she looks in on her children, her gaze softening as she sees their tousled heads peeking out from beneath the covers. Doubt slithers through her: she's about to shatter their safe and secure world, but she reminds herself that she is not to blame for this. Besides, kids are pretty resilient, given the right support. You only have to look at her and Rocco to realise that.

Closing the door quietly, she takes the stairs that lead to the upper deck and makes her way aft. It's dark outside. The boat swings on its new mooring. Surprisingly, given the flotilla of boats they've seen everywhere else around the island, there appear to be no other vessels at anchor in this narrow bay.

All signs of the party have been removed. It's as if it never happened, save for a stain – red wine, most likely – on the upholstery. She is rubbing at it ineffectually when a stewardess appears and asks her if she needs anything.

'No. Thank you.' You're never alone on a boat, even one this size, even this late. She dismisses the girl, telling her that she should go to bed. 'Everyone else has, and I'm absolutely fine here by myself.'

'If you're sure.' The girl seems hesitant, as if she knows she should stay at her post.

'Don't worry. If anyone asks, I'll tell them I insisted you clock off for the night.'

'Thank you.' The girl slips away into the shadows and Melissa breathes out.

The wind has picked up, tugging at her hair, which has come loose from its ponytail. Something rattles on deck, an irritating, repetitive ting of metal on metal.

When her father revealed the state of the company's finances she only allowed herself a second to rail at the injustice of it all, then cut that train of thought off before it could take hold. She's never seen the point of self-pity. It's the worst kind of character weakness and achieves absolutely nothing.

She stares into the blackness, her laser focus for once failing her. She's always been able to come up with a solution for any problem, no matter how impossible it might initially seem. So surely, if she just thinks about it hard enough and for long enough, she'll be able to find a way to get Thyssen out of trouble.

'Can I arrange for some tea, perhaps? Or a blanket to keep off the cold?'

She startles. She had thought she was alone on deck, but Walker stands in front of her now, his expression unreadable in the dim light. She should be surprised he's still up, but somehow she isn't.

'Really, I'm fine,' she says. 'In fact, I should probably go inside. It is a little chilly.'

A strong gust buffets them both, causing Walker to stagger slightly.

'Did you need something from me?' she asks, confused. Why is he lingering?

He clears his throat and alcohol fumes waft towards her. 'Walker, are you *drunk*?' she asks.

'Never,' he insists as he slumps down onto the cushion, uncomfortably close to her. 'You and me, we should talk,' he slurs, leaning in.

She recoils. 'You should leave, before you say or do something you will regret.'

He laughs, but the sound is bitter and humourless. 'What do you know about regret? Daddy's favourite, aren't you? Protected from reality at all costs.'

'I have no idea what you're talking about.' No one speaks to her like this and gets away with it. 'But you're on thin ice right now, believe me.'

He leans in, the whites of his eyes threaded with red veins, reflected in the moonlight. 'You have no idea what kind of man your father really is, do you? You can't begin to fathom what he's really capable of.' He wipes his nose on the back of his arm. She's never seen this side of him, wouldn't have thought it possible. He's usually so *correct*. 'Wake up, honey, and smell the roses. Ask your daddy about his side hustle.' Walker taps his finger on the side of his nose. 'The one that makes the real money.'

Despite his overfamiliarity, she is intrigued. 'If you have something to say, spill it.'

He needs no further encouragement. 'Your darling father is part of a little *contraband* smuggling network.' He sighs. 'It was all going swimmingly, too.'

She doesn't question how he knows this – Walker is closer to her father than almost anyone, even family, it seems, and it does make sense. Hadn't Evan himself just admitted to another income stream?

'Smuggling? What kind of smuggling? And why are you telling me this? Why now?'

'He has to shut it down, if it's not already too late,' Walker insists. 'The cops are already sniffing around. When they came to the boat this morning, they asked some fairly direct questions. There have been a number of unfortunate mistakes.'

'You mean the dead woman?' Melissa asks. 'How has she got something to do with this? Wait.' She swallows. 'I'm not sure I want to know. And I still don't understand why you would come to me.'

'You're the only one who can persuade him that it has to stop: he listens to you.' He leans in closer, forcing her back onto the cushions. 'Because if he doesn't, we could all be in real trouble.'

HellFire99: If they'd been on deck and were able to swim, they would have all survived. It wasn't *that* far to the shore.

Chapter Sixty-nine

THE DECKIE

Piper climbs the stairs to the deck above, making her way to the guest cabins. The floor rocks beneath her feet; the wind has picked up, the first sign of the coming storm. She steadies herself with one hand against the wall and continues on.

She moves swiftly towards the door of the final cabin. She's only got another few hours on the yacht, if that; she has no doubt that Liam will report her to Walker.

It has to be now.

She doesn't bother to knock. Instead, she turns the handle slowly, grateful for the luxe fittings; the mechanism is as smooth as butter. Opening the door a few inches, she leans forward and peers into the room.

It's dark. There's a humped shape on the bed.

As her vision adjusts, she can make out a pair of splayed legs and, half-hidden by a pillow, the curved outline of a head.

Julian. She'll start with him.

Satisfied that he is asleep, for now anyway, Piper takes a step forward and pushes the door shut behind her. It closes with a soft, satisfying click.

She is about to pull the pillow from under his head when the yacht shudders. She only just stops herself from falling against the dresser.

When it's stable again, she reaches over and yanks the bedcovers off. He's completely naked.

Good. That will put him at a disadvantage.

He stirs, hands blindly reaching, and then he jerks awake, eyes widening in surprise.

'What the fuck? What are you *doing*?' He scrambles to cover himself.

'Hello Julian,' she says, sliding the Stanley knife from her pocket, the one Johannes had given her to open the boxes on her first day on board, and pointing it at him. 'I wouldn't try anything stupid if I were you. I'm stronger than I look.'

Predictably, he's a coward underneath the bravado. He shrinks back until he's flat against the far wall of the cabin. 'What do you want?'

'I need you to answer a few questions. Does the name Alexandra Smith ring a bell?'

He shakes his head, looking confused.

'No? Then let me remind you. Lexie – as you might better remember her – was a deckhand on the yacht on which you and the Thyssens spent spring break three years ago. Ring any bells now?'

He says nothing, and so she continues.

'Lexie was the diver you said was "messing about". Remember when you told me what happened when we were at the bar? She was the one you asked to swap your oxygen tank and regulator with, knowing full well that as she was a deckie and you were a guest, she couldn't refuse your request. You swapped the reg that your best friend Rocco tampered with, with Lexie. And you remember what happened after that.'

She watches carefully, but his response is not the one she is expecting. There is a shift in his body language, a slight relaxation that hints at something she can't quite decipher.

'And who told you?'

'Lexie did.' Piper nearly chokes on her words, but she won't let her grief get in the way, not now. 'Why did you do it, Julian? Was it because you'd do anything Rocco asked of you?'

'Rocco was hungover that morning; he almost didn't make it on the dive. He got there as we were about to leave.' A half-smile plays about his lips. 'He wouldn't have had time to mess with a regulator.'

'So, if Rocco didn't tamper with the reg, then who did?'

'Lexie was obsessed with Rocco; she wouldn't leave him alone. She had some kind of pathetic crush on him. Made a complete fool of herself, if you must know. He was embarrassed by it.'

'You're a liar. She wasn't like that, not at all. She told me that it was Rocco who wouldn't leave *her* alone, that she was afraid of losing her job if she told anyone how he was harassing her.'

'Rocco was too good for her; she wasn't in his league at all. Why do you care so much, anyway?'

'Lexie was my sister.'

'Your sister?' Julian looks at her in disbelief. 'What the fuck?'

As he speaks, a piece of the puzzle slots into place.

'You were jealous, weren't you?' she says. 'Jealous that your best friend liked someone else, that you couldn't have him all to yourself? Surely it wasn't the first time?'

Julian sneers, but her words have landed.

'So, what was it about her that bothered you? Was it that he seemed serious about a girl, even if she wasn't into him?'

Julian's mouth tightens, but he doesn't reply.

Now it all makes sense. 'It was *you*, wasn't it? You couldn't stand to see your best friend with someone else, so *you* tampered with the reg, and then forced Lexie to swap with you.' She is practically shouting at him now, certain she's right.

Julian finds his voice. 'There was a full investigation; it was a tragic accident. What proof have you got? Her word against ours? Don't be ridiculous, who would believe it?'

'Did you know that Lexie died because of what you did?' Piper spits at him.

'She *what*?'

'Yes. She died. A few weeks after the accident. A silent cardiac arrest. They couldn't find any direct evidence that it was related to the dive accident, but you'd have to be an idiot not to believe that it was.'

She's satisfied to see a look of horror cross his face.

'What? Didn't anyone bother to tell you?'

Julian, perhaps feeling that he can easily overpower her, lunges towards her, reaching for her wrist, but Piper is too quick. Even in the small cabin she manages to dodge him, slashing at the air to keep him at bay.

'Are you fucking insane?' He shrinks back again.

'I just might be,' she replies, her arm outstretched, the point of the knife aimed squarely at his chest.

'What the fuck do you want?'

She grits her teeth, the knife shaking in her hand. 'What I want is for you to feel even an ounce of the fear my sister felt when her regulator failed on that dive. You should be made to pay for your stupidity.'

Julian lunges for her again and this time manages to knock the knife out of her hand. He's almost on top of her when the entire cabin shifts violently to one side, throwing them both against the wall. On her knees now, Piper scrambles for the door. Without a weapon, she's no match for him.

Julian, probably due to the amount of alcohol sloshing through his system and the fact that he'd been off balance, isn't so fortunate. He catches the back of his head on the corner of a mirror and slumps to the floor.

His eyes roll back in his head, only the whites showing.

He's out cold.

The yacht lurches again, righting itself, and Piper staggers to her feet.

Julian is motionless, staring unseeing at the ceiling. She doesn't bother to check if he's still breathing, if his heart is still beating. Part of her hopes it isn't.

She can hear someone shouting in her earpiece but can't make out the words. The signal is full of static.

She'd better get the hell out of there. But before she leaves, she takes a last look at him. 'That's for you, Lex,' she says.

From a distance comes the drumming of rain.

Chapter Seventy

THE PATRIARCH

The chef, his white jacket crumpled and stained with food, his hair lank and greasy and falling into his eyes, stands before Evan. His chin is raised and his shoulders tensed as he braces himself against the wind, which has begun to gust heavily.

Irritation flickers across Evan's hawkish features. What the hell does this punk want? At this time of night? He ignores the flare of heartburn now searing his throat. 'Speak up then.'

'I apologise for bothering you, sir, but I thought you might like to know what I've recently learned.' The chef speaks quickly, his words running over each other, as if he knows Evan will cut him off given half a chance. He has an accent, Scottish, Evan thinks, though he doesn't particularly care. From what he can tell, the crew is made up of a mongrel of European nationalities, their only commonality being their age – no one over thirty – and attractiveness. 'The operation … the import–export business … it doesn't sit right with me. If we are busted, I could lose my visa. I wouldn't get another job.'

Evan needs another complication like he needs a hole in the head. 'I have absolutely no idea what you're talking about,' he lies. How has this pipsqueak found out? He staggers as an even stronger gust of wind unbalances him, grabbing the handrail to steady himself.

'I'm trying to warn you. I – I suspect the captain is running the operation.'

He imagines the chef is referring to the importation of contraband wild Russian caviar that Evan set up a few years ago as an amusing little sideline. Walker arranges for shipments of black-market Beluga to be delivered overland to a European airport, generally one with less stringent oversight of private aircraft, or one that's at least open to the requisite bribes. There, they are loaded onto the Gulfstream among the general provisions required of such a jet, flown back to the United States and distributed to a network of restaurants prepared to pay for under-the-table delicacies. Captain Bird has zero knowledge of the operation, but he's not about to tell the chef that.

He's not sure how the chef has cottoned on, but then perhaps Evan shouldn't be surprised that he might recognise the illegal product. After all, they've been serving it almost every evening since arriving on board; Rocco and Julian have been gulping it down in great globs, the philistines. Evan's hand grips the railing as the boat shifts with the wind once more and he clenches his jaw as the stench of body odour reaches his nostrils. Combined with the near-constant heartburn, it's making him feel decidedly nauseous. He doesn't have to fake the look of pain he gives the chef.

'The thing is, I don't believe it's simply illicit caviar importation.'

'Oh yes?' Evan feigns surprise. Not all the shipments, including the delivery made to *Ambition* earlier this month, contain illegally harvested fish eggs … Evan wonders how the chef has worked this out. Those cartons were supposed to be kept separate, stowed in a hidden compartment below the laz.

'I opened a tin that definitely didn't contain caviar.'

'Oh really?'

'More like Bolivian marching powder. *Cocaine.*'

Evan frantically calculates the cost of this revelation. He clears his throat. 'Thank you for bringing your concerns to me. This is an extremely serious matter. Do you have the evidence?'

Liam nods. 'The tin is at the back of the stores.'

'Well, you'd better get it for me. Be assured, I'll get to the bottom of this. If what you say is true, I shall report the captain to the authorities.'

Liam's body language says that he is not convinced.

'You won't tell her it was me you heard it from?'

'I promise, I will handle it discreetly. The last thing we want is publicity of any kind,' Evan says.

There's no relief on Liam's face.

'I *swear* no one will find out that you came to me with these suspicions.' The lies come easily, and he's gratified to see that finally the chef appears to be reassured.

The chef is the one who will have to go, not the captain, of course. He'll be given a payout, enough to ensure his silence, and a glowing reference, but Evan doesn't want him on the boat a day longer than necessary. Let Walker worry about replacing him; Evan's got enough on his mind.

The boat rolls to port, buffeted by an even stronger gust. Spray skitters off the sea, dampening them, and Evan tastes salt on his lips. Fat drops of rain begin to spatter the decking.

They are both thrown off balance, and Liam's body slams against the railing, the only thing between him and the yawning dark of the water beneath them. 'Ah, Jesus, fuck!' He rebounds and lands awkwardly against Evan. The horrified look on the chef's face is priceless; if Evan wasn't staggering under the weight of the man he'd find it almost comical. He pushes Liam off him and as the boat rolls to port again, even further this time, they both fall towards the railings.

The boat should not be wallowing so much, even in this gusting wind. The thought that the stabilisers might be compromised flits through Evan's mind, but things are happening so fast, he doesn't have a chance to properly consider the idea. The force of their momentum combined with his awkward position means they both lose their balance again. Evan doesn't even have time to be surprised at how easily things can go so catastrophically wrong as the chef falls overboard, sinking into the ink-dark water.

Evan scans the surface for the man who was beside him only seconds ago.

Rain hammers down now, and the wind churns the surface into choppy waves.

It's as though Liam wasn't ever there, has been swallowed whole by the sea.

He should call for help, find a lifebuoy or something.

Then an alarm begins to sound, making shouting useless.

lordofherrings: The crew would have known immediately that something was wrong. The question is, did they save themselves or did some of them try and save the family?

mightymouse: Could you swim through a three-hundred-foot maze, in the pitch black, debris everywhere, without panicking? I'd like to see you try.

Chapter Seventy-one

THE DECKIE

Piper tries not to panic, telling herself that even if a storm has hit, the yacht is built to withstand far heavier squalls than this. She wrenches open the door, letting it shut behind her. Her plan is to go to her cabin and grab her passport and wallet, maybe a change of clothes, before heading to the water toy storage to launch a jet ski and get to shore. She couldn't stand to spend another minute on board: she's done with these toxic people. Confronting Julian had been cathartic, but she doesn't have the stomach for anything more – she realises now that nothing will ever bring Lexie back. Besides, if she stays until morning then she'll really be in trouble, for she has no doubt Julian will report her to Walker, and possibly even march her straight to the authorities.

She hurtles down the stairs, taking them two at a time until she reaches the lowest deck. She hurries to the end of the narrow corridor, takes a few precious minutes to locate her belongings, stuffing them into a dry bag. She tries to hurry but everything seems to be happening in slow motion.

She is passing the lazarette when the sound of banging reaches her. The lights flicker and then go out, but she already has her hand on the door.

She opens it. The stale smell of sweat is almost overwhelming. The lights flicker and then dim, but there is enough illumination to make out an old mattress on the floor, a couple of ripped-up cardboard boxes printed in an unfamiliar alphabet. Behind them is what looks to be a dry bag the size and shape of a small backpack.

The yacht tips again and she is thrown to the ground, landing mostly on the stinking mattress but bruising her knees. The boxes slide sideways and a tin rolls towards her, hitting her in the face. She grapples to get hold of it, recognises the raised lettering on the tin. Caviar, just as Liam had said. The banging starts up again, though it is harder to hear now that an alarm has begun to wail. It is coming from somewhere beneath her.

She'd like to ignore it, but she can't.

She crawls around the laz, her fingers snagging on a ridge along the floor. She traces the square outline of what can only be a small trapdoor. She puts her ear to the floor; the sound of banging is louder now.

Scrabbling to find a way to open the trapdoor, she calls to whoever is there, 'I'm going to get you out, don't worry.' She has no idea how. She feels around the perimeter of the opening.

There's a bolt. She hooks her finger through it and strains to pull it loose but it won't move, and her finger feels like it will break with the effort. It's no good. She needs something stronger. She reaches into her pocket, finds the metal ballpoint pen from her welcome pack and threads it through the handle. Adopting a rower's pose, she braces her legs against the wall, praying the metal holds.

Chapter Seventy-two

THE YOUNGEST DAUGHTER

Kitty is cradled in a hammock, rocking gently as a cool breeze floats across her body. The distant rush of water is a lullaby in her ears.

Her mother leans towards her, offering raspberries, each one a jewel on her fingertip. She takes one in her mouth and sucks gently on it, feeling the fruit explode on her tongue in a burst of sweet-sour flavour. She's never tasted anything quite so sublime. The sound of waves fades and bells begin to chime, distantly at first, then growing louder …

She startles awake, pulled from her dream by a ringing with the insistence of a school bell. She sits up, blinking in the darkness. The noise stops as suddenly as it began. She listens, straining for a clue as to what might be happening beyond her cabin. She hears nothing at first, then the ringing starts up again, louder now, with siren-like whoops overlapping it, the sounds coming to a crescendo.

It could just be another false alarm, something in the galley again. She considers ignoring it, thinks how much easier that would be, to lie down, roll over and go back to sleep, pretend it's not happening. Surely, the dreadful noise will stop again soon?

Instead, she slides wearily out of bed, more worried now, for the sirens have increased in intensity. As she opens the door of her cabin the boat suddenly tilts on its axis and she's hurled against the far wall of the corridor, her head slamming painfully into the edge of a picture frame.

Everything goes black.

Chapter Seventy-three

THE SURVIVOR

She's feeling a little better, the thumping headache easing. There are times when it seems to have disappeared entirely. She still has no idea how long she's been here: it could be as little as a couple of days or as long as a week. The fact that the hospital food is starting to taste okay surely means she's in danger of becoming institutionalised.

It occurs to her now that, apart from the sub-inspector, who keeps asking questions she can't answer, she's had no visitors. Not a single one. She will ask the nurse why that is.

She hasn't told anyone, not Luis, not the doctor, but snatches of memory have begun to return, though she still can't remember her name, where she's been, nor how she got this monstrous bump on the head. Last night there was an image running through her brain: small children dancing, twisting and turning to music. She woke with the sound of their laughter ringing in her ears. She's missing someone, people she loves perhaps, but she can't picture their faces, can't find their names in the endless empty drawers inside her head, where her memories were once kept.

She presses the bell to summon the nurse and then it hits her. 'My children. Where are they?'

'*Qué?*'

'My children,' she insists. 'Carter. Bailey.' She's shouting now in her desperation to make herself understood. 'What has happened to them?'

The nurse gives her a concerned look and hurries from the room.

If she wasn't hooked up to so many goddamn tubes and beeping, blinking machines she'd run right out after her.

A tall, thin man with a beaky nose and a serious expression enters, obviously summoned by the nurse. Melissa is silent as he checks the monitors, then comes over to her.

'You were asking about your children?' he says. 'This is very good. Can you tell me your name? What month it is? Do you know where you are?' He flicks a small pen light between each eye, watching her carefully.

'Just tell me they're okay,' she pleads with him.

'They're absolutely fine. There is nothing to worry about.' His pager beeps and he checks it before apologising. 'I'm sorry, I am needed elsewhere now. You're doing really well. It's a very good sign that your memory is beginning to return.'

He's been gone a full minute before Melissa realises she didn't ask him about Angus.

Then it hits her – Angus was the person who wanted her dead.

Chapter Seventy-four

THE DECKIE

What the hell? Piper nearly gags at the smell as the trapdoor opens, seeing the frightened expressions of two women cowering in the darkness, the terrified whites of their eyes. God knows how long they have been kept down there, but judging by the smell, it's been a while, and sanitation has been rudimentary.

They immediately begin shouting at her in a language she can't understand, reaching out, gasping for air, desperate to escape the tiny space.

For a second she is too shocked to move. Who locked these women in here? Was it Rocco and Julian? Walker? Evan? Melissa? Liam? Were they *all* in on it? What the hell have they done?

She leans in and offers her hands to one of the women, grabbing her wrist and nearly wrenching her arms out of their sockets as she hauls her out of the coffin-like compartment. No sooner is she free than the yacht slews wildly to port and they are thrown against the wall. They'll both be a mess of bruises later, but there's no time to worry about that now.

As she drags the second woman into the laz, both women start wailing so loudly that Piper has to shout to be heard over their cries. 'It's okay, I'm going to help you,' she says, first in English and then in broken Spanish.

They don't appear to understand her and Piper puts her finger to her lips, shushing them. The thin fabric of their dresses is torn and filthy, their long hair matted and greasy. She grabs one of the women by the shoulders, gets right up in her face. 'Quiet!' It finally seems to work.

Motioning for them to stay close, Piper goes to the door and peers out. The yacht is heeling to starboard now and she braces herself against the doorframe to keep from falling. There is shouting coming from somewhere, but she can't see much in the dim light. She has no idea what's going on to make the yacht so unstable, but all her instincts are shrieking at her to get out on deck where she can try to work out what to do next. They may only have a few minutes. She thinks of Bailey and Carter in their cabin somewhere above her and prays to god their parents have come for them.

Her earpiece screeches again and she hears the terrifying call to abandon ship.

Making a split-second decision, she drags the women down the corridor until she reaches a hidden door with a wheel lock on the outside. Spinning the lock, she holds the door open while the women go ahead of her. She is at the top of the ladder that leads down into the narrow space when the yacht lurches again and she is thrown to the ground, a rag doll tossed aside. Her shoulder crunches as she lands with her full weight on it. Stars form in front of her eyes and she is momentarily winded.

The women are screaming and jabbering incomprehensibly, and when she finally rights herself, her arm hangs at her side.

Chapter Seventy-five

THE DETECTIVE

Maria is wearing a low-cut top and leaning over, beckoning to Luis, calling his name softly, swaying her hips as she walks backwards into a halo of light. Somewhere, music is playing. All he wants to do is follow her, but his body has the weight of lead. His legs won't obey him. He tries to call out to her to slow down, to wait for him, but no sound comes.

The music gets louder, annoying now, and he wakes with a jolt, realising he is sprawled across the full width of his queen-size bed, covered in a film of sweat and completely alone.

The music jangles again and his phone lights up with a call. It's still dark outside, and as he grabs the phone he sees the time: 3 am. He's been asleep for less than four hours.

'There's been an accident. The inspector wants all hands available over there now. It's serious.' It's Maria. Luis shakes his head to try and clear the image of her from his dream.

'Of course.' His voice is thick with sleep. 'Where? What's happened?' His first thought is that it's likely to be a crash, possibly involving several vehicles, judging by Maria's sombre tone. He's come to know Mallorca's winding mountain roads and can easily imagine a car or a truck tumbling over any one of the thousands of precipices or blind bends that can take the unwary by surprise. But as Maria relays the details, he can't believe what he is hearing. 'Could you say that again?' he asks, still not sure that he's understood.

'I'll pick you up in ten minutes,' she says after repeating the news. He's sufficiently awake now to appreciate her succinctness.

He's waiting undercover in front of his apartment building, sheltering from the rain, when she pulls up eight minutes later. 'It'll take us about forty-five minutes to get to Cala Torta if we step on it. Air Sea Rescue is already operational.'

'Got it. Do we know how many were on board at the time?'

'Nine family members, plus a friend of the family and the nanny. And then there's the crew – according to the customs declaration, there should be twenty-six of them on board.'

The yacht, *Ambition*, is the one he'd been on his way to the night before. 'Any survivors?'

Maria makes a left, narrowly missing speeding through a red light, before replying. 'Uncertain.'

'Do we know what caused it to capsize?'

'A freak windstorm blew through the north of the island at about two-thirty am.'

'Any other boats in the vicinity? Any others capsize?'

'Negative. It's a nature reserve and it seems they had the cove to themselves.' She pauses, bites her lower lip.

'What is it?' Luis asks. There's something she's not telling him.

'The thing is, Cala Torta is known as a sheltered cove, even if the wind is coming from the north, which it was, which is almost certainly why the captain chose to anchor there. *Ambition* was unlikely to be affected, let alone capsize. The upside is that any survivors should have been able to swim to safety. If, that is, they had time to escape.' She inhales and then lets out a slow exhale, obviously trying to calm herself. 'Apparently, there were children on board.'

'I remember.' Luis had seen two youngsters when he interviewed the captain and the owner the day before. A baby, too. 'Perhaps there was something wrong with the yacht?'

'It's a brand-new vessel. Launched only six weeks ago.' She shakes her head. 'It doesn't make sense.'

They speed through the darkness, windscreen wipers flashing in front of them, each lost in their own thoughts. At such an early hour the road is virtually empty of traffic. The police radio erupts with a burst of static from time to time, and as they approach the area, they hear that so far two people have been winched from the water and transported to Palma hospital, and several others are sheltering on the beach, being attended to by paramedics.

'Did he say several or seven?' Luis wonders.

'Several,' Maria replies. 'But it's anyone's guess if that means more or less than seven.' They pull up alongside three emergency vehicles and after stopping briefly for an update, Maria leads them towards the path that goes down to the cove. 'They don't know much more than we do. It's about a twenty-minute walk this way.'

Luis peers through the darkness at the rough road, nearly blown sideways by the wind that whips off the coast. The rain, at least, has eased to a faint drizzle. 'We can't go any further by car?'

'Not unless you've got a four-wheel-drive.' Maria flicks on a powerful torch and together they begin to jog, stepping carefully to avoid the rocks that litter the path. The rotors of a helicopter whirr overhead.

It's growing lighter, and by the time they reach the cove they see a small group of people, including a couple of paramedics and two local officers, at one end of a beach a couple of hundred metres long and ringed by rocky cliffs.

Goats bleat eerily in the distance.

It's still too dark to be able to do a head count and, anyway, some of the survivors might have already been taken away by the helicopter they heard earlier. It's more than an hour and a half since the first report of the incident. Surely anyone who was able to would have swum ashore some time ago.

Maria heads towards the group as Luis stops for a moment and scans the choppy, dark water. There is absolutely no sign that a yacht was ever anchored there.

Chapter Seventy-six

THE SURVIVOR

Melissa is desperate to see her children. She's been imagining the worst, picturing her daughter in a coma, despite the doctor's reassurance that Bailey is fine. She begs the next nurse who comes in to check on her and is appeased by a promise that someone will bring them within the hour. She makes a note of the time on the clock on the wall – she'll hold them to it. 'And my husband?' she asks, but the nurse has already left.

A few minutes later, the door opens again. Anticipation bubbles up within her, joyous and life-affirming. She can hardly breathe. Is it them?

'Hello.' The voice is deep, the accent familiar. 'I won't stay long. I wanted to see for myself that you were okay.'

Her eyes fasten on him. 'Toby!' She's unaccountably pleased to see him. 'What are you doing here?'

He ignores her question. 'How are you, Issa?' he asks gently, pulling up a chair to sit beside her, taking her hand and squeezing it.

'Well, I'm not going near the water again for a while,' she says, forcing a smile. 'They tell me I nearly drowned. How are you? I missed you at the party.' It's a ridiculous thing to say given the circumstances, but he's caught her unawares and she's absurdly flustered. She decides to blame it on the painkillers.

He spreads his hands. 'Emma wasn't feeling well. Apologies.'

'Don't be silly. Sorry, I don't know why I even brought it up. Just as well you didn't come.' She tries to make light of it, then frowns. 'Though it's a shame you didn't get to meet my family.'

'Oh, Issa,' he says, his voice heavy with sorrow. 'I'm afraid Angus …'

She gasps and puts her hand over her mouth, wincing at the pain that the movement causes. She has a sudden image of Angus's expression of withering disdain, the way he patronised her, imagining himself cleverer, better educated.

She should feel loss, but shamefully her overriding emotion is one of relief.

'And everyone else? Is everyone else okay? No one's told me anything,' she says. 'What the hell happened? I don't remember very much after the party, but apparently there was a storm and the boat went down?' Her head has begun to throb with the effort of trying again to recall the events of that night. She's heard nothing about her father, Rocco or Kitty. Sandrine. Oh god, little Max.

'I don't know the details, but yes, apparently a squall came in from the north and *Ambition* keeled over. They think the stabilisers must have failed, the bilge pump too, causing it to capsize and sink. It would have all happened in a matter of minutes. Perhaps an electrical short circuit?' He spreads his hands. 'It's not really my area of expertise.'

'But the boat was brand new.' He also hasn't answered her question about survivors, she notes, afraid to ask again in case of what she might hear.

'The salvage process is ongoing. The water in the cove isn't deep, so it shouldn't be too tricky an operation.'

'Okay.' Her mind clicks into gear, assessing if they will need to file suit with the boat builders. She stops herself. What is she thinking? This is not the time for that. She needs to know what happened to everyone else on the boat. She's barely taken in the news that Angus didn't make it.

'There's another reason I'm here. I figured you could use someone with legal experience.' He hesitates, then looks her straight in the eye. 'I'm sorry to involve you now, but the Issa I remember would want to know.'

She gives him a tiny nod.

'It would appear that someone on board was running an illegal operation.'

'What kind of operation? Who?'

In a few short sentences, he tells her what he's found out.

'That's absurd,' she insists. 'Dad can put them straight on that count. Nothing would have happened without him knowing about it, and he'd never stand for such a thing.' She is adamant but doesn't meet his eyes.

'I'm sorry, Is ...' He looks at her with such sympathy that she immediately understands what he's finding so hard to tell her.

'Dad?'

He nods. 'Still missing.'

She pushes down the surge of panic, taking control of the situation. 'Toby, I need your help.' Her voice shakes, but she swallows hard, fighting back the tears that threaten to spill over. 'I have to see my children. They are what matters now. Everything else is tomorrow's problem.' She swallows her fear for her father, sure if they haven't found him by now that they are looking for a body. 'Can you take me to see them and find me a laptop and a cell phone?'

'In that order?'

'Of *course* in that order.'

Chapter Seventy-seven

THE DETECTIVE

Luis turns to his right, alerted by a muffled shout from further down the beach.

'They've found a body.' Maria has appeared at his side, speaking quietly.

'Who?' he asks, walking purposefully towards the shore and thinking of the other bodies that have washed up on Mallorcan beaches in recent weeks.

'Not sure. Male. Middle-aged, wealthy judging by his wristwatch.'

'So, one of the family.'

She gives a sharp nod. 'There was a cocktail party on board earlier in the evening, but the guests had left the yacht by about nine-thirty pm, and the captain made the decision to move moorings, even though it was late at night. She said she was seeking shelter from the approaching storm.'

'Okay. Who is still unaccounted for?'

She consults a note on her phone, the light illuminating her face. 'Among the men? Evan Thyssen, the yacht's owner. Melissa Silk's husband, Angus. A twenty-two-year-old male guest, Julian Cushing, and two deckhands who are also in their twenties.'

'Shouldn't be too hard to work out who it is then.'

* * *

The body washed up on the beach is quickly identified by a crew member as Angus Silk, husband of Melissa, Evan Thyssen's daughter. Rescue services erect a temporary screen around the body and Luis is relieved to learn that the children have already been taken to hospital. No one, but especially not young children, should have to see the body of their drowned father.

Dawn is breaking, revealing the full extent of the chaos on the beach. Flotsam and jetsam from the yacht – life jackets, ropes, sun loungers and deckchairs, cushions, a large table lamp, surprisingly still intact, various items of clothing – are all scattered at the tide line. Luis is about to turn back and go in search of Maria when his toe stubs something that's been tossed onto the shore. He bends down and picks up a small round tin. All kinds of detritus from the yacht will wash up here over the coming weeks, including fuel and waste. It's an environmental disaster, and one that will affect this pristine cove for months to come. It's disgraceful that those responsible will likely never be held to account.

His gaze travels the length of the beach and he sees that there are, in fact, quite a number of similar tins rolling around in the waves. He walks on and picks up another, weighs it in his palm. This one feels different, lighter somehow.

Maria rejoins him. She, too, has a handful of cans. 'Too many for personal consumption?' She holds up a tin, shows him the branding. '*Ikra.* It's the Russian word for caviar.'

'Get anyone who's available to collect them, can you? Seems there was more going on here than a family vacation.'

'Yes, sir.'

'I'll make sure the coastguard knows the bay is off limits until further notice.' Luis looks back at the path. 'And send someone to wait at the top – no members of the public are to be allowed down to the beach for the rest of the day.'

'Got it.'

Luis spots Inspector Vidal picking his way across the beach and goes to meet him. He seems animated, perhaps energised by an actual disaster. It's distasteful. 'The captain was asleep at the time of the accident. There is no sign of the officer who was supposed to be on watch. As bad luck would have it, two of the three engineers had the night off and had gone ashore. Then, because of the urgency of the decision to relocate, a plan was made for them to return to the yacht first thing in the morning. We'll question everyone again at some point, but it's important to get their initial reactions. I've got my other officers taking statements from those still here.' He stops, seeing what Luis is holding. 'What have you got there?'

'Can't be a hundred per cent sure, sir, but at a guess I'd say they could have been smuggling black-market caviar.' It's a practice Luis has come across once before, in a restaurant in Barcelona. 'It's a bigger problem than one might realise. I've got the team collecting all the tins that have washed ashore.'

'Good.' The inspector gives him a tight smile. 'There are two survivors who we can't identify. They're not crew, and they don't speak much English. All they can tell me is that they are Russian, but that they came from Slovenia. None of the others seem to know who they are.' He points in the direction of a couple of women sitting on a rock slightly apart from the rest of the group, huddled together under a blanket. 'You speak a few languages, don't you?'

Luis shrugs. 'A little English, some German, Italian.' He pauses, thinking. 'Maria speaks some Russian, I believe.'

'See if you can find out who they are and what they were doing. According to the manifest filed with the port authority, they weren't supposed to be on board, not even as housekeeping staff.'

Chapter Seventy-eight

THE YOUNGEST DAUGHTER

Kitty's chest is as sore as if it has been scoured with a broom and she is queasy from the gallons of water she must have swallowed as she escaped the sinking vessel.

Hours earlier, she had been thrown across the floor of her cabin. When she came to her senses, she'd scrambled along the corridor in the pitch dark, opening the first door she came to and pulling Bailey and Carter from their beds, hustling them towards the stairs. She says a prayer of thanks now that she had been assigned the cabin next to theirs. She did her best to keep them calm, pretending that it was all a game the grown-ups were playing, and that they had been allowed to join in. Bailey wasn't convinced, but Kitty didn't give her a chance to argue, pulling them both to the swim deck.

Johannes was there, shouting at them to come and get a life jacket. There was a bone-chilling grinding noise as well as shouting coming from all parts of the boat as it listed precariously to one side. Bracing herself, she fastened Carter's jacket, still pretending it was a game, though neither of the children were buying it. She almost had him secured when he caught sight of his mother and wriggled out of Kitty's arms, running towards her.

Kitty did up her own jacket and grabbed Bailey, who was now wearing her life jacket and looking at her with a terrified expression. 'It's going to be okay, I promise. Are you ready?'

Bailey nodded bravely.

Holding tightly onto her niece, Kitty jumped into the darkness.

* * *

Someone – she is too out of it to know who – has placed a towel around her shoulders and although the early morning isn't cold, she can't stop shivering. She stares blankly at the scene in front of her, not really taking it in.

'Here, drink this.' A cup of something brown and hot is thrust at her. Obediently, she takes a sip. It's sickly sweet, probably tea, but it at least stops the shivering.

Kitty almost doesn't recognise Sandrine, who after being given the all-clear by the paramedics, staggers towards her. She has dark shadows under her eyes and her normally glossy hair is bedraggled, coated with sand. She's wearing an orange sweatshirt with holes at the elbows and the words 'Sunny Day' emblazoned across the front that must have been given to her by someone, and is carrying Max, who, unbelievably, appears to be asleep, his face nestled in her shoulder. Sandrine collapses awkwardly on the sand next to Kitty and wraps her free arm around her, placing a kiss on her forehead. '*Ma chérie.* You're okay,' she says, her voice hoarse.

'I am?' Kitty doesn't feel even slightly okay.

'You are,' Sandrine says. 'You are safe.'

'How did you …? With Max?'

'The alarm woke me, and I went to Max. Amber already had him up. One of the deckhands was at the swim platform and he put us on a jet ski, pointed to the shoreline and told us to go. I've never driven anything so fast in my life.' She shakes her head as if she still can't quite believe it.

'What about Bailey?' Kitty asks, her breath catching in her throat. 'I had hold of her hand, but I lost it. We were so close to the shore, but she slipped away from me.'

'She is safe, darling. She and Carter have been taken to the hospital to get checked over, but they are unhurt. Amber went with them.' Sandrine hugs her tighter. 'Melissa as well.'

'Oh, thank god.' Her breathing returns to normal. 'Rocco too?' She can't bring herself to utter Julian's name, feeling sick as she thinks of him.

'I think so.' Sandrine is evasive. 'I haven't seen him yet.'

'What happened to—?' She is interrupted by the whomp-whomp-whomp of a helicopter sweeping low over the water, searching for survivors.

Sandrine shrugs. 'She sank. That beautiful boat sank like a stone.'

'And Dad?' The beach beneath her legs is shifting, as though they were still out on the water. Kitty feels woozy, as if none of this is real, as if it is just a bad dream instead of a living nightmare. 'Where's Dad?'

Sandrine stares out to the sea. 'It's as if it never even existed.'

* * *

'Excuse me?' A dark man wearing black trousers and a white shirt is standing in front of her. Before she has a chance to wonder why someone would be dressed like that on a beach, he points to her neck. Instinctively, she wraps her arms tighter around herself. He kneels so his brown eyes are level with hers. When he speaks, his voice is soft. 'Miss, I am so sorry for what has happened, but may I see your necklace, please?'

'My necklace?' *What does he want with that?*

'Yes. Please.'

'Why? Who are you?'

'I apologise. My name is Sub-inspector Luis Perez. I am here to help. You are ...?'

'K-Kitty Levine. My dad is Evan Thyssen, have you seen him?' Slowly, she lowers the towel so he can see the necklace. 'I didn't steal it, if that's what you're thinking.'

'I am not thinking anything, and we're doing all we can to find your father, I promise. But perhaps you can tell me where you got it?' He pauses. 'It's not yours, is it?'

She dips her head and when she raises it again, she is surprised to see a flicker of satisfaction lighten his features.

'You're not in any trouble, I promise. Can you tell me where you got it?' he asks again.

'I didn't steal it,' she repeats. 'I found it. On the boat. I thought perhaps it belonged to one of the housekeepers. I was going to give it back, I swear.'

'It's okay, I believe you. But it may be important. Can you give it to me now? I think I know who it might belong to.'

She nods slowly. 'I guess.' It isn't really hers, after all. She reaches for the clasp, the towel slipping completely off her shoulders now, undoes it with shaking hands and passes it to him. She's about to ask him if he's seen her brother, when she catches sight of a dishevelled figure limping up the beach.

Rocco.

She's never been so pleased to see him.

Chapter Seventy-nine

THE DETECTIVE

Luis pulls an evidence bag from his jacket, slips the necklace inside and seals it. Dropping it into his pocket for the time being, he walks over to where Walker – the man he had spoken to just the day before – is standing at the water's edge. He's been checked out by the paramedics and is suffering no obvious ill effects from his swim to shore.

He turns, hearing Luis approach. Luis stops, takes a pen knife from his pocket and uses it to lever one of the tins open. Making sure Walker is watching, he dips a finger inside, scoops out some of the contents and raises it to his nose, then the tip of his tongue. Definitely fish, almost certainly illegally imported. He shakes the cluster of grey eggs off his finger and picks up another tin, weighing it in his palm. It's several ounces lighter than the first one, he'd swear on it. And when he compares the two, there's a subtle difference in the labelling. Something you'd have to look at closely to spot.

Luis places the first tin on a nearby rock and proceeds to open the second one, stopping as soon as he sees that it contains a cellophane-wrapped puck of compressed white powder. Bingo! His intuition is proved right; he doesn't need to taste the contents to know what it is.

Maria approaches and Luis hands her the tin, nods towards Walker. Her mouth falls open as she sees what it contains.

'Mr Walker, I need you to accompany me to the station,' he says. 'We'd like to question you in regard to the illegal importation of a banned substance found on board the vessel *Ambition*.'

Chapter Eighty

THE DECKIE

Focused on escape, Piper urged the women to follow her down the ladder and into the narrow space. Essentially a long service tunnel, this was the nerve centre of the yacht, the part that the owner and guests almost never see. The lighting there was on a different electrical system and although dim, was thankfully bright enough that they could see where they were going. Gesturing for the frightened women to stay close, she crawled through the passage, which ran all the way to the yacht's aft, glancing back every so often to check they were right behind her. Ducking her head, she passed the fresh water tanks, then the fuel tanks, the sanisplit, hot water system, fire detectors, HVAC (heating, ventilation and air conditioning) and sprinkler systems. It was easily forty degrees in the tunnel and she could feel the sweat gluing her shirt to her back.

She had no idea what was happening above them, refused to let herself think about it. She had expected to run into at least one, possibly two, of the engineers, and hadn't quite formulated a plan as to how to deal with that, but astonishingly there was no one there. It made her task easier.

Without warning, the yacht lurched to starboard again, throwing them against scalding metal pipes that ran the length of the tunnel. Her shoulder took the brunt of her fall and she screamed in pain. An alarm began to bleat.

The plans she'd studied of the similar yacht showed the HVAC and stabilisers on separate backup generators. If she turned off the power, and its backup, it would create a diversion, allowing her to get the women off the yacht without risking detection. She couldn't risk turning off the backup to the stabilisers, not given the storm that had hit.

She halted as she reached the HVAC system and searched for the right switch, blinking sweat out of her eyes, her breath coming fast.

Seconds ticked by. The two women began shouting at her, but she tuned them out.

She had to concentrate. She tried to picture the plans, the layout of the electrical system.

One of the women pulled at her arm, but she shook her off. She located what had to be the switch, took a deep breath, praying she was correct, and flipped it to off.

All of a sudden, the low lighting went out, plunging them into total darkness. The alarm was silenced.

So far, so good.

It would take precious time for anyone to work out what the problem was, and she and the two women would be at the yacht's aft long before then. 'Come! Come!' she said, urging the women, still not sure they understood her.

The yacht lurched again and they were forced to crawl the final few yards in darkness, one of the women so close behind that Piper could feel her breath on her legs.

They emerged from the service tunnel at the aft, a short distance from the swim platform and Piper halted, checking they wouldn't be seen.

After the sweltering heat of the tunnel, the night air was sweet and deliciously cool, but there was no time to appreciate it.

Gesturing for the women to be quiet, she pointed to the dark water and mimed a diving motion, but they only looked back at her with terrified expressions. Piper gestured towards the dark mass of cliffs, thanking fate that they were at least facing towards the shore and not out to sea.

She mimed again for the women to jump but they remained frozen on deck. *Oh Jesus. Can't they swim?*

She passed one of them the dry bag that she had retrieved from the laz and gave the bag containing her possessions to the second woman. With luck they would provide some flotation. 'Jump!' she hissed, but they did not move. Grabbing each of their hands in frustration, she pulled them into the water with her.

The long jump forced all the air from her lungs and the water was shockingly cold. She couldn't hold on to the women's hands. As she bobbed up above the surface she took a breath, casting around frantically for them.

Oh, the sweet relief when she saw that they were only a few feet away, both clinging to the dry bags.

She stroked over to them, wincing at the pain in her shoulder, choking as she swallowed a mouthful of water from the chop kicked up by the wind and the rain. 'Kick!' she shouted, pointing to the shore. 'Kick!'

* * *

It feels as though all this happened in another world now, as she huddles on the shore, sitting on the dry bags and shivering beneath a shiny, tinfoil blanket.

The yacht wasn't supposed to sink. Turning off the power and backup generator shouldn't have affected the stabilisers. Did she get it wrong? Or was the vessel wired differently than she thought? She's horrified that she could have caused so much destruction, not to mention possible loss of life.

She's tried to take stock of who's safe and who is yet to emerge from the water, relieved to see Tamara and Ruby clinging to each other, but the beach is more crowded now and her head is throbbing. She puts a tentative hand to her forehead and feels the pulpy mass that has begun to swell there. Her shoulder is also killing her and she wonders if she's broken her collarbone. The medics haven't seen to her yet, preoccupied with the children – she almost bent double with gratitude when she saw they were safe; she couldn't have lived with herself if they hadn't made it.

The police have questioned her, but she's kept her answers short, saying simply that she left her cabin and, disorientated in the dark, was trying to get on deck when she heard banging. She told them she found the women locked in the lazarette and so led them on deck where she persuaded them to jump into the water and swim to shore.

The two women are being interviewed separately. Piper is counting on the fact that the women wouldn't have known where they were on the yacht, and that the darkness and confusion was such that they cannot tell the officers anything of consequence. Even if they can recall the details, all they saw was her flip a switch and the lights go out.

* * *

More police arrive and they help the survivors up the narrow track from the beach. A paper cup of sweet, milky tea is thrust into her shaking hand and she has to concentrate to stop it from spilling onto the sand. Ambulances are waiting up on the road and when she gets there she is checked over by a paramedic, who says her collarbone is only bruised and puts a dressing on her grazed forehead, then deems her well enough to be taken to a hotel. Somehow, she still has the dry bags with her, collecting them from the two women as they stumbled ashore. No one bothers to ask her about them; there is too much else going on.

Chapter Eighty-one

THE DETECTIVE

Luis makes a final visit to the hospital. Melissa Silk has recovered her memory and will soon be cleared to leave. He wants to question her one final time before she departs the country. He's gathered the statements from the survivors, including allegations made by the yacht's chef, Liam Kelly, who says he confronted Evan Thyssen on the night of the disaster about the cocaine he discovered, that the boat started rocking violently and Kelly was knocked overboard. Kelly said he was able to swim to the shore, where he sheltered when the storm hit.

Kelly claims that Evan denied all knowledge of the operation, was happy to believe Kelly's initial assumption that it was the captain who was running the operation, but the more Kelly thought about it, the more he was sure Evan was lying. He said that from what he had observed, Mike Walker was across everything that took place on board *Ambition*, that no one even sneezed without him knowing about it.

If Kelly is correct, and Walker was central to the caviar/cocaine smuggling, then he had to be involved in the other, far more serious operation as well. The two were undoubtedly linked.

Luis referred the matter to his boss, voicing his suspicions as to the involvement of various other parties, but Inspector Vidal dismissed him. 'You're drawing conclusions based on the flimsiest of evidence,' he said. 'Where is the proof? One lousy statement from someone with an axe to grind? We have a suspect in custody, that's enough.'

But Luis isn't satisfied.

He stands at the doorway to Mrs Silk's room. She's sitting up in bed, a laptop in front of her, squinting at the screen, her fingers flying over the keys.

He needs to tread carefully. '*Señora*? Mrs Silk? Would you have a minute?'

She looks up, quickly masking a flash of irritation. 'Of course.'

'I understand you and the children are leaving tomorrow.'

'I am anxious to get them home,' she says. 'For us all to go home. To try to rebuild our lives.'

'I won't keep you,' he says, drawing up a chair to sit by the bed. 'But I'm afraid I have some difficult questions that I must ask.'

Melissa shrugs and flashes him a weak smile. 'I'm used to those.'

It wasn't until Maria had the chance to find an interpreter to interview the two women who weren't supposed to be on board *Ambition* on the night of the accident that Luis was able to make the connection between them and the two bodies that had been found in the weeks before. The women from *Ambition*, Alina and Nadia, said they had been in Slovenia before arriving in Spain. The first woman – Krystina – had also been there.

Slovenia is a known people-trafficking hub, a fact Luis and Maria both realised at the same time.

He takes a punt. 'It's about your father. It has come to light that Evan Thyssen might have been involved in an extensive trafficking operation. Both of the Russian women from *Ambition* have reported being promised money, and said that they were held captive for days on end, on board both your family's yacht and another vessel.'

'That's completely ridiculous!' She almost shouts the denial. 'The only women I saw on board were some party guests – and the crew, of course. You think my father was involved? This is a dead man you are talking about, remember. Where is your proof?'

'I understand that.' He searches her face for a sign that she's lying, covering up for her father, but her expression is indignant.

'Sub-inspector, I can hazard a guess as to who is making the allegations – is it Mike Walker? I heard he had been arrested. No doubt he's trying to spread some of the blame, not that it will do him any good. I knew my father better than almost anyone and he was an honest, upstanding citizen who had never been accused of any wrongdoing in his life.' She turns back to her screen. 'Now, if this is a fishing expedition, you've come to the wrong place.'

He sees her hands trembling, whether with rage or fear, he's not sure.

'I'm sorry,' he says, getting up from the chair. 'I had to ask.' He's not surprised at her denial, nor the vehemence of it. By all accounts, she idolised her father. Betraying him is the last thing she'd be prepared to do. He almost admires her loyalty, misplaced though it might be.

He stops as he reaches the door, turns back to her. 'Safe travels home,' he says.

She meets his gaze, unflinching, cold as ice. 'Thank you.'

Sure as shit, if Mike Walker was central to the human-trafficking racket, then he was doing the bidding of someone higher up, and that someone was almost certainly Evan Thyssen.

Mrs Silk either knows nothing about her father's involvement, or she's a damn good poker player. He may never find out which.

FIVE MONTHS LATER

www.newyorktimes.com
25 November

Thyssen Confirms New CEO

Beleaguered property company Thyssen Properties today confirmed its new CEO, Melissa Thyssen-Silk. Ms Thyssen-Silk has been acting in the role since the death of her father in a tragic yachting accident in Europe earlier this year. Ms Thyssen-Silk also lost her husband in the accident, which was found to be the result of catastrophic failure of the yacht's stabilisers, combined with an unseasonal windstorm that hit northeastern Mallorca in the early hours of 1 July. A lawsuit naming the yacht's builder, Larsbergen, alleging criminal negligence, is pending.

Chapter Eighty-two

THE DECKIE

Piper puts all her weight on the lid of her suitcase, attempting to close the zip with both hands.

'Need any help?' Her dad must have heard her struggling. He stands in the doorway, a mug of tea in one hand. 'Made you a cuppa before you go.'

Piper finally manages to close the case and takes the mug from him with a grin. 'Thanks.'

'How long is the flight?'

They've had this conversation before, along with the one that usually starts, 'You can't keep away, can you? Even after everything that's happened.' But despite her father's concern, her mind is made up. 'Nearly nine hours to Antigua.' It's blowing a gale outside, unrelentingly grey in the way that only Britain in winter can be. She can't wait to feel the sun on her skin again, and golden sand between her toes, and to be able to dive into crystal-blue water. 'It's only for five months, Dad. Then I'll be home again. It'll fly by.'

He doesn't respond; they both know she won't stay home for long. The call of the ocean is too strong.

She's desperately, desperately sorry about what happened in Mallorca, of course she is. Julian's body, along with those of Evan Thyssen and Angus Silk, was recovered by divers a couple of days after the accident. It was never her intention to put lives at risk, and she has no idea how the yacht came to sink. Turning off the power should not have cut the stabilisers as well.

Nevertheless, the chaos of that night still wakes her, gasping for breath, in the small hours as she relives the plunge into the darkness and the frantic swim ashore. She suspects the nightmares won't stop for a while. It was a terrible accident, and she can't be expected to take the blame for that. Especially since, as it turned out, there was so much more going on.

Her eyes flick to the wardrobe. It's still there: the dry bag, the one from *Ambition*'s laz. She hasn't told anyone, not even her father, what she found inside.

Bills. A big stack of hundred-dollar bills.

Not enough money to never have to work again but enough to put a down payment on a small apartment, to take her father on holiday, perhaps fly him out to the Caribbean when the worst of the British winter begins to bite. It'll never bring Lexie back, nothing can do that, but it is enough, if she is careful, to make a difference to her life.

'And someone is going to meet you there?'

'Yes, Dad, my friend Liam, remember?' She hasn't told him that Liam was one of the chefs on board *Ambition*, nor that he knew Lexie, doesn't want him to worry.

She thinks Liam must have felt sorry for her, after everything that happened, and after he heard about Lexie ... He got in touch a few months ago and they started texting, chatting, FaceTiming, and haven't stopped. He's more fun now, less stressed, and when he said he was heading to the Caribbean, and that there was a job going if she wanted it, she hadn't needed much persuading.

'Try and stay out of trouble this time, hey?'

That makes her smile. 'I'll do my best, I promise.'

Chapter Eighty-three

THE TROPHY WIFE

'Rolling.'

Sandrine strolls casually along an empty street, trailing her hand along a railing. It's just past daybreak and they've been shooting all night. Her toes are numb, her fingers blue and bloodless, but it's the first time since the nightmare events of last summer that she's felt that things are going to be okay. It's only a small part, but the feeling of finally doing what she loves again is almost overwhelming. Tears threaten to spill over and she blinks them away. This is a melancholy scene, one that comes right at the end of the script, but she's not been directed to cry.

'And … cut. That's a wrap for today. Thanks everyone.'

As the team begins to dismantle the lighting rig, Sandrine walks over to the production vans where Max and his nanny are waiting for her.

Chapter Eighty-four

THE DETECTIVE

Luis arrives at the door of his family home in Sant Cugat, the Barcelona suburb he grew up in. He's unaccountably nervous but does his best not to show it, wiping his palms on his trousers and clearing his throat. '*Mamà?*' he calls, being sure to clean off any mud from his shoes before he steps onto the newly polished floor. The smell of garlic and tomatoes wafts towards him. She is preparing lunch.

'*Hola, inspector!*' His little brother doesn't miss an opportunity to tease him about his recent promotion, joking that he is the 'youngest in all of Spain'.

Luis pretends to be embarrassed but secretly he doesn't mind the fuss. He was assigned to the Balearic Homicide Unit and was instrumental in making the connection between the yacht and its involvement in trafficking, not only cocaine but also young women.

The operation had been a slick one: the women would fly in on tourist visas, attracted by the promise of an all-expenses-paid luxury trip. They were picked up from the airport by a driver and delivered to one of a number of yachts in the Med. The women weren't stupid – they soon cottoned on to what was expected of them, and for the most part had no choice but to go along with it.

The trouble arose when a couple of them found out that the holiday was only the first part of an arrangement that saw them transported afterwards to Ibiza or the mainland by boat, where they were kept as sex slaves, rotated on and off yachts as required. The money they'd been promised was withheld, so they had no means to escape. He was able to deduce that the two women whose bodies washed up that summer had tried diving overboard in an attempt to get away, but were most likely poor swimmers and never made it to shore.

The necklace had been a crucial piece of evidence – the two young women rescued from the yacht had also been wearing necklaces with their first initial on them. He was able to determine that they had been some kind of twisted gift from their handler. And so Luis was able to prove there was a link between the two women from the yacht and the dead women, between *Ambition* and the trafficking.

Captain Bird was cleared of any involvement, but they were able to prove links between Mike Walker and Slovenia, the country where the women were trafficked from. The painstaking work of uncovering the operation has been lengthy, grisly and heartbreaking, and is still ongoing.

He's back in Palma now, and he's been happy enough to be in the city again, but his family have been even more delighted, especially by the person who accompanies him to lunch today, the *chica encantadora*, as his father calls her.

'Maria! Luis!' His mother appears, all smiles. '*Entra! Entra!*'

www.seemallorca.com
Breaking news
30 November

A pre-trial hearing was held today in Barcelona in the matter of British-born Michael Walker, 56, accused of four charges of human trafficking and one of cocaine importation. Mr Walker is pleading not guilty to all charges.

The Cuerpo Nacional de Policía will allege Mr Walker was part of an organised crime syndicate that profited from trafficking women from its headquarters in Russia to Mallorca, Ibiza and Barcelona for over a year. To date, Mr Walker has refused to name any of his partners in the operation.

Chapter Eighty-five

THE YOUNGEST DAUGHTER

Kitty threads her way through the crowded coffee shop, spotting Rocco at a table near the back. He's got his laptop open in front of him and a notebook at his side. She greets him with a kiss. 'How are you?'

'I'm taking this new class on global biocultures, specifically sociocultural theories of biocultural process.' He is fizzing with positive energy, waving his hands as he speaks and beaming at her. 'It's blowing my mind, Kit.'

'I wish I knew what any of that meant.' She wrinkles her nose at him and sits down, pinching off a tiny morsel of the pastry that sits uneaten in front of him.

'Help yourself. I'll order another. And coffee's on its way.'

'No, that's okay, I'm not super hungry,' she says, popping the crumb of pastry in her mouth, savouring it. She's getting better at eating foods she once saw as forbidden, and a few months ago managed to confide in her mom about the trouble she's been having. 'We're all works in progress, darling,' her mom replied, hugging her so tight Kitty could hardly breathe. Her mom's been doing a lot of that since the accident. Kitty doesn't mind it so much anymore.

'You coming to Melissa's tonight?' Rocco asks.

'It's Wednesday, isn't it?' Ever since they returned to New York, the three siblings have got into the routine of meeting for a weekly dinner together. Nothing fancy – champagne and caviar have been replaced by pasta and pizza, and they eat early so Bailey and Carter can join them.

Kitty thinks it's probably saved them all.

Chapter Eighty-six

THE ELDEST DAUGHTER

Melissa glances up from her laptop and out the window on the sixty-fifth floor of the Thyssen building. The company used to occupy eleven floors of this building, and although she's only been able to hold on to four of them, the naming rights remain. Despite the bleak November day, the unforgivingly grey sky, there is a lightness in her heart that she hasn't known for years, possibly not since Carter was born.

It's been five months since the accident, the likes of which she hopes never to have to live through again. Grieving the loss of the two most important men in her life, comforting children who have lost their father and grandfather, attempting to resurrect a company in crisis, while also putting together the pieces of a broken family, has been almost too much to bear. She's often surprised that she's still standing.

She has successfully steered the property empire back from the brink of collapse, drastically downsizing headcount, renegotiating existing loans and getting out of leases for the controversial Rawson development at Hudson Yards. For a long while she wasn't sure if she'd be able to pull it off, but after a series of meetings with Thyssen's bankers and by bringing in a new investment partner, it looks as though they might scrape through.

The children have been amazing, largely thanks to a wonderful new nanny, and Melissa's rule that she's always, without exception, home in time for dinner with them.

Today, the board formally confirmed her as CEO. She can't believe she's done it – she's the youngest head of a major US property development organisation, and one of only a handful of females. After celebrating with a glass of champagne, she left the board meeting to return to her office. She has one more thing to do before leaving for the day.

She will likely never know whether her father was involved in, or even knew about, the horrific treatment of the young women trafficked for entertainment and sex, not forgetting the two who lost their lives in the waters surrounding Mallorca that summer, but she has her suspicions. Nevertheless, when she discovered the extent of the operation she made a vow to atone in some way.

She clicks on the Hope for Justice website, a charity that helps identify those at risk, supporting survivors and preventing exploitation. Navigating through the screens, she sets up a monthly recurring donation, an amount that she calculates represents ten per cent of her personal income. When the business is back on a surer footing, she plans to raise the subject of greater corporate support with the board.

It's not much, but it's a start.

Acknowledgements

A finished novel is never a solo effort, and despite the fact that only my name is on the cover, there are so many others who have shepherded this to publication and made it far better than I could ever manage on my own.

Among the many to whom I am indebted are:

Stephanie Thwaites at Curtis Brown UK for her positivity and continuing faith and belief in me as a writer. It's a privilege to have her in my corner.

Pippa Masson at Curtis Brown Australia for her level-headed insight and market acumen.

Carolyn Mays at Bedford Square and Anna Valdinger at HarperCollins Australia for their enthusiasm for the characters (especially the vilest ones!) and setting (and not thinking it totally ridiculous when I said I'd watched far too many episodes of *Below Deck* in the name of research) and their invaluable commentary on my initial draft.

Whip-smart editors Madeleine James and Vanessa Lanaway who generously pointed out my errors both large and small (any remaining are entirely my own), and who have polished my prose until it shines.

And finally, an enormous thanks to my readers, whether you've come along for the ride from my historical novels or are just discovering how much I love a deep dive into character, motivation, misdirection and suspense in crime fiction. I am profoundly grateful to anyone and everyone who decides to give their valuable time to something I've written, and I hope I've given you something escapist and enjoyable.

If that's the case, please tell your friends – spreading the word is the best, most helpful thing any reader can do for a writer whose work they love and helps to make it possible for us to keep writing!

About the Author

Photo credit © Jed Grace

Kayte Nunn is the internationally bestselling author of seven novels, most recently 2025's *The Palazzo*. They are available worldwide in English, and have been translated into eleven languages. She was brought up in England, lived in the US for a number of years as a child and now calls the Northern Rivers of NSW, Australia home.

kaytenunn.com

If you loved *The Yacht*, why not try Kayte Nunn's thrilling destination murder mystery *The Palazzo*…

They're all killers, but only one will resort to murder. The stunning new novel from international bestseller Kayte Nunn, for all fans of Lucy Foley and *The White Lotus*.

Successful beauty entrepreneur Vivi Savidge is about to celebrate her fortieth birthday at the Palazzo Stellina, a historic former convent in the foothills of the Italian Alps.

Vivi's little sister is flying in from Brisbane with her sixteen-year-old twins in tow. Her ex-colleague and his new husband are coming from Boston, and old university friend Caroline is driving from Turin. Every one of them is hiding a shameful secret.

Amid a suffocating heatwave, the holiday ignites an explosive cocktail of obsession, jealousy, and greed. Before the week is over, secrets will be exposed and the gathering will turn deadly, leaving one victim, a handful of suspects, and a murderer in their midst.

* * *

'A brilliantly twisty thriller in a beautiful setting. I couldn't put this down'
Pip Drysdale

'Will whisk you away from everyday life and immerse you in the Italian mountainside, which turns out to be as deadly as it is idyllic' **B.M. Carroll**